2024

THE OATHBREAKER'S DAUGHTER

THE DRAGONKNIGHT TRILOGY
BOOK 1

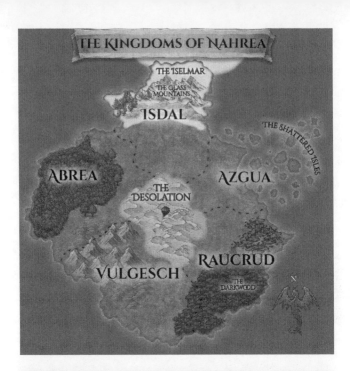

Upcoming Novels

Bound By Flame (The Chronicle of Thyss)* (7/24)
Wolves of War – A John Hartman Novel (10/24)
Book 2 of The Dragonknight Trilogy (2025)
Spectres of the Black Sun – A John Hartman Novel
Advent of Judgement
The Horizon's Edge
Mirrored, Darkly
Fractured Descent

Other Novels and Works

Blood and Steel (The Cor Chronicles Vol. I)*
Fire and Steel (The Cor Chronicles Vol. II)*
Darkness and Steel (The Cor Chronicles Vol. III)*
Gods and Steel (The Cor Chronicles Vol. IV)*
Blood Betrayal (The Cor Chronicles Vol. V)*
Blood Loss (The Chronicle of Rael)*
Tendrils in the Dark – Eight Tales of Horror

*Denotes a novel of Rumedia.

The Oathbreaker's Daughter

The Dragonknight Trilogy
Book 1

By

Martin V. Parece II

ISBN: 9798878225892

I dedicate this novel to my wife who, when I said I would be writing a young woman main character, said, "Well, good luck with that."

Prologue

The Arrest of Jenna's Father

Jenna sat in her father's lap for a time as he rocked her tenderly in the wooden chair he had made over the summer. He stared into the fire, his arms wrapped around her, while she laid her head against his chest, listening to the beat of his heart. He still smelled like boiled leather, like his armor, but it didn't bother her at all. In fact, Jenna had come to enjoy the smell, so attached to him as it was in her mind. He was a giant to her, as all fathers did to their little girls when they were small, with straight brown hair that curled as it grew longer, a brown that matched his trim mustache and goatee.

They needed the crackling blaze in the hearth to keep away the chill of late autumn. Northern Abrea grew colder faster than the rest of the nation, being so close to Isdal, but it meant more to Jenna than warmth. She never understood why at her young age, but her father only came home to them after dark, and in the spring and summer months, the days were long. The shortness of daylight in autumn and winter meant she would have more time with her father, even if only a few more hours.

Her mother glided into the room, as she always seemed to when Father was around. She was a young woman, thin and graceful, a beauty that could have married any man in any of Abrea's villages or towns. Luxuriously soft, brown hair with a hint of curl framed her lovely face and set off the slight traces of green that tinged the inner ring of her brown irises.

"I think it's about time for bed, Jenna," she said, her voice almost inaudible over the fire.

Jenna almost imperceptibly tightened herself in her father's lap, to which he replied, "A few more minutes yet."

She savored those minutes, allowed her father's embrace to wash over her, a shield of warmth and love that protected her from the marauding, brutish warriors of Vulgesch, the wolf packs and polar bears of Isdal, or even the vile assassins and necromancers of Raucrud. Jenna knew he would always be there for both her and her mother, defending them and Abrea with a bow, steel, and his dragon. Though King Rendor ruled, her father was the true king in the eyes of his five-year-old daughter.

After some time, his embrace slacked, and he whispered into her ear, "Off to bed now."

She mumbled something, really nothing more than a wordless moan as she wrapped her arms around his muscled torso. Jenna never wanted to let go. She knew he would be gone when she awoke with the sunrise. Sometimes she would try to stay awake all night, to catch one last glimpse of him, say one more goodbye before he left, but those nights, she seemed to fall asleep even faster. She resolved herself to rising earlier, because sometimes she awoke before the sun, but those times he had either already left or still slept next to Mother. She would always fall back to sleep before he awoke.

"No more of that, Little Dear," he said as he stood, the small girl still in his arms. She felt the power of his body, the strength, as he did so. He was a warrior, a Dragonknight, a man who spent his entire life training and fighting.

He carried his most delicate possession across the small den toward her bedroom, and Jenna twisted a bit to rest her head over his right shoulder. Her eyes

2

scanned the room, stopping briefly on her mother who blew her a kiss goodnight, but then moved to the door of their home, or rather, the items next to the door. A heap of blackened, boiled leather armor sat there, a quiver full of arrows leaning casually against it. A steel longsword gleamed unevenly in the firelight, its smoky black hued steel betraying its origins in the forges of Vulgesch from where came the best steel in all the world.

Last was the longbow. Taller than some men, Jenna knew her father could end an enemy from hundreds of yards away with a single arrow. All of Abrea's Dragonknights, including King Rendor himself, carried bows crafted from the Great Tree. This one carried etchings and reliefs of wood nymphs, pixies, and a dragon, all caught in mid-flight.

The bow passed from her sight as he carried her into her darkened room.

Jenna felt the snoring of the huge, green beast behind her home; he arranged himself in a ball not unlike a common cat, with his enormous, triangular head resting on folded paws. Just a few weeks ago, Father introduced her to the dragon, and she reached out and laid a tiny hand on one of its hooked claws, a claw that was the same size as her entire body. She gazed into its eyes as it regarded her, and where other people sensed fear at the creatures that could crush someone with a mere step or eviscerate a foe with one swipe of those massive claws, she saw only a deep wisdom and the love of the forest.

"What's his name?" she had asked.

"I call him Titan."

Jenna cocked her head a bit, her brow knitted in some confusion and replied, "That's what you call him, but what's his *name*?"

Father hadn't understood the question, and she didn't understand why.

He lovingly laid her down on her bed of skins and woolen blankets, but she wrapped her arms and hands tighter around his body when he tried to pull away. Other children saw their fathers every day, for hours and hours, to the extent that both tired of each other's presence, although children of Jenna's age rarely recognize such. Jenna was lucky to see him more than a few hours once per week, and she loathed letting him go, for she knew she wouldn't see him again for days at least. And days or a week felt much like an eternity to Jenna.

"Don't go," she implored. He shushed her softly as he extricated himself from her embrace and pulled a blanket up over her body. She worked her arms out of the blanket and clasped her hands across her stomach.

"I have to, Little Dear, but I'll be back again to see you soon," he replied, caressing her cheek with a thumb. He had a kind face, free from scars of battle, with slight lines of sadness around his eyes and mouth, the latter of which he tried to cover with his dark brown goatee. But Jenna could always see the sorrow in the deep brown of his eyes, though she didn't understand the cause.

"When?"

"Just a few days," he promised, and he leaned over to press his lips to her forehead.

He left the room, pulling the door shut behind him, and Jenna stared at the ceiling and listened to the dragon. Its breath came and went like some smith's giant bellows, and it seemed to shake their small home each time it exhaled. Still, she found it somehow soothing; other children had their mothers' lullabies, but she had the comforting snores of a dragon.

Even still, she threw back the blankets and leapt out of bed. She padded over to her door, her bare feet making no sound on the animal skin that carpeted her floor, and she gradually eased the door open a crack.

4

Soft orange light from the dying fire spilled through that crack, and she put one eye to it to see her parents. Jenna saw them in an embrace, kissing. She opened her mouth and stuck her tongue out in revulsion, stifling the "blah" sound that often accompanied such a reaction, and then returned to bed.

She had just begun to dream when a far off thumping sound disrupted her sleep, some image in her mind fading as she was pulled back to consciousness. The thumping grew more insistent, and she recognized it as someone pounding on the outside door of her home. There were shouted words also, and they sounded angry, but Jenna still wasn't awake enough to decipher them. The splintering cracks of wood, sudden like a crash of lightning, caused her to gasp and bolt upright in bed, as someone burst in the door.

Again, she jumped from her bed and rushed to the door, opening it just enough to see. The light from the fireplace was all but gone, but there were five or six men in her home. All wore armor and were armed with swords, and several carried torches that flickered smokily. Her father wore his breeches and no tunic, unarmed, while her mother lay on the floor with nothing but a blanket wrapped around her, her dark hair spilling about her shoulders.

Something was wrong with the dragon. He no longer slept, but instead stomped in the open yard behind the house. It seemed almost nervous, like that of a deer when it knew a predator was about or perhaps a spooked horse. He shook the house with each impact of his immense paws on the ground as they lifted and fell in an uneven staccato. She understood how he felt – something bad was happening, and he didn't know what to do.

"By the order of King Rendor, I place you under arrest, Sir Timbre," gruffly said one of the men, drawing Jenna's attention back to the scene beyond her room.

"No!" her mother screamed. She climbed to her feet and almost lost her meager covering in so doing. "He's done nothing wrong!"

"You're charged with breaking your Oath, betraying both your King and the Brotherhood."

Jenna opened the door a few more inches so she could see the speaker. He was tall, well over six feet, with dirty blond hair and a clean-shaven face. His black leather armor seemed more intricate than the others, with brass rings inserted all over it, and sigils signifying his place. Her eyes widened when she realized that he too was a Dragonknight, perhaps of the First Circle, and slung across his back was a longbow not unlike her father's.

"You can't!" Mother shouted.

Jenna agreed. They couldn't take him. He was a good man, and he loved her. They had no right! Why didn't he do something? He was a warrior, a Dragonknight. He could fight them. He would fight them. Why didn't he have Titan save him?

"Tim," sighed the other Dragonknight as he cast his eyes downward. He brought them up to her father's face, and added, "You're my friend. Please don't make this any more difficult. You know what you've done."

Jenna's father almost shrank before her eyes. If he had any thought to fight or even argue, all his resolution had fled, almost as if he agreed with the accusation, as if he knew any resistance was pointless. It would only endanger those he loved. He had done his best to protect them, to make sure no one in the order – not his king, his commander, or his friends – knew of his wife and child, but deep down within his heart, he had known it would only be a matter of time. His final act of protection would be to go to his fate without endangering them. He stepped forward.

"No! You can't!" Jenna's mother again shouted, but this time at her husband instead of the armed men in her home.

He turned to face her, and in contrast to her raised voice, he whispered, "I must. We both knew this day may come. I only wish we'd had more time."

Father kissed her mother then, but Jenna didn't turn away as she had before. Tears began to track down her face, though she still couldn't comprehend the scene entirely. Mother cried; Father looked like he wanted to.

"Come, Tim," said the blond man, and after a long moment, her father broke away from the embrace. He turned slowly and headed for the door leaving the house, the men enveloping him as an escort as he neared the door.

Realization struck Jenna, and she swung her bedroom door open. It banged into the wall with a sharp report, and she burst forth with all the fury of the summer storms. She shouted at the men, "He's my father! You can't take him! Daddy, don't let them! Don't go!"

Of the men who had come to arrest her father, only one was a Dragonknight, and the others appeared to be plain soldiers of Abrea's armies, those who likely knew what it was to be a father. Several of these men shifted indecisively at Jenna's attack, looking at the little girl, then their leader, and then at last to Sir Timbre himself for some sort of guidance or support against the onslaught. Their relief was palpable when he turned and knelt before her. He put a palm on each of her cheeks and used his thumbs to wipe away her running tears. He leaned forward and kissed her forehead as he had done before, as he always did when saying goodbye, before pulling back to just look at her. His brown eyes reflected calm serenity, and she realized she no longer endured the agitated thumping of the dragon outside. She could see the many things he wanted to say, but after the space of a few breaths, he seemed to settle on, "I love you, Little Dear."

Jenna broke into sobs then and somehow eked out, "I love you too, Daddy."

She didn't know how long he held her in an embrace, only that too soon he was gone. Whooshes of air sounded from outside, a familiar sound as not one, but two dragons lifted from the ground. Jenna and her mother held each other through the night and well past dawn, sharing their sorrow. Her father's longsword lay next to his armor where it had clanged to the floor amidst the forced entry of his captors.

Later, Jenna realized that the blond Dragonknight had taken her father's longbow as he left the house.

Chapter 1

The Announcement

When the rider trotted into the village right before midday, everything seemed to stop. Vendors and their customers deep in negotiations trailed off in mid-sentence, and old women tending flower or vegetable gardens in front of their homes paused to gaze upward as he passed. A blacksmith ceased pounding glowing iron, and a wagon driver hauling grain from the northern plains pulled his horses to the side to allow the man by. Even Brasalla, seated on a bench before all the village children grew silent and pensive. Jenna was no longer a student at twenty, at least not in the ordinary sense, but an aid to Brasalla, something she rather enjoyed as the older woman entered her golden years. She glanced up at the sudden silence to find all eyes facing toward the village center.

The rider was of no great stature, though he rode a regal black stallion, a powerfully built creature that seemed more built for action than a jaunt through the woods. He wore no armor over his deep green, woolen tunic and brown, soft leather breeches, and a golden hilted rapier hung sheathed from the right side of his saddle. A quiver hung on the opposite side, and a fine longbow lay across the horse's hindquarters. But it was the rider's cloak that made everyone stop whatever task in which they were involved. He wore a cloak of fine black silk - the finest black silk that was only harvested from the silkworms of Darkwood - emblazoned with the golden seal of King Rendor.

He had been tasked with delivering a message from the king to all the villages south of Highton and Great Tree, and this place was just one like so many others. A well-traveled dirt track, the road he traveled from north to south, created the primary thoroughfare amidst clusters of small homes built of stone with shingled rooves of wood. Many had small wooden fences, some newly whitewashed while others had grayed from exposure to sun and rain, and almost all of them had their own flower and vegetable gardens. The sun cheerily poked rays intermittently through the towering canopy of mighty oaks and ancient pines, and a cool autumn breeze completed a pleasant day.

He halted in the village center, and sat upon the horse in silence, the well-disciplined animal standing at perfect attention. The rider was middle aged, with a full head of almost black hair and a handful of silver streaks. He looked as if he kept his face clean shaven but hadn't had the opportunity to clean up for several days, patches of black and gray growth spreading across his face.

He waited until he was certain he had the attention of everyone within earshot before he reached down to a scroll tucked into the front of his belt. His message had not yet preceded his arrival at each village, though that would change within a week, as news, either terrible or important, would spread faster than the king's emissaries could deliver it. He removed and unfurled it, holding the parchment by the top and bottom edges as it tried to roll itself back into its previous form. The rider began to speak in a rich, deep voice that seemed that it would carry for miles. He appeared to read, but as Jenna observed and listened, it was clear to her that the rider had memorized his announcement well in advance of his arrival.

"I bring tidings of great sadness. It is with much regret that King Rendor informs the people of Abrea of the death of Sir Garond of the Second Circle. A

Dragonknight for some forty years, Sir Garond represented the best virtues and traditions of the Brotherhood, and his stalwart dedication to both his king and the people of Abrea will be keenly missed. Sir Garond will be interred six days hence in the roots of the Great Tree as befitting his station.

"Of course, the Brotherhood cannot suffer such emptiness, and Sir Garond's mount requires a new master. With glory unto the name of Sir Garond, King Rendor announces that Trials will commence in seven days at the Great Tree. All boys and young men between twelve and twenty years of age are encouraged to test their strength of arms and will at the Trial Grounds, and may the Brotherhood find one worthy of earning Sir Garond's mount."

With an almost theatrical display of somberness, the messenger crisply rolled up the scroll and placed it in a loop at his belt. Without looking up to meet the eyes of anyone around him, he took back the horse's reins from where he had draped them across the saddle horn, and soothingly urged the animal forward on his way through the village. He kept his eyes locked straight ahead, not deigning to look at any of those around him, as if making eye contact with any of them would be too painful to bear. Jenna thought the rider might have had a storied career on the stage.

A growing murmur of whispered voices replaced the deafening silence that preceded his proclamation. Villagers spoke in hurried tones to one another, their previous business forgotten as their voices raised in excited discussion. The death of a Dragonknight was a terrible affair to be sure, but the opportunity for Trials! That so rarely came about; it would be a glorious spectacle. Jenna's attention snapped to the children arrayed before her and Brasalla and found them to be in the grips of the same excitement as the adults nearby.

She couldn't blame them; it was infectious, and her mind reeled with the news.

She heard one of the boys, a boy named Stonn, rasp excitedly to a friend, "I'll be twelve the day after tomorrow. I can go!"

His mate seemed less enthusiastic about Stonn's chances and guffawed with an eye roll, but the idea struck Jenna like lightning. Her eyes widened as the dust settled in her mind, revealing a possibility. She glanced at Brasalla, realizing that the older woman had been watching her appraisingly for several seconds. Along with the usual wisdom, Jenna's teacher's eyes now carried a knowing sadness, an understanding of what was forming in Jenna's mind, and Brasalla simply shook her head almost imperceptibly.

"I suppose that should be all for the day. Run home, tell your parents the big news, if they haven't heard already," Brasalla said to the assembled children. They scrambled to their feet and were hauling off before she even finished speaking the words, leaving her alone with Jenna. The older woman turned to her and said, "I know what you're thinking."

Seeing no point in arguing, Jenna stood and reached out to grasp the older woman's shoulder. "This is it!"

"This is what?"

"My chance!"

"Your chance. To do what? Jenna, you've grown into a strong warrior, and I know you'll make a celebrated Protectress, if you would but accept the truth of that. But this is something you cannot do."

"And why not?" Jenna asked, lifting her chin defiantly. "I'm a better shot than any boy in the village. I can handle a sword well enough. I -"

"You are a girl, a young woman," Brasalla rebutted with finality. "This is not a point of debate. Women cannot forge the Link of a Dragonknight to his

12

mount. There has never been a woman Dragonknight for this reason. It is not just an unfair rule."

"I am strong enough. I can do it, and I'm twenty. I'll not have another chance."

"I believe you can do almost anything," Brasalla agreed with a nod, "but you cannot deny what you are."

"A girl," Jenna spat, almost petulantly.

"Yes, a girl, and what that means."

"It's bullshit."

"Yes, it is. I don't disagree with you on that, but it just is," Brasalla replied in a matter of fact tone. "Would you like to train today?"

Jenna turned away sharply to run the back of her wrist across her eyes as if merely clearing them of some dust or windblown debris. "No, I think I'll go home and help Mother."

Except her mother wasn't home when Jenna arrived at their quaint three room cabin on the edge of the village. She glanced around, her eyes lingering on the longsword of smoky Vulgeschi steel almost forgotten as it leaned in a corner by the front door. Her mother's longbow, quiver, and pack were missing, indicating to Jenna that she had most likely gone out for a hunt. Odd, because she usually would have left before sunrise and been back well before noon.

Jenna closed the door behind her as she left the house, going around to the small clearing behind it, so like a home she remembered long ago, where a dragon had once alighted and slept. She crossed through this and entered the forest where it started less than a hundred feet from the cabin. She moved slowly, silently, with her eyes and ears open to the slightest noise or sign. After a few tentative steps, she found it, nothing more than some displaced leaves where a foot had tread, and she penetrated deeper into the tree cover.

The sounds of the forest greeted her as she moved past shrubs, trees, and fallen leaves, following

13

the human spoor left behind by someone who clearly could hide it, should she so desire, but had made no attempt to do so. Even still, the shallow, scarcely visible imprints of soft leather boots indicated a quarry that acted stealthily as part of her nature, and Jenna knew she followed her mother. After an hour or more of following the careful trail, she lost it as it purely vanished at a narrow brook that babbled merrily as the water moved past long smoothed stones. Jenna assumed her mother had to cross the stream, but she could find no sign on the other side, which could only have one meaning. Her mother had found a beast to hunt. Jenna should have turned and headed home then, but then again, such would have been opposed to the very essence of her soul. She wanted to find her mother, just to prove that she could, and she wanted to see what animal was worthy of such a protracted stalking.

She crossed the stream noiselessly and moved into the brush on the far side, starting up a long ridge that gently sloped upward and to the south. This she climbed less stealthily, her left foot having settled on a loose patch of wet leaves and sliding out from under her. She avoided falling to her knees or worse, sliding down the embankment, but the noise disturbed a few birds overhead. Cursing her clumsiness, Jenna continued the trek upward until she crested the hill, and she looked around intently as she searched for any sign of her huntress mother.

A muffled snort grabbed her attention to the right, and she spied a mammoth boar as it rooted into something under a bush less than twenty feet away. For the second time in a few minutes, she cursed herself again, realizing that she had brought no weapons with her. Of course, her mother had the longbow, wherever she was, but she could have, should have taken her father's sword of fine Vulgeschi steel. While fighting the animal, at least six foot in length and over two

14

hundred pounds, with something as close as a longsword wasn't her preferred way of dealing with it, any weapon was better than bare hands. Jenna kept her wits, and as silently as she could manage, she began to back away. If she could extend the distance between them a bit, she could make her escape or even climb a tree. Boars were not like bears. If you climbed a tree to escape a bear, it would either climb after you or knock the tree down, whereas a boar would eventually lose interest and roam away.

Jenna had only backed away about six paces when a figure exploded from the brush to her left, wrapped a calloused hand about her mouth and pulled her down into the brush. Her initial reaction was to struggle and cry out, but with her mother's face hovering inches from hers, she mastered the impulse. Her mother placed a single finger to her lips, to which Jenna nodded her understanding, and then the finger pointed out through the brush and at the boar. The animal had stopped its rooting and lifted its head to the air, drinking it in with huge snorts of its snout.

"It smells us," Mother whispered in a voice Jenna could have mistaken for the wind. She, with a smooth, slow motion born of decades of practice, reached to her back and pulled an arrow which she nocked onto her longbow. "My first shot will do little good, and I will get one, maybe two more as it charges."

"The eye?" Jenna asked.

"The eye."

As her mother drew the bowstring back, the rushing anxious energy of the hunt ran through Jenna's blood. A slight sickness touched her stomach, and every nerve burned with its own, individual fire. Both stood steadily as the boar breathed their scent – Jenna, to be ready to dodge away if necessary, and her mother to pull the bowstring as taut as possible. She loosed the first arrow, and it whistled through the air to strike the

15

animal's hindquarters. It squealed like a common pig, turning in the blink of an eye while the huntress reached for another arrow, and the creature charged.

The first shot should have slowed the beast, but no one made that clear to the boar as it rushed onward with bared tusks. The second arrow was perfectly aimed and would have felled the animal right through its right eye, but for a reason only known to the universe, it lifted its head as the arrow struck. The missile impacted the boar's right tusk instead, caroming into the woods wildly and eliciting a disgruntled noise from the animal. Moving faster than a blink of an eye, Jenna's mother had a third arrow and pulled back the string just as the boar reached them. Jenna dove to her right while her mother stepped to the left at the last moment, the arrow went astray of the target, pounding into the boar's flank as its massive head swept the huntress' legs out from under her and continued to run past.

Jenna scrambled to her feet amidst the detritus of the forest. Time had slowed in a bubble that surrounded her while everything else continued as normal. Her eyes sought her mother some six or eight feet away, and the woman clutched at her thigh, red blood welling up between clenched fingers where the boar's tusk had rent a gash. The longbow had fallen, or been flung from her, and even if Jenna could reach it in time, her mother's weight pinned the quiver of arrows somewhere underneath her.

"Mother!"

Jenna reached the fallen woman's side as the sound of the boar's breathing and snorts pulled her attention away. The animal had stopped, turned, and stamped one of its cloven hooves on the ground once and then twice before urging its back legs into motion in another charge directly at Jenna. Fortunately, it moved more slowly than the first charge, as the wounds from two arrows, though not immediately fatal, slowed it

16

down. Jenna's mother acted without thinking, yanked her dagger from its sheath and tossed it upward with a slight arc toward Jenna, blade straight up in the air. Jenna caught it by the hilt in a smooth motion, and it threatened to slide from her hand, the hilt slick from her mother's own blood.

Jenna stood to face the onrushing boar as her mother rolled out of the way. As large as it was, it came at her low to the ground, and in this she saw her chance. Its speed waned, blood loss sapping the animal's strength, and she crouched as it came close, her legs like coiled steel springs. She watched the gap lessen as it closed to under ten feet far faster than she expected as wounded as the boar was. It halved the distance again before she could blink, and as the boar threatened to bowl her over, Jenna launched herself in the air in an attempt to sail over the animal. She almost made it, as the tip of her boot barely caught the arched back of the boar, and this flung her forward to land on her chest as the boar attempted to skid to a halt amidst fallen leaves and other forest debris.

Fortunately, she extended her arms right before hitting the ground, leaving her with skinned palms that would burn later; if she hadn't, the impact may have knocked the breath out of her lungs, stunning her so she couldn't move. Jenna acted fast, jumping to her feet and turning to find the boar only a few feet away as it turned ponderously to its left to again face its antagonists. She charged right at it, correcting to her right at the last moment, and fell upon its back. She wrapped her left arm around its thick neck in the hopes she could hold on for just a few seconds. The boar outweighed her by at least double, and its earthy musk filled her nostrils. Her right hand plunged the dagger into the boar's thick hide over and over. It squealed a high pitched song of battle and death as it fought against her, bucking and swinging its huge bulk around to dislodge the terrible attacker that plunged cold steel between its ribs, into its neck, its back, and anywhere else it could strike. She clung to it desperately, her legs locked around its enormous body. After five or six blows, the boar's blood ran hot over the dagger's hilt and Jenna's hand, and it shook its immense frame in one final desperate attempt. The strength of her arm failed, and unable to keep a grip on the blood slicked dagger, the boar flung Jenna off its back and over the embankment.

She flew weightlessly through the air for a breathless moment before landing on her side and rolling sideways down the slope as children often did for enjoyment. She completed only three or four such somersaults before her flailing arms caught at something, an exposed tree root that brought her to an halt. In a daze, she half crawled, half clambered fifteen feet or so back up the slope, terrified as to what she may find when she reached the crest. The world spun as she reached the top of the low ridge, and Jenna dropped to one knee, more to steady herself than out of exhaustion. The boar lay on its side, where she'd left it when it threw her, and it still breathed, though death was somewhere close. Her mother limped toward her, bow in hand and a piece of her tunic torn off and tied about her wounded thigh, blood spreading and soaking through the wool.

Despite the gash that needed close attention and soon, her mother beamed at her from behind disheveled, near black tresses streaked with gray, "You killed it, and with a dagger! So fierce! Such a tale to tell!"

Jenna sighed as she climbed to her feet, the world settling into calm as she replied, "Didn't have much choice. It would have killed you."

"Or you."

"I'm sorry. I may have damaged the meat with all that."

"We'll make do," her mother laughed.

Jenna moved to her mother's side, wrapping the woman's left arm about her neck and shoulders. "Let me help you home. We'll see to the leg, and I'll send someone back for the boar."

Hours later, Jenna cooked a stew of vegetables and slices of pork belly over their fire as her mother leaned back in a rocker, her leg outstretched across a footstool. Upon returning home, Jenna had gone to retrieve Brasalla from the cottage she shared with Wheelbarrow Man, as Jenna had decided she would always know him. Jenna pretended not to notice the muffled sounds emanating from the cottage, and the two oldsters volunteered nothing about it, acting as if they'd been interrupted doing nothing so important as a game of dice. The retired Protectress came at once to tend to her mother's wound, while Wheelbarrow Man went with Jenna back into the forest to retrieve the boar, and he had been all too happy to work on the butchering of the animal in return for a share of it.

As Jenna stirred the hanging pot, her mother ventured, "So, what had you coming out to the forest to find me?"

"I thought you may need my help."

"You're a poor liar, Little Dear," her mother responded, but she softened her words with, "but, as it turned out, you were right. I'm grateful for your help; you've become such a strong woman."

"If I hadn't distracted you, you would've killed that boar with your second shot."

"You didn't distract me. I just missed."

"You'd have been fine. You didn't need me."

"This old woman still has some tricks up her sleeve," her mother smiled, "but I'm glad you were there. I might have been hurt much worse."

"You're not that old," Jenna chided, lifting a wooden spoon from the stew to check the taste.

"Perhaps not," the woman sighed, "but this will hurt for a time."

"It's getting hot in here," Jenna said as she stood from the stewpot and busied herself for a few minutes throwing back shutters about the house. A breeze kicked up, nothing too tempestuous, but a gentle cross breeze of cool air that both vented the heat from their home's main room but also spread the mouthwatering emanation of cooked pork throughout the house and beyond. As Jenna returned to the fire, she brought with her a pair of bowls and spoons, and as she served her mother something to eat, she decided that it was time to chance it.

"I did come to find you. There's news, and I've made a decision," Jenna explained, tension in her nerves and muscles building even as she said these few words.

Her mother's face flashed through emotions from surprise to mild suspicion to hopeful expectancy as she pulled her long dark hair back and knotted it around itself behind her head as if it were bothering her. She leaned forward in anticipation and asked, "I assume it has something to do with being twenty? Please tell me you've decided to join the Protectresses before it's too late. They need good women, especially in the south."

Jenna averted her eyes as her mother spoke, first to one side and then down into the depths of her own bowl as she turned the food over itself with a spoon. After a moment of expectant silence, she looked up at her mother and answered, "No. I'm going to Highton."

"Highton? What for?"

"A rider came this afternoon," she started to explain, "Sir Garond of the Second Circle has died. There will be Trials to replace him."

"And what does this have to do with you?" her mother asked, the suspicion having returned and laying plain across her face. "You don't think…?"

"I'm going to compete. I'm as good as any boy. Brasalla has trained me well. I can win."

"No, you can't. First of all, they won't even let you in the Trials. *You're a girl.*"

Jenna's eyes flashed angrily, and she spat, "A few minutes ago I was a strong woman."

"That's not what I meant," her mother sighed, turning her head back and forth while shrugging her shoulders.

Jenna argued on, "Then, I'll go as a boy. I'm not as… rounded as other girls. I can hide under layers of thick clothing, cut my hair, rub dirt on my face to look like I'm from the forest."

"And how long do you think you'll get away with it? There'll be thousands of people there, hundreds, maybe thousands of boys there to compete in the Trials. You don't think *anyone* will recognize you for a girl? You won't even be able to relieve yourself."

This gave Jenna a slight pause, but as her mind was made up, she pushed forward, "I'll figure it out. I–"

"It doesn't matter," her mother interrupted with a raised voice, "even if you manage to fool all those boys, all the other people who came to see the Trials, the thousands of people who live in Highton, the Dragonknights *and* King Rendor, you can't succeed! The dragons meld with their riders, and we can't make the Link."

Jenna shook her head in vain disagreement, "We don't know that. We've been told that. For hundreds of years, we've been *told* that women can't make the Link, but how do we know? When's the last time a woman was allowed to try?"

"Why try? It's the way it had been for… a thousand years. It's a known truth throughout all of

Nahrea. If you were to ask your mentor, Brasalla, what would she tell you?"

"She has nothing to do with this."

"What would she say?" her mother asked again. Jenna fell into silence as she stared at the rugged floor, unwilling to answer the question, and her mother pressed on, answering the question herself, "She would tell you it's impossible. Why must you do this? Why must you rail against that which you can't change? Why is it so important that you be a Dragonknight? Why not join the Protectresses? You are so strong, a fine archer and fencer. They would be honored to have you as their numbers have shrunk the last few years."

"I am not you, Mother. Nor am I Brasalla," Jenna responded almost petulantly, and neither of them dared to speak as the words seemed to hang in the air before them. Jenna turned her attention to her stew, continuing to turn it over and over but not eat, while her mother only sat it to the side and stared unblinking into the fire which slowly died. After a few minutes, Jenna placed her bowl on the floor and moved to her mother's side, kneeling.

She took the woman's calloused hands in her own and peered into the depths of her eyes, speaking with a lowered voice as if sharing a secret, "Mother, I am going to tell you something no one else knows, something I've never told anyone. It's about Father and his dragon, Titan."

"I'd rather not speak of him," she replied, and her eyes became suddenly glassy.

"I know it troubles you, and I'm sorry," Jenna said, and she truly meant it. But her mother needed to know. "When Father first introduced me to the dragon, I was not frightened in any way."

"You've always been brave, downright incorrigible."

Jenna smiled and nodded her head at the compliment, but she continued on, "But it wasn't that. I felt something when I touched the dragon. Father told me his name was Titan, but I knew that wasn't true. Somehow, I knew the dragon had his own name, and when I asked Father about it, he didn't understand. Some nights, after the two of you had gone to sleep, I snuck out my window and went to the dragon, and sometimes, I even dozed off amidst his paws. I could feel him, almost hear him in my mind."

"We believe the dragons to be telepathic. That's how they communicate with their riders once the Link is forged," her mother reasoned. "You probably just felt his mind reaching out to yours."

"No, it was more than that," Jenna disagreed, shaking her head.

"Little Dear…"

"No! I sensed his mind, his feelings, but they were unclear, probably because I hadn't been Linked to him. But doesn't that mean I can be?" Jenna asked imploringly, tears welling into her eyes.

Her mother shrunk as if a tremendous weight had been placed upon her while they looked into each other's eyes before replying as delicately as she could manage, "Little Dear, I don't think it means… anything. I admit that I never felt any such thing, and I even rode Titan with your father many times as a Protectress. I don't pretend to understand the magic that links a Dragonknight to his mount, but I think it likely you were just somehow caught in the middle of that energy.

"I don't know, but I know one thing. There has never been a woman Dragonknight anywhere in the world, and I don't believe there ever will be."

"Then, I'll prove it to you and the world," Jenna retorted, standing from her crouch and releasing her mother's hands as she turned away. She ran a sleeve across her eyes, wiping away the tears that threatened to run down her face, embarrassed that she showed such weakness like a common six year old girl. *No one will ever see me cry again*, she decided.

"You can't go. Please, I can't lose you, too. If they discover you, they could imprison you. Or worse."

"Fine," Jenna replied, picking up her bowl and taking it to a basin on the other side of the house. She stared down into it, watching her undulating, wavy reflection – her father's deep brown eyes and matching straight hair and her mother's understated nose and pretty, well defined cheekbones and jawline.

"Jenna."

"I said fine!" she shouted at the ceiling. She dropped the bowl into the basin without emptying its contents, strode across the room to her bedroom, and slammed the door behind her.

When the moon had risen high into the night sky, a lone figure slipped out of a house on the edge of a village and skulked away toward the road that led to Highton. She had used a dagger to shear the hair from her head, as close to her scalp as she dared, and it had been a painful, messy process that left her with a number of long strands that she would cut later but for now hid under a common cap. She carried a longbow in her left hand, its ammunition loaded into a quiver upon her back, and a sheathed longsword hung from her left hip. If she were to draw that sword, there would be no mistaking the workmanship and smoky steel forged only by the artisans working with dragon fire in Vulgesch.

She also carried a knapsack with a number of hardtack biscuits, a small amount of pork pulled from a recently killed boar, and a number of nuts and berries. The journey to Highton would take days without a horse, and she might have to scavenge for additional food as she went. As she reached the village edge and entered the forest, she shifted the pack, hoping to redistribute the weight so that it didn't pull on the thin wool fiber that she'd wrapped tightly around her chest to hide certain features.

Chapter 2

Journey To Highton

Jenna couldn't have asked for better weather as she made her way north toward Highton. At this time of year, storms often blew through quickly with a whimper, dropping only light rain and leaving behind a sense of clean renewal in the forest, but even these made no appearance. The sun gleefully shined down into the forest, touching the ground where it could, and the days warmed nicely from the overnight chill. In this part of Abrea at this time of year, people always awoke to white puffs of air from their exhaling lungs, vapor that ceased appearing after the sun had been up an hour or so.

Still, the day reminded her of another so many years ago.

"Who can tell me why we are so blessed to live in Abrea of all the five kingdoms?" asked Brasalla as she met the eyes of the dozen children of various ages who sat arrayed about her, some on the limestone benches upon which children had sat and learned for decades, a few others cross legged on sparse grass.

She was pretty, beautiful as middle-aged women went, with what had once been light skin and dark brown hair, the former of which had darkened while the latter grew lighter from decades exposure to the sun. Her face showed lines of worry or grim determination around her eyes and the corners of her mouth. The whispered rumor among the children, a well-known fact with the adult villagers, was she had once been a strong warrior, a Protectress of the wilds. The earthen toned, loosely fitting dresses she often wore obscured a fit frame and lithe muscles, that she betrayed when she helped up a fallen child or scooped one into an embrace. But her left arm, having been severed above the elbow, lent the most credence to the warrior story. After all, any such injury could only happen in battle.

Having not received an answer, she repeated, "So? Who can tell me?"

"The weather," responded a voice, and Jenna turned to see a man pushing a wheelbarrow about to overflow with various colored taproots.

"No, Azgua has wonderful weather," Brasalla disagreed with a slight shake of her head, "warm sunshine and cool ocean breezes washing over the islands and coast."

Wheelbarrow Man stopped a moment. He set his vegetable conveyance down and scratched the side of his head. "Then it must be our majestic forests and our bountiful plains," he ventured, before adding with a wink and a mischievous smile at Brasalla, "the great beauty of Abrea."

She returned the smile ever so slightly, as she continued to rebut his assertions, "But Isdal is such a sight to see, with its shimmering, frozen lands that stretch for miles and reflect the sun in such a dazzling way. And one has truly never seen majesty until presented with the volcanoes of Vulgesch that provide obsidian and iron as bountifully as Abrea grows your dirty vegetables."

Jenna smiled and snorted at this, and most of the other children snickered and laughed. None were old enough to truly understand the conversation, but Jenna perceived something passed between the man and Brasalla. She couldn't quite put a finger on it.

"Hmmmm," he mused, "nothing good to say about Raucrud?"

A grimace shot across Brasalla's face. It passed quickly, disappearing as abruptly as it had come, but she felt it somewhere deep in her being. Those watching may have thought bile had risen in her throat and touched the back of her tongue before being swallowed back down. The air almost seemed to darken as a cloud passed in front of the sun overhead. She nearly whispered in reply, "I don't think so."

"Well," he replied, nodding, as he gripped the handles of his wheelbarrow and continued on his way, "I don't know what else to say. Fare thee well."

"Well then," Brasalla drew their attention from the interruption. She squinted when the sun returned as did her smile, slight as if reliving a fond memory. "I'll have to thank him later for coming by. Does anyone else have an answer?"

"Our Dragonknights?" Thom asked.

"But the other nations have Dragonknights as well," Jenna pointed out.

"Yes, but ours are the best," he argued.

"Then why haven't we conquered all of Nahrea?" Brenton blurted in challenge, silencing Thom in a heartbeat.

Jenna disliked Brenton. The same age as she and Thom, he was taller by half a foot, and much thicker, than most boys his age, and he knew it, too. Of course, the whole village knew he fancied himself a warrior. He used his size to bully himself to a leadership position, lording himself over half the village's children, and the other half did their best to avoid his attentions. He had a broken nose that never healed right, and the bumps and blotches of adolescence covered his cheeks and forehead. Last, a shock of red hair adorned his head that didn't seem to match his face for some reason she couldn't explain.

"We could if we wanted to," Thom answered uncertainly, "It's just not our way."

"It will be when I become a Dragonknight and reach the First Circle."

"No, we don't conquer," Thom asserted.

Before the argument could continue further, Brasalla interrupted, "That's correct. Abrea doesn't make war on the other nations for land or money or what they own. We fight to defend ourselves, and that's all. And our Dragonknights are the pinnacle of our warriors, as are the Drakriders of Isdal, Drakkritt of Vulgesch, Dragaval of Azgua and even the Balacav of Raucrud. All-out war amongst the nations would bring death and devastation to Nahrea. None of the nations would allow it to happen.

"Remember your history, Brenton. Some one thousand years ago, we warred with our neighbors. The wars went on for years, decades. The dragons flew about untamed, either ignoring or destroying as they pleased. Maltos, the king of Azgua, and King Fathen of Abrea learned to communicate with the dragons. Our two nations allied, and soon Dragonknights flew above our armies in battle. Isdal retreated to their icy castles in the far north, where our armies and dragons could not follow. The armies of Vulgesch and Raucrud fell before us, but we were betrayed.

"An errant mystic from Azgua struck a deal with our enemies. He taught them the way of the dragons, gave them the powers they needed to speak and negotiate with the beasts of their lands, and the Dragon War began. While the mystic was slain by King Fathen, and his name is lost to history, his legacy lives on in the Desolation at the center of Nahrea. The war culminated there, in one immense and last battle, that left hundreds of miles a barren wasteland. Nothing has lived there in hundreds of years, and nothing ever will."

"We weren't strong enough to win," Brenton decided.

"No, we weren't," Brasalla agreed.

"We will be... one day."

"No, Brenton. There are just over a hundred dragons in the world, twenty five native to the lands of each nation. No weapon forged by man can slay them, and we're not even sure they can slay each other. The destruction they would wreak... That is why the kings all meet at the center of the Desolation. They air out their grievances between the nations, between each other. They negotiate treaties and agreements, use each other as neutral arbiters in their debates and conflicts. We say it is done there because it is neutral ground, and there is nothing left there to destroy should they begin to fight. But the truth is that the great sand dunes and emptiness of the Desolation humble the kings, even the blustery rulers of Vulgesch or the snakes from Raucrud. The Desolation reminds them why we cannot war."

Jenna glanced at Brenton, and she could tell the boy had not been convinced. As Brasalla spoke, his unblinking gaze had hardened, and his face seemed to be set in stone. She thought his chin jutted outward a bit as he clenched his teeth.

"Back to my question, who can tell me why we're blessed to live in Abrea?" Brasalla paused as she glanced around, awaiting an answer, but none seemed forthcoming, either for the lack of one or the fear of being judged incorrect in front of one's peers. She finally answered the question for them, "Because here in Abrea, we are free. We choose our paths through life, whether it means being a warrior, a carpenter, smith, or even farmer of taproots. We have our own homes, our own land, and we choose our own husbands and wives, should we desire one at all. Our lives are ours to do with as we please. What is it, Jenna?"

Jenna started and sat up erect. Her face must have betrayed her thoughts to garner her teacher's attention, and she didn't realize she'd been wearing them so plainly. She remembered her father, and

30

somehow, Brasalla's statement didn't seem to marry with her memory. She shook her head somewhat to indicate that she had nothing to say, but urging looks from the others as well as Brasalla finally forced her to answer, "Is that really true?"

"Of course, it is. Surely, we have laws, but those are meant to protect everyone's freedoms from the rare few who would take advantage of them."

"Yeah, but everyone can't do everything. Girls can't be Dragonknights," Thom interjected enthusiastically. He seemed to be coming to Jenna's aid, offering his support to her question, and yet his words burned like a knife twisting between her ribs.

Brenton whispered amongst several of his cohorts but was silenced by a stabbing glance from Brasalla. She quietly acceded, "That is true, but that is a limit of our gender, as well as the laws of Abrea. It is almost midday, so we should be done for now. Tomorrow, I'll spend more time explaining how the other nations rule their peoples differently, and you will all understand more clearly."

No sooner had she said the words than Brenton and a few others, members of his retinue, shot to their feet and disappeared through the village. Jenna looked around, and with the grumbling in her stomach, decided to head back home. Brasalla's face wore an expression that seemed as if the adult wanted to speak further, but Jenna wanted nothing more than to leave. She started down the dirt track through the village, and Thom fell in right beside her.

"What do you want to do?" Thom asked, his voice full of excitement at the prospect of hours of free time.

"I don't know."

"Do you want to go down to the river and fish?"

"No."

This silenced Thom for a moment, but he quickly recovered with, "How about we go to my house, and you can help me practice my swordsmanship?"

"No."

"Or we can go to your house, and you can show me how to use your mother's bow?"

"No," Jenna replied, more forcefully than she meant, exasperation evident in the way she drew out the response, but it had the desired effect as Thom fell silent.

Jenna took a turn to her right, cutting between two cottages and through a copse of elm trees, a favorite shortcut of hers. She and her mother had moved to the village a few years ago, putting a small home on the very edge of the forest, away from most of the other inhabitants. Jenna had come to know the forest well, but also, she knew every rock, tree, and fencepost in the village itself.

"Uh oh," Thom muttered.

Jenna stopped in her tracks when Brenton and three younger, smaller boys popped out from behind a hedgerow only a few yards away. She eyed him suspiciously, noting the smirk that he made no attempt to hide or subdue. Most of the village children made use of the time-honored tradition of avoidance rather than confrontation with Brenton, and Jenna reacted no differently now. Without betraying her urgency, she continued toward him a few paces, then turned to her left as if that had been her intention the entire time and she obviously wasn't plotting a course away from him.

"Where ya' goin'?" Brenton called after her as she continued away from him. As she wouldn't pay him the complement of looking over her shoulder at him, Jenna heard but didn't see Brenton and his boys scramble into action.

"They're running around the other side," Thom whispered.

"I know."

Sure enough, Brenton and his boys emerged from a tiny alley of sorts created by the rear fences of two houses a few feet in front of Jenna and Thom. "I said, where ya' goin'?"

"Home," Jenna replied.

"Just home, huh? Don't do that. Stay an' talk."

"No," Jenna's tone held the same tone of finality she'd used with Thom a few minutes earlier. She resumed her walk, sidestepping left to go around Brenton, but the boy fleetly adjusted to block her path.

"Oh, you're not leaving yet," he said with a hint of cruelty.

"Just let us go," Thom implored from a few feet behind Jenna, though his voice seemed to waver.

"Not yet. Not until we talk about how Jenna wants to be a Dragonknight," Brenton explained. As he said it, her face hardened, and her eyes narrowed as they stared into his. Her mouth became a thin line as her lips pressed together. "Oh, that's it. You do, don't you? What do you know of Dragonknights? Girls can't join the Brotherhood; they're not strong enough."

Jenna paused, having been reminded for the third time in one day, for some reason that made no sense to her, that she could never be what she believed in her heart was her destiny. She was young, but she was already tired of people saying such things. She answered him, "I am."

Brenton laughed heartily, loudly enough to be heard for a hundred yards or more. As he did so, he leaned back toward the other boys, and they joined in, mocking her with every "ha" and chuckle. A red-hot fire lit in her chest, an anger, an indignance at the boys' scoffing, while a sick feeling began to form in the pit of her stomach. She began to breathe heavily, the air passing noisily in and out through her nose.

Brenton stopped his laughing, leaned toward her marginally and challenged, "Prove it."

"Cut it out, Brenton," Thom called, still safely behind her.

"I said, prove it," Brenton repeated quietly, and when she did nothing, he reached up and slapped her on the cheek. The blow stung the tiniest bit, but it was so fast, so unexpected, that she hardly saw his hand move.

"Hey!" Thom finally moved to action, but as he came forward, the other three boys mobbed him. One tackled his legs, while the other two went for his arms. All four went down in a heap in the grass, and all Thom could do was watch.

A second blow struck Jenna's cheek, this one harder than the last, and the flame in her chest erupted into rage. Jenna had never fought anyone before, and she brought her open hand around in a sweeping arc aimed at Brenton's face. He deftly avoided it and used her momentum to turn her around, entangled his arms in hers and then pushed her down unceremoniously to the ground. The boys began to laugh again. Jenna had seen boys get into fights before, and she matched what she had seen, balling her right hand into a fist. She began to stand on her feet and pulled the fist back to deliver a blow, but Brenton reached out and pushed her back down to the ground. It seemed almost lazy, as if she wasn't even worth a real expenditure of force.

This time, he chuckled and said, "You're not so strong."

But he was, and she hadn't expected that he could handle her so effortlessly. She had no chance; he was so much larger, stronger, and much more practiced, if not faster. Was he right? Was she weak? Tears welled into her eyes, causing the edges of her vision to blur as she looked down at the grass and dirt underneath her hands and fingers. She balled them up again, the green blades of grass between her fingers tearing from the ground.

"Oh, what now?" Brenton asked as he stood right over her.

Jenna lifted the weight of her father's sword once or twice, and her mother had taught her the longbow so that she could hunt. Maybe Jenna didn't really know how to fight anyone, as she never had to, but even at her age she realized one weakness, one tender point all boys had. She pivoted her torso to her left and brought her right fist straight up between Brenton's legs. All the air blew out of the boy in one great rush as he grunted and bent over forward, almost going to his knees.

"You… little…" he breathed between spasms that spread across his groin. Pain blossomed on his reddening face, but so did an unmatched rage. Lightning quick, he jabbed a fist forward right into Jenna's nose, and she went down to the ground in an instant.

"Let's go," he called weakly to his underlings, and he limped away as majestically as he could manage with them in tow.

Jenna lay in the grass, crying into the dirt. Hot blood ran down from her nose, across her lips and threatened to leak into her mouth. She already choked from the sobs. She couldn't even think, didn't know what to think. She was defeated, controlled, unable to fend for herself. She would never be a warrior, much less a Dragonknight like that. Thom settled on the grass next to her, and he laid his hand on her back in as comforting a manner as he knew how.

"Are you okay?" he asked softly, but the only answer he received was her shaking her head from side to side as she sobbed. He sighed, "I'm sorry. I'm sorry I didn't help. Sorry I couldn't help."

She swallowed her sobs then, the anger returning to burn out the misery. She rubbed her eyes with one hand as she sat up, pushing the tears away as she wiped her nose on her other arm, smearing blood all across it and her face. Jenna moved away from him, shaking his hand from her and looking at him with revulsion.

"I didn't ask for help," she sneered.

"I know, but…"

"But nothing. Don't you ever help me," she spat, and she climbed to her feet. She began to walk away toward home, leaving him bewildered on the ground behind her, when she came face to chest with Brasalla.

"A warrior knows when they need help," said the one-armed woman. Jenna didn't answer, didn't know how to answer such a statement, she just stared back pridefully as the blood dripped down across her lips. The teacher continued, "You have fire, Little Dear. I know who you are, who your father was. Regardless of his crimes, I mourned him."

Jenna set her jaw defiantly, almost grinding her teeth at the red hot flame that suddenly rebirthed in her chest. The tears pushed back into her eyes, and she willed them not to fall even as the bleariness threatened to overwhelm her vision. The mention of her father, and even the mere suggestion of his crimes, always wrought such within her. She replied, "Don't ever talk about him like that."

Brasalla smiled, that fleeting, enigmatic smile she sometimes showed for a second before it vanished as abruptly, and she kneeled down enough so her face would be level with Jenna's. "There it is again," the one-armed woman said with a knowing smile, "that fire. Tell me, Little Dear, are you going to fight everyone, every time even the smallest slight is paid your way?"

"If I have to."

"Fire is powerful, Little Dear, but it is not enough. Untamed it is destructive, dangerous even to itself. The smith uses fire, forces it with control and discipline to make steel, but when a fire breaks out in the forest, it must be contained quickly. Otherwise, it will burn and burn and burn until there is nothing left, and then even the fire itself dies. I can teach you discipline; I can teach you to fight and to use that fire to temper yourself into steel."

"You?" Jenna virtually snarled, her anger and indignation still driving her as blood began to trickle from her nose again, mixed with snot and tears that she could no longer restrain. "What do you know of fighting?"

Brasalla's face hardened and she said, "Little Dear, you are bright, but you need to look beyond what you see. The hearts and pasts of those before you are often different from what they show." With a pause, she added, "Do you think I lost this arm in a teaching accident? I was once a Protectress of the Second Circle. I can train you if you'll allow yourself to learn."

Jenna could say nothing; she didn't trust herself to speak for fear that she wouldn't be able to say a coherent word. She gazed down at the ground for a moment and ran the back of her hand across her mouth and left cheek. She then looked into the kind eyes of Brasalla and wordlessly nodded.

"Very well. Let me take you to my home to clean you up. Can't have you going home like that," Brasalla said, wrapping one arm around the girl to lead her back toward the village center. She added over her shoulder, "Go home, Thom."

Jenna stopped and looked up at Brasalla as a realization hit her. "You saw the whole thing, didn't you?"

The woman nodded and added, "Yes."

"Most grownups would have stopped it," Jenna half accused.

"Yes, they would have," Brasalla agreed, "but our greatest lessons in life come from our failures not our successes."

"What lesson?" Jenna asked, again furiously holding back tears.

Brasalla placed a caring hand on the young girl's shoulder and answered, "You can't win a fair fight against a more powerful opponent – someone who's bigger, stronger, and more experienced than you. You have to find another way to win. Fair fights are for suckers."

"So, like when I punched him in the balls?"

A wild grin broke across Brasalla's face, and her eyes lit up for a moment as she said, "Yeah, that was a good shot."

Less than enjoyable at the time, the memory of that day always brought Jenna a satisfied smile. It was the start of years and years of hard training with a sword. For obvious reasons, her mentor could only do so much when it came to the use of a longbow, instructing rather than showing, and besides, Jenna's mother taught her the use of the bow since she was even smaller and younger. Over the weeks, months, years that followed, hard callouses formed on Jenna's hands, and she learned how to use her smaller stature and natural quickness to avoid more than parry. While other children ran to play as part of one game or another, she attacked marked courses through the forest involving muddy ridges, steep inclines, and crossed narrow logs felled across streams, their decaying bark slick with moss.

Strength built in her limbs, wiry sinews hidden beneath the common wool tunics and trousers she wore.

The clothes she explicitly chose that were either for boys or slightly too large for her frame to hide her development, both muscular and feminine, would serve her well in what was to come, just as they had caused the roving eyes of boys about her age to stare at other girls. With a little dirt smeared on her face, easy enough to do on the road, and her bobbed hair pushed up under a common cap, Jenna was sure she could pass for a somewhat younger boy if no one paid her too much attention.

To this end, she turned off the road as soon as the sun rose the first morning, choosing instead to make her way through the lower wooded areas of Abrea's forests. She knew this type of terrain well, and her soft leather boots stepped across holes filled deceptively with decrepit leaves or avoided disguised tree roots that reached out to grab the unwary. Jenna travelled as speedily through the woods as others may on the road, which she knew always wound north only a few hundred yards to her right, and it kept her away from the curious looks and questioning conversation of fellow travelers, of which there would be many the closer she drew to Highton. She wanted no company, except that of other woodland creatures, which included the many chittering squirrels and songbirds as they sang their high pitched melodious tunes to any who cared to listen.

Chapter 3

Arrival at Highton

Jenna arose from her bedroll in the woods away from prying eyes. The first rays of sunlight struggled to pierce the green canopy overhead, warming the tops of the trees enough to cause a hint of steamy fog as dew burned off the leaves. She looked about as she stretched, confident that she had stayed far enough into the woods to avoid most of those traveling to the Great Tree. She figured she had an hour or so before the boys gathered for the trials, more than enough time to make her way to the Trial Grounds.

Forcing herself to a sitting position, Jenna stretched to ease the kinks out of her muscles and joints, relieving the stress they endured from another night's sleep on the forest floor. Of course, she had slept outdoors many times, and sometimes for up to a week, but the night had been unusually chilly, the ground here colder and harder than a mossy bed she may have ordinarily chosen.

She reached into her pack and retrieved a bit of hardtack. She chewed absently, staring out into the forest at nothing in particular as the early morning birds chirped overhead. Her mind wandered to home, and doubts and questions began to fill her thoughts. Really though, what was she doing? This is stupid. A woman has never been a Dragonknight; why did she think she was so special? If a fierce woman such as Brasalla couldn't do it, why could she? What of Mother or Brasalla? Were they searching for her? With her mother's skills, they would have been able to track her by now, despite Jenna's head start. Why haven't they tried to take her home yet?

She stopped chewing as her jaw hardened with resolve, and Jenna pushed these thoughts out of her mind. She stood and began to roll up her bed into a tight cylinder of wool and fur. Tightening thongs around it to hold its shape, she crammed it into a plain, brown leather pack. Normally, Jenna would be inclined to find a small stream or creek to wash away some of the dirt, grit, and smell from travelling, but she wished to waste no time. Also, the idea that prying eyes might spot her and betray her gender to others at the Great Tree made the thought impossible.

Strapping on a belt, heavy with her father's Vulgeschi steel longsword in its plain, brown shagreen sheath, she struggled for a few minutes as she adjusted the angle at which it hung as the sword's point tended to drag the ground due to the length of the blade. Jenna considered the longbow and the quiver full of arrows. Opting to carry the bow, she slung the quiver diagonally across her back so she could reach back with her right hand and grasp the fletching as she had so many times. The quiver's strap crossed her chest in a certain way, but she had made sure to conceal the obvious signs of her femininity. Last, she shouldered her heavy pack, the leather strap pulling backward against her left shoulder as she parted the brush in search of the road.

But she never found it. Within minutes she walked among other travelers, many of whom poured water on smoldering campfires, packed up supplies into packs or knapsacks or practiced with swords and bows. She walked through camps consisting of families, or even several families, who traveled to Highton to watch their sons and brothers compete for one of the greatest honors in all of Abrea. Jenna needn't have found the road; she merely followed the ever increasing quantity of those who clearly had no home in Highton until she found the city itself.

Jenna had never been to Highton, and when she finally pressed her way through the mass of her fellow transients, she stopped and gaped in awe at the marvelous sight. Dozens of trees, none less than ten feet thick, towered a hundred feet in the air above her, and that was where Highton was located. Bridges, ropes, lanes, and avenues crisscrossed overhead, connecting all the trees of Highton, and the city's homes, inns and taverns, markets, and even workshops for smiths and other artisans were part of these connections. Highton had at least four distinct levels, as far as Jenna could tell, though she had no idea of the significance of each or what one had to offer over the other. Iron protected torches provided light throughout the city as the forest's canopy tended to block out much of the sunlight, and ladders of wood and rope allowed access to Highton from the ground. In one place, and she was sure there were more, Jenna spied an ingenious contraption featuring a wooden platform upon which sat a wagon laden with vegetables lifted by a series of gears, ropes, and pulleys from above.

In the center of Highton stood the Great Tree, the tallest and thickest of them all by far, being at least fifty feet taller than the next and perhaps eighty feet across. Everyone knew that King Rendor's palace was at the top of that tree, though try as she might, Jenna could not see it past the rest of the city. The Dragonknights also had their quarters and meeting rooms there, though on lower levels somewhere perhaps even within that massive tree. The dragons themselves stayed on the ground on the far side of Highton from where Jenna now stood. She could not see them for the intervening trees and the mass of people that roamed the area, but she fancied that she heard their deep bellows breathing somewhere beyond all the activity.

Someone bumped into her from behind, almost causing her to stumble, and Jenna immediately restrained her angry impulse. After all, she was the one standing in the middle of dozens of people moving about the area. She turned around toward whomever had jostled her, beholding an aged woman with a bent back and dirty, gray hair. "Excuse me," Jenna offered politely.

"New to Highton, are ya'?" the woman asked, her voice sounding gravelly and unhealthy. "You can always tell by the way they stop and gawk."

"Could you tell me where the Trial Grounds are?" Jenna asked, adding an edge to her voice that she hoped disguised its softness.

"They're here under Highton. You're standin' in 'em. Here for that, are ya'? Well, you had best hurry up and enter yer name on the registers," the woman said with a point to the west, "but it'll do you no good. My grandson is the strongest, and yer as small as a girl."

Before she had gotten this out, Jenna had already curtly thanked her and began moving away. The woman continued to shout at her turned back about her grandson and the rudeness of young people, but Jenna paid it no heed as she walked further into the area, following the general flow of the crowd of boys and young men. She caught glimpses of large areas being roped off, one of which was being set up as a shooting range complete with circular targets at one end. Jousting lanes separated by short fences and ropes were to the east, sending a jolt of fear through Jenna. She had trained so little on horseback.

The crowd grew louder here as the boys, none older than twenty years of age as was the limit for trials to become a Dragonknight, jabbered and shouted at one another. Some embraced or clasped each other's arms, friends or comrades of a sort, but others guffawed at such displays and gloated about their own skills. A dull roar of voices trying to be heard by ears right next to them continued to rise, and a man in a fine black cloak and common but clean garb stood upon a crate calling out to make his voice audible over the din, "This way to register. All wishing to take part in the trials, this way!"

Jenna wasn't sure how much more she could stand, for it wasn't just the noise that assaulted her ears, but also the smell. She had found that young men and boys started to change as early as twelve, and as their voices both cracked and grew deeper and their bodies grew stronger, they also began to smell most obnoxiously. It didn't help that few of them understood the need for or value of bathing. But also, Jenna keenly realized that the longer she stood amongst large numbers of eyes, the more likely it was that someone may spot her or reveal her secret. That would not do, so she endeavored to keep her eyes straight forward and avoid contact with any of the others as they took halting steps forward in the undulating mass that began to coalesce into single file lines.

An hour or more had passed, and Jenna's line hadn't moved more than perhaps thirty feet. She passed the time by counting the heads of boys in front of her but gave up when she surpassed three hundred. Every boy in Abrea must have come for the Trials, and why not? She couldn't blame them; after all, she was here after being told her entire life that girls couldn't be the only thing she ever dreamed of being. As she stepped forward again, excitement ran up her spine in a shock as she could see the end of the line if she craned her neck – a series of makeshift tables set end to end at which sat men and women, each with a long scroll, pen, and ink set before them. She was only six away!

The boy, man really, at the front of her line righted himself from leaning over the table to write something on the scroll before him. The unruly, bright red hair caught Jenna's attention, and she shrunk away

44

as the young man turned. She hadn't seen him in four or five years, not since he had left her village to go apprentice with a smith in another town, but Brenton's pockmarked face with its crooked nose was immediately recognizable. He was even taller than before, now well over six feet, and she could see thick muscles cording their way under his ill-fitting clothes. She thought he could pick her up by the neck with one arm, and Jenna cast her eyes downward to make certain she didn't draw his attention. Brenton walked past her without a second glance and joined hundreds of others in waiting.

She stepped forward again. Within minutes, she was next in line, watching impassively at a boy of no more than twelve as he leaned over the table and scratched something onto the registrar's scroll. Sweat began to bead on her brow, and she felt as if she could no longer stand still. Would the man behind the table have a keen eye and know she was a girl? What if he asked her where she was from? What should she say? What about her name? Her face flushed red as she realized she hadn't picked a boy's name to go by. She could just leave now. Step out of line and go home; no one would be the wiser.

She might have done it, too, except for the sudden deep drums that sounded well above the gathering cacophony below Highton. All craned their necks to look upward, simultaneously ceasing most of the chatter and noise on the ground. With the attention of those below gained, the drums Jenna could not locate sounded one more time, reverberating through the air and her guts. A host of wind instruments of various pitches joined the vanishing drums, making it clear to everyone in and below Highton that an announcement was to be made and causing quiet whispers to rumble through the crowds. A lift similar to, though much smaller than the one she saw earlier came into view, lowered from one of the higher levels of the city, and as it dropped below the lowest level of Highton and came to a halt some twenty feet above the assembled hundreds or even thousands of Abrea's people, all sound came to a halt.

Jenna had never seen King Rendor in her life, as he tended only to visit Abrea's larger cities, and she had never been to Highton. But the appearance of this man left no doubt as to his station. She was unsure as to his height, for he seemed to tower over everyone in a way that may have been an illusion as he hovered so, but he was surely tall. He wore blackened boiled leather armor about his torso and legs, embedded with metal rings the dusky hue of Vulgeschi steel. He stood with an upright longbow in his right hand almost as if it were a staff, and it was almost as tall as he. A huge sword hilt, long enough for three or four of her hands if she had so many, extended from behind his left shoulder. A long, but neat, brown beard with a shocking stripe of gray right of his chin hung down to his sternum with matching hair that fell past his shoulders as it bled into a black cloak of heavy furs. At this distance, she could see few details of his face, but it was the gilt wooden circlet on his head, crafted from the highest bough of the Great Tree so they were taught, that completed his identity.

"I see you," the king called forth, his deep voice booming across the grounds, "all of you, my good people of Abrea. You have come to Highton from across my kingdom due to a time of grief, to help the Dragonknights mourn the passing of a great man, a Dragonknight. He loved this kingdom, he loved you all, and I loved him as a brother. Tonight, we will lay him to rest in his place below the Great Tree. All of you, my wonderful people, are welcome to attend and pay your respects," King Rendor ended this almost softly, with his eyes cast downward at his feet.

After a brief pause, a silence that no one would dare break, the king continued in a more uplifted tone,

"But tomorrow we celebrate Sir Garond as all boys and men of Abrea from twelve to twenty contest with each other for the good Sir Garond's seat in the Second Circle among the Dragonknights. Make no mistake, the Trials will not be easy – they will test your strength, your abilities with both sword and bow, and your will, among other things. The Trials are not for the faint of heart, the weak, or those who are not willing to do whatever is necessary to succeed, but the reward is the greatest curse I could ever bestow on anyone. The *one* who prevails will live the rest of his days in servitude to Abrea, spending every minute of his life studying, training, and learning the ways of the dragons. Until his life ends, he will spend it in service to me or my successor and to the kingdom of Abrea. He will know no wealth, except that of knowledge. He will know no love, except that of his Brethren. And he will know that any day he could be called to die upon the back of his dragon for his nation. This is the prize that one among you, sons of Abrea, will claim within days.

"Enjoy the rest of this fine weather day, prepare yourselves and mourn with the Brotherhood and all of Abrea tonight. Tomorrow, the Trials begin."

As he uttered these last words, his lift began to rise again, passing the lowest level of Highton amidst a creaking of ropes and a clattering of gears, and it was then that Jenna spotted the rest of the Dragonknights assembled on the walkways of the city. The nineteen of the Second Circle stood a level below their four lords of the First Circle. The quiet reverence turned to exhaled awe as the rest of the crowd also saw the Brotherhood, and as the king continued to travel upward out of sight, they returned to the tasks at hand. Boys in line began to turn back to face the registrars, and Jenna suddenly spotted an old friend as he turned to face her.

"Next. You boy, next!" called an impatient voice behind her, and Jenna turned to face the registrar, praying to the spirit of her father that Thom hadn't seen or recognized her. As she stepped forward to the rickety, makeshift table and the long scroll upon it, the unkempt bearded man asked, "Your name, boy?"

"Timbre," Jenna answered without a second thought.

"Can you write?"

She almost scoffed indignantly as she replied, "Of course, I can."

"Then write," he grumbled, forcing a quill into her hand about to drip with fresh ink. "And your age."

She leaned over the scroll, surprised at the number of names already written on the parchment. She paused a moment to look, finding the name of Brenton some seven above, confirming that the red-haired young man was in fact who she believed. At the sound of a sigh from the little man on the other side of the table, Jenna scrawled the name Timbre just below the last boy's name, though she made sure to angle the letters a bit, hoping the writing appeared more hurried as was often the case with boys' penmanship. Next to that, she almost added her real age of twenty, but then wrote sixteen after thinking of the woman she'd crossed paths with earlier.

The gruff man handed her a blue bit of cloth and said, "Tie it around your right arm. Wear it at all times. Yer blue one hundred forty two. Next!"

Jenna stepped to the side as she struggled to tie the cloth about her arm before deciding she'd do so once out of the press of all the boys in line. She turned to leave, heading away from the lines toward more open air where perhaps she could breathe a bit again, but she didn't go far before a hand shot out to grab a loose bit of her sleeve. She met the eyes of Thom as she halted, and her hard gaze alone made him release her so she could stalk off in quiet annoyance.

Seeing Thom so unexpectedly brought back a memory of one particular day some ten years ago. Perhaps, she mused, the encounter should have stirred up feelings of bitterness and resentment, and the memory of that day he left her and the village, she thought forever. Strangely, it was the day on the fence that came to mind.

Sunlight filtered down through the trees overhead, and a light breeze came in from the east, causing Jenna's hair to wave about her as she walked. The village had awoken at dawn, as it always did, the people attending their various duties and chores. Some smiled at her as she carelessly flitted about the dirt roads and paths toward the benches at which she and the other children met for learning, but most ignored her. Thom appeared from her left, from between two houses and fell into step with her.

"What do you think she'll talk about today?" he asked.

"I don't know."

"I hope it's over fast. I want to get back to my sword training."

"Swordsmanship," Jenna mumbled as she leaned over to pick a small orange flower, really nothing more than a weed that had somehow found a way to root in the well-traveled path.

"Huh?"

"It's called swordsmanship or fencing," she repeated.

"What difference does it make?"

"None, I guess. You really should spend more time on archery," she chided. She avoided looking at him, but she could feel that his eyes hadn't left her face since he first spoke to her.

"Bows," Thom almost guffawed, "Bows are a girl's weapon. A man wields a sword."

"You're not a man."

"I am, too!" he squealed indignantly, and he promptly dropped both the volume and register of his voice. "Well, I will be soon, but you'll always be a girl."

"True," she conceded with a purse of her lips, "a girl who can put an arrow between your eyes at a hundred yards. What good would your sword be then?"

This silenced Thom for a moment as he searched his ten year old brain for a retort of some kind, some grand answer that would again make the sword mightier than the bow. He failed to notice that Jenna no longer walked alongside him. He had continued another fifteen feet or so before he realized it, and he turned to hurl his comeback at her, "Your bow won't matter when I'm five hundred feet in the air on the back of my dragon!"

She ignored him. In fact, it seemed that she had lost all interest in the conversation, ignorant of Thom's continued existence. Instead, Jenna stood staring at the picket fence around Old Grable's home and meager yard. For years, the ancient man had grumbled, complained, and fussed at the children of the village as they passed his home every day to learn, and finally he grew tired of them stepping on his grass, picking his flowers or trampling his vegetables. The fact was none of these things ever happened, but in Grable's mind, they were the most important of transgressions, so he erected a wooden picket fence. It stood some six feet tall, more than enough to keep out children or even the prying eyes of all but the tallest of men. Each picket had been sharpened to a point, much like the protective walls of the villages near Vulgesch, ostensibly to keep birds from perching atop them. Though the birds didn't seem to mind, and the skewers had dulled over time.

"What are you doing?" Thom called to her. "We're gonna be late."

The corners of Jenna's mouth turned upward mischievously as a notion formed in her mind. She kicked off her sandals, letting her feet and toes feel the dirt underneath. She reached down and picked them up with her left hand as she considered the fence.

"Come on!" Thom almost whined, before he shrugged and started to turn away.

Jenna took several large strides, almost reaching a full run in a few steps, and she leapt upward to seize the point of one of the pickets with her right hand. Her right arm was always stronger than the left, as it was the one with which the drew her bowstring, and she grunted as she pulled herself up, her bare feet scrambling for purchase against the smooth wood planks. Splinters found ways to drive through the skin on the bottoms of her feet, thick from always traveling the forest and the trees barefoot when her mother wasn't looking, but she ignored these painful distractions, finding her way to perch at the front corner of the fence, looking down on Thom below and heedless of the villagers gaping open mouthed.

She held her arms out to either side to balance her as she unfolded her legs to stand atop the pickets' points, though the weight was uneven due to the shoes in her left hand. She tipped that way for a moment, then over corrected and tipped to the right before steadying herself with a self-appreciating smile. Jenna began to walk forward, traversing the top of the fence as if it were a tightrope.

"What are you doing?" Thom repeated.

"Balancing," she replied as if it were the most obvious of answers. She crossed more than ten feet, having almost come up even to him on the path below. "Balance is important to ride dragons."

"You can't be a Dragonknight," Thom replied with a furrowed brow and a slight shake of his head, to which Jenna stopped her approach. "You're a girl."

"Hey!" shouted a voice from Jenna's left, a voice like rocks being ground together. She glanced over to her left and saw Old Grable standing in the doorway to his house. "What in damnation?!" he called as she tumbled off the fence to her right.

"Watch out!" was all Thom could say before she slammed into him from above, and they went down in a heap of arms and legs. Choking dust kicked up from the path, and a couple of the villagers charged to the children's aid, calling "Oh my!" and "Are you all right?"

Laughing, Jenna jumped to her feet, her shoes lost and forgotten somewhere in Grable's yard. She grabbed Thom by an arm with both hands and strained backward for leverage. "Come on, stand up!" she ordered him as he found his feet and began to stand. Thom joined in the near hysterical laughter as they ran off up the road, leaving behind a barking old man, bewildered villagers, and some who shook their heads at the whims of children.

Chapter 4

A Confrontation With an Old Friend

After accepting a small amount of bread and cheese being handed to contestants of the Trials, Jenna made her way away from the thousands of competitors and spectators. The longer she stayed amongst them, the more uncomfortable in her own skin she began to feel. She wanted to squirm as eyes stopped on her face with wondering squints and sometimes roamed across her. Perhaps it was all in her mind, her own anxiety at being discovered before she had the chance to prove that she could join the Brotherhood of Dragonknights.

She sat cross legged, alone in the woods, perhaps two hundred yards from the Trial Grounds, while a thousand thoughts and questions ran through her mind. She couldn't even consider one before another came to the forefront. Would they change the name? Could it continue to be a Brotherhood? She certainly wouldn't press the matter; they could call it whatever they wanted if she had what she knew was hers. If she didn't win, she could accept that she wasn't the best. But despite what the law said, despite the belief that women couldn't form the Dragonlink, if she passed or won every Trial, they must give her the prize. Mustn't they?

As she lost herself in such ruminations, she reached to her head to scratch an itch that annoyed her from somewhere under her somewhat pilfered cap. In so doing, she let some of her sandy brown hair down across her face before swearing and brushing it backward and under the cap again. Unaware, she hadn't heard the brush off to her right separate and the soft footstep of someone coming close.

"I knew it was you," called a voice. It was deeper than she remembered, though not quite as deep as the bass she heard rumble in other men's voices.

Jenna did not turn toward the voice, and she even turned her face away toward her father's sword, *her* sword, as it lay on her spread out bedroll. She would not let the weapon touch the ground. Ever. She asked with an almost disdainful sigh, "What are you doing here, Thom?"

"No, the question is what are *you* doing here?" His tone was not what she expected – it contained more concern than accusation, and he moved around to stand right in front of her, though her face still pointed down and away from him. "Your father's sword? And your mother's longbow? Does she know what you're up to?"

"None of your concern."

"How can you say that?" Thom asked, squatting down. "We're friends. We've known each other since we were little."

At this she turned her face toward him, as he shifted to plant one knee on the ground while leaning on the other. As she looked over him, she realized how much he had grown since she had last seen him those years ago. He was taller than she remembered, over six feet and at least six inches taller than she. His frame had widened from either growth, training, or perhaps both. He wore a tunic of thick padded cloth dotted with copper rivets, and she could tell that a fit, muscular torso had begun to build underneath it. His face had thinned somewhat, revealing a strong chin and razor jawline that was not unattractive with his unruly, short blond hair, passed to him by his grandmother whom Jenna had heard was from Isdal to the north.

He shifted, and Jenna ripped her eyes away with a blush, realizing she was staring.

54

"We *were* friends. You left. Remember?" she accused, returning a hard gaze to his eyes.

"That's not fair. I couldn't pass it up. My father worked hard to get me the chance to serve Sir Garond's house. To serve a Dragonknight, to train with his men-at-arms, to see how he lives? I joined the Northern Cavalry, under the command of Sir Garond himself. Wouldn't you have done the same?"

"I wouldn't have been offered that chance," she replied, accusation and a hint of petulance plain in her voice. "So now here you are, at the Trials for his seat in the Second Circle."

"As are you." Thom's voice had changed, acquired an edge to indicate he grew tired of her implications. "I have done nothing wrong. I am here by right, but you... What do you hope to accomplish here? Women, girls, can't be Dragonknights. It has been that way for hundreds of years. What do you think will happen if they find out? At the least, you'll be kicked out and sent home. At worst? I don't know."

"Who's gonna' tell them?" Jenna fired at him, her cold gaze again meeting his eyes as her words pierced him like a poisoned arrow. "You?"

Thom tilted his head for a moment, anger flashing across his face and through his blue eyes for just a second before it was gone. He blew air out of his nose in a sort of hurried sigh, and he stood to his feet. He walked the way he'd come, leaving Jenna's field of vision as she did not turn her head to follow him with her eyes. At the last moment, he stopped and said, "You know, I'd always wished that maybe you'd visit me in Sir Garond's house at some point, but you never came. And I couldn't leave. I'm not going to rat you out. Like I said, we're friends, but I will promise you one thing. We both wear blue armbands, which means we might face each other in one of the Trials. If that happens, I won't hold back. I will win."

"Good luck with that," Jenna almost mumbled, the words hanging dead in the air as he headed back through the shrubs for Highton.

Chapter 5

Day One, Archery

She realized she dreamt, of course, as it was a dream that Jenna had come to have over and over and over ever since she was a little girl. The dream often varied a bit sometimes, perhaps reflecting her mood regarding a day's happenings, but the setting and generalities were always the same. She knew herself to be little, maybe as young as five and wearing but a linen sleeping gown. She again lived in her old home, the one her father used to come to see her and Mother, his giant dragon always curled up in a ball like an enormous housecat in the yard behind the house. She lay in darkness, the middle of the night in summer. The air had cooled, and the house's windows were unshuttered to allow through a pleasant breeze. The moon was but a sliver in the sky overhead, shedding but scant light across the forest and into Jenna's home. She listened to the sounds of the house and the forest beyond the clearing – an owl hooting in the distance, deer moving peacefully through the woods, and a rodent of some kind scratching at the ground outside her window.

But what drew Jenna's attention was the sounds of the dragon, and she stood from her bed to gaze at him through the open window. Titan, as her father had called him, was little more than a voluminous mass of shadow in so little light, but if she moved just right, she could catch a glimmer reflecting off his deep green scales. His nostrils, each as big as her face at least, whistled just audibly as he exhaled through them, followed by an immense inhalation of air like that of a thousand smith's bellows all at once. He was glorious.

Jenna turned toward her door and very nearly left her room to go outside by way of the door in the house's main room. She stopped for fear of waking her parents, so she instead turned back to the window. She placed her palms flat on the edge of the frame, pushing down while hopping upward in one motion to sit backward on the right side of the windowsill. In an oft practiced maneuver, Jenna then rotated to her right and pulled her legs up, while folding them to squeeze through the window and then letting them dangle outside the window as she completed the turn to look. A slight duck of her head, followed by a gentle, controlled slide on her bottom off the window's edge, and her feet lightly touched the ground outside her bedroom.

Titan slept two dozen paces away, and the air moved around her as he breathed peacefully in and out, the currents substantially warmer than the cool night air and tinged with an unpleasant stench likely from his last meal. Barefoot in dew moistened grass, a feeling that she enjoyed to this day, Jenna padded softly over to the dragon. She made almost no noise at all, and the dragon showed no signs that she had broken his repose.

She saw him more clearly as she approached, holding her hand out before her to touch the dragon as she closed the distance. Like all of the dragons of Abrea, Titan's scales were of a deep green, even deeper than the green of the forests and more like the darkest of emeralds. He had expansive wings that now shone black as night but daylight would reveal to be a dark, leathery brown, and these were daintily folded into his back. The myths told them Abrea's dragons naturally protected their wings when they weren't in use, as they were the only one of the five dragon breeds born without them. He had the thinner body, neck, and tail of his kind, especially when compared to the giant brutes of

Vulgesch, depicting a sort of elegance, grace, and agility not seen in the dragons of the south. His head, shaped somewhat like a dog's with a rounded forehead and long, narrow snout, lay comfortably atop two paws folded over one another. One such paw could crush her small child's frame, and no doubt Titan could swallow her whole.

And yet with such thoughts in the back of her mind, Jenna came close to the dragon, wishing nothing more than to lay a hand upon him. She had never come this close to him without her father present, standing but two feet away from the creature, her open, upright hand hovering only inches from the scales of his face. She held there for an unfathomable amount of time before she finally broke from the trance, steeled herself, and laid her open palm about midway down the right side of his snout.

Titan's scales were shockingly cool; she didn't know why, but she expected them to be burning hot to the touch, even though fire was the domain of the dragons from the south. The feeling sent a shiver up her arm and down her spine, through every inch of her body and even to the tip of each individual finger and toe. Gooseflesh rose on her arms, and her hair may have stood on end if not for the weight of its length down past her shoulders. She held the pose for minutes at least, enjoying the sensation, a fulfilling wonderment that washed over her as she touched the dragon.

And then Titan's left eyelid lifted lazily, revealing a white orb with a brown iris that focused, dilated, and focused again as it took in this tiny being that stood only a few feet from the eye itself. The dragon did not move as it regarded her quietly, and as she gazed longingly into that one eye, she realized that the iris was not brown, but rather hazel with hints of green at the edges that merged into gold near a slit shaped pupil.

"Hello, Titan," Jenna said in a soft, hushed tone, and her hand still gently pressed against his snout.

The dragon did not answer, and yet as she looked into that eye, she felt as if an answer should have been forthcoming. She could see something glint there, an intelligence that willed itself to the surface, powerful and yet gentle, a force of nature yet restrained. She wanted nothing more than to hear this incredible creature's thoughts, for she felt so certain that he had his own, but nothing issued from the dragon. Her sense of his intelligence, of his nature, disappeared as quickly as it had come as he closed his eye again and began to snore.

She dropped her palm from the dragon as her father's voice called urgently from behind her.

Jenna awoke to the sound of Highton's drums, their deep bass thrumming through the air and trees around the city. The sun began to rise over the horizon, the drummers announcing that to all around Highton to make sure they rise and ready themselves for what the day would bring. She wasted no time getting herself together and making her way towards the deep and constant tattoo. Underneath the city, feasting tables had been set out all over the forest floor, no doubt left from last night's mourning of Sir Garond, but now hundreds, perhaps thousands, of people milled about as cookfires provided a breakfast for the masses much like they would a marching army.

Jenna partook, but carefully avoided as many people as she could, choosing to eat alone behind one of the many trees that held Highton aloft. The food, though relatively plain, was hardy enough – two pieces of lightly charred bread, a few slices of ham, a hunk of cheese and a small wooden bowl of what she thought passed for porridge. Having eaten hardtack, nuts, berries, and whatever else she could easily find in the forest, she'd built quite an appetite and tore into her breakfast in a way that Mother would have found most distasteful. It didn't matter. She'd seen men eat much the same way many times, and she was supposed to be one after all. After returning the bowl, she found a relatively quiet place to sit and wait.

The sun was almost halfway to its zenith when the drums began again, calling for attention. A man was lowered from the lift that carried King Rendor on the previous day, and Jenna recognized him as the rider that had brought news of Sir Garond's death. He hung over the assembly of boys and men, many with family members, friends, or even wives with them, until not a voice dared to whisper. At a wave of his hand, the drummers above ceased their pounding.

"Welcome, sons of Abrea, to the Trials!" he exclaimed with arms that rose to the heavens as he spoke. The crowd broke into cheers, whoops, and hollers as almost everyone bellowed their excitement. Jenna did no such thing, suddenly wondering if breakfast was such a great idea after all. Perhaps she ate too fast, or maybe it was nervous anxiety, but she was fairly certain she was about to be sick. The man lowered his arms and held out his hands for silence.

He continued as all settled, "Today and tomorrow, you will be tasked with displaying your skills in combat. Your strength, agility, and endurance shall be tested by four different Trials. You will be judged by the Dragonknights, the Brotherhood awarding points in each test by your performance. Failure at one does not necessarily preclude participation in the others. In some tests, you will compete directly with other members in your color group, whereas in others, you will be judged individually. At the conclusion of these Trials tomorrow, only the top fifty participants will be allowed to continue.

"The Trials will begin in twenty minutes. Each group is to assemble at the following Trial Ground. Red – Duels. Green – Horsemanship. Blue – Archery. Yellow – Gauntlet. Good luck, sons of Abrea!"

Jenna smiled despite herself as the announcer was lifted back up to Highton. She couldn't have asked for better luck to start the Trials, and the roiling motion in her stomach began to abate as she watched the crowds separate and begin to congeal into their color groups. She could be one of the first to shoot, using her skills to establish dominance early. She made her way to the shooting range ahead of most of the boys wearing blue armbands and her heart leapt at what she saw; she couldn't have asked for a more perfect opportunity.

She filed in behind twenty or so others, ropes and stakes creating a single file line that went left some twenty paces before turning hard on itself and running back the other way. The line did this some six or seven times before an exit that allowed access to ten marked standing positions, a target of painted hay a mere thirty or so yards off. Jenna noted the slight breeze blowing from the northeast, measured with her breath how the sun warmed the air in the shade below Highton, and she knew that this shot would be all too easy. How many attempts would they receive? She only needed one; after all, there was no way to beat a bullseye.

As the line filled up behind her, Jenna became aware of spectators above, leaning against and over the railings to call out to their favorites, most likely their sons and brothers, maybe even young husbands. As she glanced over them, she noted at least four Dragonknights of the Second Circle spread throughout the area overlooking the shooting range, each of them holding a scroll in one hand.

She brought her eyes back down and started as she realized that another Dragonknight stood at the head of her line, preventing the contestants from approaching the shooting line. He may have been the tallest man she had ever seen at perhaps seven feet in height. He held a longbow almost like a staff and wore the black leather so common to the Brotherhood with a hooded cape. Sigils across his armor and hood indicated his seat among the First Circle – one of only four besides King Rendor – and most of his features were hidden except for the oiled, black beard that hung from his chin and the glinting in his eyes as he appraised those in line. He could only be Sir Tullus, a Dragonknight for over thirty years and legendary not just for his giantlike height, and Jenna turned to face straight ahead, hoping not to be scrutinized too closely.

An amazing, deep voice boomed from beneath the hood, as the Dragonknight stood back away from the throng of boys, "As you may have surmised, I am Sir Tullus of the First Circle. Here we shall test your skills with a bow, one of the most important weapons to a Dragonknight."

He moved so quickly that Jenna wasn't sure that she hadn't blinked, as Tullus spun while drawing an arrow from his quiver, set his feet, nocked the arrow and fired. The arrow streaked, whistling as it cut the air and impaled a yellow songbird that had been flying overhead some hundred yards away. A small girl ran out from somewhere behind the trees, picking the dead bird up by the arrow's shaft and holding it aloft for all to see. A reverential hush came over everyone present.

Tullus turned back to them and continued, "That shot was nothing. On the back of the dragon, such a shot is much more difficult, and you will need to make every single arrow find its mark without fail. Your Trial is simple. You will take one of the ten positions on this firing line. A target is just ahead. When I call your number, fire your shot. You will each receive three. You will be judged not only on accuracy, but also the strength and speed of your arrow. Know one thing – fail to hit a target all three times, and you are eliminated from the Trials completely."

This last caused a bit of a stirring, both amongst the Trial participants and those watching up above. Apparently, if one couldn't show the most basic skill in archery, the Brotherhood didn't consider that boy worthy of consideration at all. Jenna shrugged it off. She'd practiced with the longbow every day since her childhood scuffle with Brenton and quite a bit before as well. If a boy couldn't hit a bale of hay less than a hundred feet away three times in a row, he probably didn't have what it takes.

And yet they say girls can't become Dragonknights...

Sir Tullus let the first ten boys out of the line, the rest filling the gap and allowing the line to advance. He called out the number on each boy's armband as they took positions before he turned to look down range. Starting with the leftmost boy, he called down the line one after the other, first with the boy's (or man's) number, followed by, "Fire!" Jenna noted with interest as the different contestants produced mixed results. Three missed their first shot entirely, and two of those would go on to miss their next two, either due to total lack of skill or nerves as Jenna thought in one case, causing Tullus to call out their disqualification from all the Trials. Of the eight remaining, two young men struck the white center of the target, four had varying degrees of success and the last... well, his arrow struck the target and bounced off. Cheers called down for some, while guffaws or dismay fell for others. Tullus called for the next two shots from each in the same manner, and then bellowed into the trees, "Judges, record your scores." To those who completed the Trial, he said, "You are free to stay and watch or do as you will. Blue's next Trial will be at the horse runs this afternoon. Next ten!"

Jenna counted those in front of her and pursed her lips in dismay. She would not make it into this group but would in fact be first in the next. This put her uncomfortably close to Sir Tullus for more time than she would like, and the eyes of that archer were known to be the sharpest in Abrea. She considered moving backward in the line a bit, but the apprehension shown on the faces behind her didn't indicate this had much chance of success.

An odor reached her nose, that of urine, and she looked down at the boy in front of her. His bow was taller than him, and piss ran down his leg and puddled below his soft leather boots. Realizing what happened, he turned all around in a panic, finding several sets of eyes on him, and some of the older boys wore vicious smiles or started to mock him. Jenna's heart went out to him for a moment, but she made no move as he pushed his way out of line to run away. None of the other boys stood in his way, worried that either his cowardice or his urine might rub off on them.

Jenna stepped over the small mud puddle and closed the distance to the others filing out of the line to take their positions. Dutifully, Sir Tullus called their numbers one at a time, and Jenna breathed a sigh of relief as she noted that his focus was on their armbands rather than their faces or any other sign that may betray her gender. She just needed to prove herself to them, and then being a girl wouldn't matter anymore. She breathed deeply as she took the last mark on the far right of the range.

The conditions had stayed fair – there was but a slight breeze that would have negligible impact on an arrow fired at this range with her strength and skill. In no particular order, the archers prepared their first shot, and once convinced that all, including judges, were ready, Tullus began calling the contestants numbers in turn, as he had before. Jenna held her breath, struggling to steady sudden nerves. It was an easy shot, and yet now her wrist began to shake. Then Tullus called, "One forty two! Fire!" and she loosed the arrow without a second thought. She'd twitched a hair's breadth at the end, and the arrow went wide from the bullseye by one inch to the left.

Even amidst applause, she gritted her teeth as she looked at her feet.

But there was no time to be angry at herself. It was still an excellent shot, and Tullus had already started the order over on their second arrows. This one went as planned; Jenna thunked the arrow dead center into the target, a perfect bullseye that no one living could beat. She hazarded a glance upward as applause and cheers grew. Her group was certainly more impressive and proficient than the last, but none besides her had yet hit a bullseye.

She drew her next arrow as Sir Tullus began ordering final volleys. What could she do? She had to do something better, something dominant, but what is better than a bullseye? She could place her third arrow right in between the first two? Or perhaps plant it exactly one inch to the right of the bullseye, making a straight line across?

"One forty two! Fire!" came the command, and Jenna hesitated. Sir Tullus shouted again, "I said fire!"

Jenna corrected her aim and loosed the arrow; with a streaking whistle it went straight and true, hitting the dead center bullseye of the target three to the left of hers. Silence reigned for an intense, terribly long moment, and then cheers, claps, shouts, and stomping of feet on wood erupted from above. Jenna hung her head in silence but couldn't contain the smile that split her face.

And then Tullus' bass voice split through the crowd's noise, silencing them, "One forty two! You are disqualified!"

Jenna about turned toward the Dragonknight to argue against him. He would discover she's not a boy named Timbre, and she didn't care. He disqualified her anyway, so what difference would it make if she revealed herself now. But before she could move to argue, before she betrayed her own secret, someone from the trees above shouted, "He hit a bullseye!" Another voice called, "Twice!" A chorus of agreement exploded from the trees and Highton, and the Dragonknights above found themselves in the oddest of places. Their ranking Brother had made a decision, but even they found themselves caught up in the surge of the crowd.

"Enough!" Tullus bellowed, and all began to quiet down. "I stated the rules clearly. You must hit your target all three times, or you are disqualified from the Trials."

"No," Jenna contradicted him, her contrarian nature finding its outlet through her voice. She didn't turn to face him, for if she had, she would have seen the Dragonknight storming her way. "You said we must hit *a target* all three times."

Sir Tullus stopped dead in his tracks as he heard this. At first, some of the crowd may have thought the man would use his own bow to end one forty two, or perhaps he would just pick the boy up and bodily throw him out of the Trials. Instead after a dozen heartbeats or so passed, Tullus broke out into the loudest, most raucous laughter Jenna had ever heard. It seemed to make her teeth chatter together, and it vibrated through her ribs. The people of Highton, familiar with Tullus' good humor, joined in.

The towering man took ahold of himself long enough to say, "Well done, one forty two. Judges – record your scores! Next!"

As youngsters entered the firing range to retrieve arrows imbedded in the hay bales, Jenna turned to leave her mark on the range. Amongst her fellow participants, there were some who smiled or cheered her, but most wore smirks of disdain or disapproval. Based on her admittedly limited contact with males of such ages, she ignored it as jealousy. Even if they tried the same trick, she had done it first!

However, there was one who she spotted staring back at her who wore a genuine smile. Thom nodded as she met his gaze, his ice blue eyes twinkling with respect and maybe a hint of mischief. She began to smile back and turned her face away to hide her blush from Thom and the rest.

Chapter 6

Horsemanship

Finding anything close to solitude or a modicum of privacy was a fool's dream after her performance on the archery range. Jenna could go nowhere without people gawking and pointing in her direction, and sometimes they even clapped as she walked by. Her competitors had mixed reactions to be sure, the hostility plain on some of their faces in open challenge, but there were others, often the young boys that looked at her in astonishment or open mouthed awe. She wasn't the only one who had hit a bullseye, but she was the only "boy" in the Trials to openly break the accepted rules and secure an unmatched level of success in so doing. Everywhere she went, she pulled her cap down to hide her face in shadow. People began to gather near her to gawk, and as small children worked up the courage to approach the archer known as Timbre, Jenna turned and hurried away. The first round of Trials came to an end, and cookfires flared, the sweet smell of cooking meat permeating the air. Jenna took her portions early before the lines and crowds began to grow, before conversation, bragging, and amazed discussion of certain performances filled the air like a swarm of bees. It wasn't long before the area under Highton roared with activity and laughter, and all the while, she endeavored to stay away from as many people as she could. Even still, she spotted Sir Tullus and several Dragonknights from the Second Circle observing her from a distance.

Jenna felt like she had to pee, and it constituted the better part of an hour to find a place where she could do so in privacy; it seemed younger boys preferred to make a contest out of how far they could urinate.

When the sun moved a short distance past its zenith on its path toward the western horizon, the drums sounded from above. Dragonknights stood on tables or the city paths above, calling for the Trial participants to finish their meals and prepare themselves to assemble at the grounds. Jenna's eyes narrowed as she and the rest of the blue group were called to the horsemanship Trial. She had little experience with horses, a novice rider at best as there was little need to hunt the forest on horseback, and she wished she'd stayed closer to the crowd, perhaps listened to the boys wearing green armbands. They just completed that Trial, and she would have liked to know what to expect.

Shrugging, as there was nothing she could do about it now, Jenna made her way to the Trial Grounds, finding that some three dozen of the blue group had already arrived. The waiting area was not a winding, roped off line like it had been at the archery range, but rather a broad, fenced off pen. What looked like a jousting run, an avenue some two hundred feet in length extended straight ahead from the gate that opened inward into the pen. A gorgeous black stallion with a bolt of white on his forehead and covered in padded canvas armor waited patiently with a pair of handlers. Jenna looked down the length of the alley, expecting to see another horse at the other end, but there was none. Instead, wooden platforms of intermittent height and spaced some twenty five feet apart lined either side of the run. Some were purely lying on the forest floor, while others stood almost to the lower level of Highton, some twenty feet in the air. Men and women with longbows filtered into the area, taking up positions on the platforms as more of the contestants made their way to the pen.

Jenna focused on one over halfway down the horse run as he nocked an arrow into his bow. The arrowhead had been replaced by a blunted piece of metal, much smaller and less dangerous at first glance than what would normally be in its place. What is this? She began to listen to the buzzings of those behind her, as it seemed that most of those who remained in the blue group had arrived.

"This one's impossible," whined a smaller boy, while a deeper voice said, "It'll be easy to get hurt here."

This was replied to with, "I heard a kid died here this morning."

"Did not," contradicted a deeper voice.

"Did to. Gregor saw it happen."

"And who the shit is Gregor? You just met him an hour ago."

This seemed to end the conversation, at least for now, but other similar discussions were being had behind her. Though, those assembled ahead of her evaluated the scene in silence, sometimes with a point and a hushed whisper to a fellow. Jenna examined them and found no boys among them; they were all grown men or teenagers with wide shoulders and strong limbs, the smaller and younger boys having filtered to the back of the pen. They paid her no mind, even though she had palpably won the last Trial in everyone's mind; they had their own opinions about what it would take to win this contest, whatever it may be.

As it tended to do with young men, the excitement turned to boredom within ten or fifteen minutes, even as some sixteen archers stood on their places, bows and blunted arrows at the ready. The drums in Highton reverberated through the air once more, and a Dragonknight materialized from nothing to stand before the pen. He was the vertical opposite of Sir Tullus, standing under five and a half feet, close to Jenna's own height. In place of armor, he wore only canvas clothing with soft leather boots, all of it black. He had the dark brown hair and eyes so common to Abrea, and a clean shaven aquiline face. He carried neither a sword nor a bow, but two long daggers were sheathed at his belt, each guard emblazoned with the sigil of the First Circle. He made a deep bow with an arm extended out to the ground, and as he arose, his face wore a mocking smile. Jenna wasn't sure if she liked him already or hated him.

"I am Sir Malum of the First Circle. Welcome children!" he called with the grin widening, causing quite a stir among the young men before him. "You wonder why a test of horsemanship? Well, we're not yet prepared to give you a test of dragonship, for you would most certainly be killed, crushed, and eaten, and perhaps not in that order! No, a horse is the closest you will get for now.

"This is a Trial of strength, agility, and endurance. The task is simple. Sit astride Sir Noctorum here – yes, he is of higher station than you – and make it from this end to that without falling off. These fine archers behind me will each be allowed to fire three shots at you, and I promise you, they are excellent marksmen and markswomen. You will be judged on your ability to avoid their arrows, keep control of Sir Noctorum… and how you take a blow. Your Trial ends if you reach the other end or once you fall off. I promise you, this will be painful!

"Who is first?"

Villainous laughter fell from the onlookers above, and most of the contestants turned and looked at each other, hoping to see a volunteer but just finding the same trepidation. A tall, thick young man in the front pushed his way confidently past two others to make his way out of the gate, which was more than fine by Jenna. "Forty seven is the first victim!" Sir Malum called upward to additional guffaws and catcalls.

She wanted to examine how different people went about this Trial, but she was more interested in the archers than the participants. Archers often took considerable pride in their skills; in fairness most people who were good at something took pride in it, but archers were a different breed. She'd seen the light in Brasalla's eyes as the older woman watched her shoot, and Jenna had no doubt the same feelings showed upon her face – concentration and determination, followed by the light and thrill of loosing the arrow, hearing it whistle as it cut through the air, and ending with heady satisfaction when the missile struck home. Marksmen, good ones at least, made any number of minute calculations before they fired. Is the breeze steady or gusting and from what direction? What weak points are in the target's armor or hide? What direction is it likely to move and how fast? All these questions, and their surmised answers, must be determined expeditiously, sometimes within a few seconds before the archer took his or her shot. Watching the men and women with the bows trying to take down the riders would tell her more of what she needed to know than watching the riders themselves. In the end, Jenna could ride, and with agility, too, but she hadn't trained extensively on horseback. She wouldn't be able to compete with those who had, so her best chance was to anticipate the archers themselves.

The first Trial lasted less than ten seconds. A boy mounted the black stallion and walked the horse up to be even with Sir Malum as the Dragonknight held a white cloth aloft. When Malum dropped his hand, the young man dug his heels into the horse's side. He obviously thought that his pure brawn would be enough, that he merely had to withstand the blunted arrows' impacts. He tried to rush the horse through at a gallop, but his weight slowed the animal's advance. He was an easy target, plunked mercilessly over and over by the archers, until an arrow he turned to avoid taking in the face caught him on the side of the skull, and he fell off Sir Noctorum in a heap.

Another older boy went next, and Jenna didn't need him to turn around to know it was Brenton. She recognized the thick, bright red hair and the size of him from the previous day, and it didn't surprise her that he chose to go early. He'd always had an exaggerated sense of his own abilities, which meant something back home when they were all younger and smaller. Being the biggest and the strongest among children was one thing, but this... He fared better, having been smart enough to lean forward and keep his profile small against the horse. Brenton made it about eighty feet when the seventh archer on the right side clocked him right in the forehead, and with stars bursting in his vision, Brenton lost his hold and fell. Jenna noted the wry smile on the man's face as he readied for the next rider.

Boys, teenagers, and those old enough to be considered men moved forward to take their turns, though as they each tried and failed in turn, they became far less eager. A lad about Jenna's assumed age took his turn, climbing into the saddle with confidence. He wasn't as filled out as the other boys, which he perhaps thought gave him an advantage. He drove the horse faster laid forward on the steed to reduce how much of a target he made for the archers. He made it further than most, but he too fell.

No one made it to the other side, prompting Jenna to think the Trial was plainly unfair. Could it even be won? Brasalla's voice echoed in her mind, *"Fair fights are for suckers."* So, there was a way to win, there had to be, but it wasn't about strength to be certain. For that matter, pure speed didn't seem to help, either. But as the riders fell to the arrows, Jenna came to realize two things. First, the archers avoided firing shots that would hit the horse, Sir Noctorum, and they were exceptionally good at it. But second, she was certain that the seventh man on the right, that same archer, had knocked out at least a third of the now almost thirty that had tried. Avoiding that man may increase the odds...

She broke away from her ruminations as a well-coiffed head of blond hair passed the gate after the horse was allowed some minutes of rest. Jenna's eyes narrowed as she recognized Thom's fit frame approaching the horse, and he did something she hadn't seen any of the others do. Rather than at once climbing into the saddle or taking the horse's reins to walk it to his desired starting point, Thom approached the animal's head, stroking the side of his face several times. He seemed to whisper to the stallion, an odd smile playing across his lips.

"Oh, just get to it, Thom," said Sir Malum. "Your three months spent with the Northern Cavalry won't save you now!"

This elicited more laughter from both above and the pen holding those remaining to take the Trial, but the latter group likely laughed from anxiety or even fear. Thom's smile widened at the jab, but he then suppressed it as he patted the horse one last time, whispered something into its ear and then swung up into the saddle. He took more time than any of the others had, adeptly dancing the horse back and forth a bit to allow both rider and mount to get a sense for each other.

Then without warning, he bolted the animal up the lane, catching Sir Malum and the archers by surprise. Most of the first volley of arrows missed behind Thom, fired in a hurry and a moment too late. Only two managed to strike him, glancing off his shoulder and thigh. The archers rushed to prepare their second shots as the horse's hooves chewed up the ground, and Jenna stared on in excitement, pushing up to her toes to watch. She saw bowstrings being drawn, and she knew Thom's time on horseback would be short.

But then he steered the horse right, galloping hard toward the right most edge of the run, and the quick change of direction caused more arrows to go off target behind or even in front of Thom. Those on the right couldn't seem to get a bead on him as he thundered by them, and that's when Jenna realized the genius of Thom's plan – he recognized the accuracy of that seventh man on the right, just as she did. By making such a move, he forced the archer to fire almost directly at him, and Thom ducked low as the blunted arrow was released. It whistled past his right ear!

Cheers and whistles came from all around. One almost deafened Jenna's ears, and she didn't care that the voice was hers. She hopped in place, up and down, driven by the excitement of Thom's run. The archers closest to the pen holding her and the others could manage little as the horse stretched the distance between them. They fired their last shots, and a few made contact but nothing significant as Thom shrugged them off. He straightened a bit as he neared the finish line, mere feet away when a blunted arrow caught the afternoon light just before it hit him right in the back of the skull.

Thom crashed to the ground, his body falling limply as the horse crossed the finish line, and Jenna's eyes shot to the man she knew hit the shot, the most dangerous bowman (or woman) there that day. He carried a smug smile, selfish satisfaction plain at a mark well hit, and she wanted nothing more than to storm through the gate and punch him in the mouth. Thom had won. It was over. The shot was unnecessary. She began to push her way to the front intent on doing just that when Thom began to stir.

Two men secured Sir Noctorum, calming the cooling stallion, as two others ran out and helped Thom to his feet. They continued to keep their hands on him, steadying the young man as he waived his hand languidly at the crowds above and the onlookers below. A cheer thundered from all around, the excitement of knowing he had been the first to beat the Trial infecting everyone who witnessed his run, even those against whom he competed. Jenna couldn't help but scream his name once before realizing how high pitched and girlish her voice sounded compared to some of those around her. *Stupid girl*, she chided, but she simply couldn't ignore the greatness of Thom's victory as he was helped from the field.

Jenna of course hadn't done as well. She finally decided to get it over with after about ten more boys went down. Sir Malum had changed the horse to let him rest, not that it had any impact on Jenna's attempt. The archers would not again be taken by surprise, and she was pelted by blunt steel tips on her back and sides. She took Thom's approach and adapted it, charging the horse left instead of right, and then she leaned low around the left side of the horse's neck to protect herself from Seven on the Right. Unfortunately, it was her own lack of training that spelled her end, as her right foot suddenly came out of the stirrup, and she could no longer hold on as her weight shifted increasingly off balance to the left. Before she realized what was about to happen, she'd fallen face first into the dirt on the left side of the lane.

Hidden away in her private grove, away from the Trial Grounds as the sun receded into the horizon, she nursed a dozen sore spots across her body that would turn into bruises tomorrow. She'd thankfully avoided any hits to her head or face, but there were two particularly painful spots – one to her left breast that she knew would pain her for a week and another where an arrow struck the back of her right hand. She hadn't even realized the latter when it happened. Most of the damage was done to her pride, but that wound would heal over time.

"Why do you keep coming here?" Jenna asked as she heard Thom step through the bushes and shrubs.

"I brought you something to eat," he explained, and she looked up to see a smooth wooden plate balanced on the length of his right forearm with another in his right hand. They both had several slices of rare roasted beef, a bloody gravy and a hunk of bread. "I thought you'd like that."

Jenna said nothing as he took the plate off his forearm with his left hand and offered it to her with a genuine smile. She searched his eyes for a moment and took it, returning the smile just a bit. She set it in her lap as she sat cross legged, and Thom affected the same position facing her a few feet away. She reached up to the tight cap she'd stuffed over her head and fought the urge to take it off. Her hair felt suffocated.

"I'm sure it's okay," Thom offered, pointing a single finger at the cap.

"I better not," she said wistfully. "Are you all right?"

He glanced up at her, and it was his turn to search her eyes for the meaning of the question. After a moment, he answered, "Yeah, I'm okay. Head hurts. Probably will for a few days."

"I'm sorry," Jenna offered, and she meant it. "The bastard shouldn't have taken the shot. You already won."

"Doesn't matter," Thom shrugged. "Besides, now I know you don't hate me."

"I never said I hated you," she eked out around a mouthful of blood soaked bread. "I was just... angry. Jealous."

"It's fine," he said with another shrug and a shake of his head. "I forget how lucky I am."

78

"Lucky? That's bullshit. What you did out there today wasn't luck. It was masterful, amazing."

Thom hung his head, pointing his face toward the ground, but the huge smile on his face betrayed his attempts at humility. "There was still some luck in it," he said as he looked back at her, "but on the range this morning? What you did? That was no luck at all."

"Brasalla is a great teacher."

"I suppose so," Thom nodded, "but I think so is your mother."

Silence prevailed for a while as the two ate and then leaned backward, contentedly enjoying the cooler night air. The forest canopy obscured both the moon and starlight, but Highton glowed orange, a beacon in the night both above and below. The sounds of music and merriment carried in the night, but Jenna had no desire to be a part of it. Even if she weren't hiding who she really was, such public displays weren't things she enjoyed.

"Do you want me to stay with you tonight?" Thom ventured.

"I don't need you," Jenna's temper flared.

"No. No, I didn't mean that," Thom explained, his hands held up placatingly. "I just meant maybe some company wouldn't be a bad thing. We used to spend the night at each other's houses. Remember?"

"We were little then," she dismissed, but then she nodded, "but you can stay if you want."

He smiled again, not just with his mouth but with the ice blue of his eyes twinkling like stars. She didn't know how to take that smile, but she'd seen it a few times today. She'd never been alone with a boy before, at least not of age, and she wasn't sure she wanted to be. All she knew was that younger girls kissed boys secretly in the woods or behind their homes at night, and it seemed to lead to other things. Many women her age already had husbands and even children.

Jenna hastily added, "But nothing else."

"Um, uh, of course not," Thom stammered in reply as she laid out her bedroll.

An hour later, they both lay in silence, unable to sleep as they stared up into the trees. Jenna's eyes had found a break in the green leaves and needles where she could see the smallest patch of blue black sky, a few stars, mere pinpricks in the curtain of night winking through.

"Duels tomorrow morning," Thom mused.

"Yeah," Jenna whispered, wondering if he was considering whether they would face each other. If they did, she wouldn't hold back, and she hoped neither would he.

Chapter 7

The Duel

Armbands, little more than folded handkerchiefs dyed blue, filled a pair of wicker baskets as the contestants filled in an open field in the cool morning air. Jenna's eyes roamed those who remained, and as she counted, she realized that close to half of those who'd registered two days previously were now gone. Some had, of course, been disqualified during the Archery Trial, and there had been a few injured during the Horsemanship Trial, none badly that she knew of, but enough to send them home. But many others had quit after a day of poor performance, or maybe they knew they couldn't measure up to some of the feats that had already been accomplished. Jenna smiled at the thought. She was just a girl and couldn't possibly be a Dragonknight, and yet she'd already surpassed most of the field in just the first two Trials.

For the Duel Trial, a fifteen foot square area had been marked by stakes at the corners, and white lines of paint marked the square's sides, covering the ground and scant grass where pine needles and leaves had been swept away. The remaining members of Blue gathered around the square as they entered the Trial area, the vast majority of them choosing to walk the perimeter rather than crossing the lines. A number of wooden racks on the far side from where they entered held numerous swords of many assorted styles. Longswords, of course, were the most prevalent, being the most common sword found in Abrea, but there were shorter weapons, some as small as daggers, as well as broadswords with blades about double the width of a longsword, and even great, two-handed weapons. Sprinkled in amongst these common sights, Jenna saw the occasional rapier or the curved weapons found in Azgua or Raucrud, though she doubted they would be poisoned as was so often the case with the latter kingdom. All had blunted tips and dull edges, though she had no doubt that a strike could still crack skulls or break bones.

And she somehow doubted that the offerings of hardened boiled leather hauberks or padded canvas tunics and skullcaps would offer much protection from the concussion of the weaponry.

Thom stood to her left, and she rubbed her hands back and forth vigorously on her legs, trying to create enough friction to chase away the chill in the air. The night had been cold, well, cooler than expected for late summer, and Jenna awoke to find that, over the course of the night, the two had inadvertently huddled together. It was a jarring experience at first, and only the fact that Thom seemed more embarrassed than she about something kept her from laying into him. He'd jumped up and left to find the creek nearby with its night chilled water, returning a few minutes later. Even over breakfast and as they walked to the Trial, he seemed unwilling to meet her eyes for some reason.

As the last few contestants straggled in around the square, a formidable figure pushed his way through the throngs of bodies, more men now than boys, and two others dressed as commoners followed him, each of them carrying a wicker basket. This new Dragonknight wore a blackened leather cuirass inlaid with dusky steel rings and the First Circle sigil, and a smoky steel guard attached to it to cover his left shoulder while his right stayed bare along with both corded, muscular arms. He had sun bronzed skin and a full head of raven black hair that ran straight just past his shoulders. He stood in a warrior's stance on thick legs, but in addition to his

82

obvious strength, everything about his bearing bespoke a predatory cat ready to strike. The bluest eyes Jenna had ever seen examined everything.

"I am Sir Conor of the First Circle," he announced in deep baritone voice with a strength that matched the man's body. Whispers travelled amongst those assembled, for everyone had heard of the son of a Vulgeschi blacksmith who had come to join the Brotherhood. He was well known to be King Rendor's most feared fighter, his Champion in all matters in which one would be needed, as it was unheard of for the kings to engage in single combat.

"You have heard of me. Good, now shut your yapping! I am unimpressed by what Abrea has to offer. None of you dogs are fit to take Sir Garond's place, but I suppose you children are the best we can do. This morning, you will fight each other, and chance will decide who faces who. I will choose a number from each basket, and those two dogs – dogs, nay! Puppies! – will choose a weapon, armor if they wish, and fight.

"There are few rules," he continued as he counted them off with splayed fingers, "One, no blows aimed at the head. Hit your opponent in the head, and you are disqualified. Two, leave the square twice, and you are disqualified. Three, if you disarm your opponent, you must offer him the chance to yield. And four, strike a blow to the body to win."

Conor nodded at the two basket bearers, and they sunk their hands into their respective pile of armbands, turning the pieces of cloth over and over as if the wicker containers were bakers' mixing bowls. After a moment, the Dragonknight held both hands with his palms facing away to signal a stop to the stirring, after which he bent down and reached into each basket to remove one piece of cloth from each. "Thirty seven and one twelve!" he loudly read them off, and he retreated back out of the square as his basketmen attended to the readiness of the contestants.

The first four Trials blew by in moments, the duelists distinctly mismatched from the onset. A younger boy scampered away from his opponent, twice leaving the square within a minute, while one of the next combatants, matched in size but not skill, simply tagged his opponent in the chest with a faint followed by a thrust of his longsword. The battles began to grow in length and complexity as the more skilled opponents came to bear against each other, and everyone above and below watched with growing intensity – some for the spectacle, others in the hopes of picking up anything that may help in their own trial. Jenna was sure there was no small amount of wagering going on amongst the spectators in Highton.

The sun climbed into the sky on its inevitable path toward noon, and a full quarter of her group had either won or been eliminated when Sir Conor shouted, "One forty two and one thirty six!"

Something akin to a stone dropped into the pit of Jenna's stomach, a feeling in her gut she had come to recognize the last few days – nervousness, maybe a sense of dread or trepidation. Despite her successes of the previous day, she stood as if in a daze, as if she could not move or react to her number having been called. She realized gazes from many sets of eyes had fallen on her; she was well known due to the exploits of one forty two on the archery range.

Thom's whispered voice in her ear broke the spell, "You face Brenton."

She blinked once, twice to clear her eyes with a slight shake of her head, and there was the massive red haired boy as he marched to one side of the square. An attendant helped him shrug into leather armor as he pointed at a massive, six foot great sword. She turned and walked away from him to the far side of the Trial's

84

square and handed her father's sword to Thom as she tested the weight and balance of various longswords.

"Take good care of that," she growled as menacingly as she could manage.

Thom replied with the smallest of smiles and a hushed voice, "Brenton is large. He'll try to overpower you with heavy strokes."

"Good. He hasn't learned anything," Jenna concluded. Having chosen a weapon as close to her father's sword as possible, she began to step toward the square.

"Armor," he whispered urgently, stopping her with a grip on her upper arm.

"If that brute strikes me, I don't think a little padding will help," she answered, her tone grim.

"Enough talk over there!" called Sir Conor from across the square. "Talk is for lovers!"

At this, howling guffaws and fits of hooting erupted from all around. Every male around the square laughed or issued catcalls, but somehow Jenna thought some of them may have been trying too hard to be a part of the joke rather than the target of it. Abrea had no laws against such unlike Conor's homeland, his upbringing likely being the cause of the hurled insult, but it certainly wasn't as accepted as in the more intellectual Azgua. And Conor couldn't have known the incorrectness of his assumption of her gender, but it had the desired effect as her face burned red hot with annoyance at the suggestion.

She pulled away and entered the square, her sword at the ready as her opponent did the same. As Jenna looked him over, her memory of the larger boy quickly faded with the realization that he had grown into manhood. Tall with massive thews, his arms and chest almost matched that of Sir Conor despite being several years the Dragonknight's junior. He handled a huge blade easily and dexterously, though perhaps with an absence of grace. He planted his feet shoulder width apart, his boots leading up thick calves to sturdy thighs, and Jenna was sure they were capable of impressive feats of strength. If he hit her with that sword, he would break bones. As she finished looking him over, she met his eyes, and a contemptuous glare shined balefully back in his green eyes. Brenton had never had any respect for any other child back home, before he left the village, and it was plain that his haughtiness had never abated, driven on by his own sense of his muscular power.

And then for just a moment, his eyelids shut to a squint as he peered at the enemy before him, and then widened as a sudden recognition dawned on him. *Shit*, Jenna swore in her mind, knowing that the tormentor of her village's children realized who stood before him. No doubt he would stop the Trial, call her out to the Brethren for what she was – a female, unallowed and unable to compete in the Trials. What would they do to her? But, no, Brenton did no such thing. In fact, his muscles seemed to relax, and a cruel smile began to spread across his face.

"Begin!" bellowed Conor.

As expected, Brenton lunged first with a powerful thrust that would have ruptured her guts even if it hadn't broken her tunic and skin. She danced backward, aware that she was mere inches from the boundary behind her. Convinced he would strike her or she'd retreat out of bounds, he thrust again, telegraphing the attack, and Jenna deflected the blade to the left while somersaulting to the right to avoid a great sweeping, backhanded strike, the sword *whooshing* through the air. As she came up and around to land a blow to his back, he had already recovered and brought the sword down in a way intended to cleave an enemy in twain. Jenna only just brought her sword up in time, the dull edges meeting in a thunderous clang, threatening to bend the steel as metal shavings showered about.

The onlookers gasped and hooted at the brutality of the blow as Jenna was hurled onto her backside, but Brenton was off balance and over extended. She kicked her boot out, hooking her foot at the ankle to catch him right behind the knee, and he went down hard onto his back. Smaller and more agile, Jenna recovered more fleetly, thrusting her sword at his side just as he turned onto his hands and knees. Unable to rise in time to parry, he slapped the sword away with his right wrist, causing the dulled point to skate off his right thigh. Excitement flooded the crowd as murmurs weaved their way about, as no one had yet seen a combatant allow himself to be stricken! Nay, he hadn't allowed it as much as actually directed the attack so that he wouldn't lose.

Brenton rolled away, and she pursued with an overhand blow which the large man just managed to deflect from his knees. Off balance herself, she kicked out backwards with her right foot, catching him square in the chest. He hadn't expected such a move, and he fell backwards onto his back. And out of the square.

"Out!" shouted Sir Conor, and the crowd roared their appreciation at the spectacle.

They had all expected it to be another ten second duel, the fight clearly an overmatch. But, no! They had received more than any of them ever imagined, and the roar faded and was replaced with the clinking of coins as more wagers were placed. Jenna wondered how her odds looked as she glanced at Sir Conor and found his face awash with the heat of bloodlust, the love of battle.

"Return," came Conor's command as the crowd calmed, and Jenna stepped aside to allow her adversary to rise and return to the square.

As he passed her, Brenton grunted, "You're dead."

"Prove it, shithead," she mumbled back with a jut of her chin.

He stopped with his back to her for just a moment before he stiffly returned to his starting position. As he turned, she could see the anger burning in his eyes, and he adopted an aggressive stance, every corded muscle in his arms and neck bulging. Jenna realized then he would do everything he could, to not just beat her there and then, but to inflict as much pain with his winning stroke as possible. He had been overconfident at first, realizing that he had been matched with a mere girl from his childhood, but he would give it all this time.

He seemed to jump to the attack the instant the word left Sir Conor's mouth, with a lightning fast thrust followed by a wide arced swing that followed Jenna even as she escaped. Brenton recovered faster than she thought possible with lightning quick, deadly reversals that swept through the air. His giant blade whistled as he made no contact, but he controlled the entire fighting space with sheer power. It was all Jenna could do to stay away, as she couldn't hope to parry the power adequately, and every time she thought to sneak past his guard, the sword was back. But how long could he keep up such a swift onslaught?

Brenton maneuvered until he had her away from the broad sides of the square and instead backed into a corner with only two feet or so to retreat into. Jenna watched as he closed in on her, knowing that her options were limited. She'd allowed him to control the space around them in this second round of combat, and now she had nowhere else to run to. His body heaved up and down as sweat ran down his face and matted his hair. He was tired, and she could just back out of the square to avoid his next attack, forcing a third round of the duel. Then, perhaps, she could use his tiring muscles to regain the upper hand. He wouldn't expect that.

A halfhearted jab came her way, and she deflected it without difficulty, losing another foot of her ground. There was no chance at riposte; Brenton hadn't intended the attack to do anything but cause her to back away even more, and his brutish smile returned as he became more and more assured of victory. He swung from her left, and with nowhere to go, she brought her longsword up to parry. She managed to deflect the blow but not without losing her sword, the crowd ducking for cover as it sailed over their heads. They grew deathly silent as they eagerly anticipated the next move.

"Yield," Brenton commanded, his voice low. Defiance burned in Jenna's eyes as she stared back at him, unblinking and spat to the side.

Brenton shrugged as he brought his sword around in an attack that was both unnecessarily grand and overpowered. It was exactly what she had hoped for, one more arrogant move since he couldn't conceive of losing to her. She dropped forward, landing her weight on her fingertips and the balls of her feet as the sword cut the air above her. Jenna sprang to her feet and to Brenton's left as the sword went by. Before he could recover from having shifted so much weight to that side, Jenna threw herself against the bigger man's left side, causing him to overextend to his right and then tumble out of the square.

"Disqualified!" Conor announced, and the crowd, both Trial takers and spectators, roared in appreciation of her victory. The upraised voices caught the attention of the other Trials and their onlookers, of everyone above in Highton and even most of the Dragonknights as such a clamor hadn't yet been heard on the day. Jenna returned to the middle of the square and turned with arms raised overhead, catching Thom's admiring smile. Then the smile dropped to sudden concern.

An incredible force launched into her back and slammed her to the ground. It roughly flipped her over, and she realized that Brenton climbed atop her, astride her waist. His weight was crushing, and she struggled to take in a breath, much less move or attempt escape pinned as she was against the hardpacked ground where the Trials had been fought. Voices shouted for an end to it all – Thom's, Sir Conor's, and many others – but nothing contained the rage she saw in Brenton's eyes as his fist came across her face. Stars exploded in her vision, blocking out the scene as his other fist came and slammed her face to the side. One strong hand gripped the front of her tunic in a balled fist as she was hit again in the face, her nose breaking, her blood spattering the ground.

And then the weight was lifted from her. She saw through tear stricken eyes that he had been yanked backward by several sets of strong arms. Brenton still had her tunic clenched in one hand, and the force of him being pulled away lifted her from the ground. And she heard cloth rip. They dragged him some ten feet away from the square as he shouted unintelligible curses, the edges of the torn cloth in his fist fluttering like a rent standard. In a fugue, Jenna reached her hands up to wipe tears from her eyes and blood from her bent nose and mashed lips, and she began to cough as the blood and snot began to drip down the back of her throat. In her dazed state, it took her a moment to realize that sharp inhalations and gasps of air had rippled through all around her, and it was then that she realized the torn cloth in Brenton's fist was the front of her tunic, ripped away and exposing her naked breasts.

She folded her arms across her and in near panic sought Thom's face but couldn't find it amidst everyone else. For a moment, she locked eyes with Brenton, his face a mix of burning rage and cruel satisfaction, knowing what he had taken from her. She stood and tried to run from the crowd, intent on making it to her campsite, but bodies stood all around her not allowing her passage. She tried once, then changed directions to try again, but Jenna couldn't find an escape.

"Enough!" a voice thundered, rattling ribs and chattering teeth, and all eyes looked to Sir Conor. "Give her something to wear, for pity's sake," he commanded with a chin jutted toward Jenna, and then he wheeled to point at Brenton, "And you are disqualified."

"I was cheated!" Brenton argued, still restrained by three or four others, though he'd released Jenna's tattered tunic. "She had no right to be here!"

"Be that as it may, your superior muscles were defeated by her superior brains. You're not fit to be amongst the Brethren."

"I demand –," Brenton began, but his voice was cut off by the point of a sword mere inches from his throat.

No one had seen Conor move; his muscles sprang into action as fast as a striking snake, and he warned, "Demand nothing, one thirty six. You have lost, and your dishonorable display will follow you for all your days. I will speak with King Rendor, and be assured, you will never again compete at a Trial, no matter how many of my Brethren fall."

"And so it shall be," intoned a voice from above, and Jenna's eyes shot up to the king himself as he looked down upon the calmed bedlam.

His sword still raised, Conor continued with a nod, "Release him. Leave Highton now, one thirty six, and without further incident. Your Trial is over. Such is the command of the Brethren and King Rendor."

Conor's smoldering eyes locked with the disgraced Brenton's, and for just a moment, all thought the larger, younger man might make a fight of it. Relishing the chance to dispatch a pitiful foe so that he may not dishonor himself again, the Dragonknight of the First Circle grinned in anticipation, but his prey thought better of it after a second. With slumped shoulders,

Brenton dejectedly slunk his way through the crowd, and they parted expeditiously to allow him through, as if just being close to him would spread his taint.

Conor sheathed his sword, turned toward Jenna – who now had a blanket wrapped around her torso – and looked up to his king. "And what of the girl, Highness?"

Rendor contemplated this for a few seconds, his eyes searching Jenna's face as she looked back with a surreal mixture of trepidation and defiance, her tears from the broken nose and the pain of Brenton's punches threatening to blind her.

"Bring her up," the king commanded, and his regal voice carried to all the ears about Highton.

Chapter 8

King Rendor

A kindly old woman gave Jenna a shirt made of modest, white wool to wear and even held the blanket to give her some privacy as she pulled it over her head, all the while clucking, "A pretty girl like you should be looking for a husband, not fighting possible husbands with swords," and other such minor condemnations. In the end, however, the crone said, "Take care, child," with a soft touch to her face after helping her wash away the blood and applying a gentle salve to broken lips. The nose would have to wait, though she had packed it to staunch the bleeding.

Sir Conor escorted her into the heights of Highton. He said nothing to her, his blue eyes smoldering with some inner fury while his face betrayed nothing. He leaned against the backside handrail of the lift, his weight causing it to list while Jenna held the railing tightly as they rose further and further into the air. Perhaps many people would have found the height dizzying or the rocking of the small platform sickening, but Jenna felt no such way, her eyes wide as she took in everything, her damaged face almost forgotten but for the ache.

Well over a hundred feet in the air, the lift came to a halt, swaying a few inches back and forth before a wooden bridge some ten feet across that spanned a forty foot gap between the Great Tree and one of its lesser neighbors. The bridge had its own handrail, about three feet tall, and Conor, in a well-practiced maneuver, vaulted out of the lift and over this rail with phenomenal dexterity. He turned and held his hand out to Jenna, but she scarcely realized it as she looked to the north end of the bridge.

It ended on an expansive, wooden platform of ancient boards long sealed with the products of Azgua's alchemists, protecting them from both fire and the elements for generations. The platform extended east to west some fifty feet, other bridges heading off in those directions, and twenty feet from the edge of this bridge began the most wondrous building Jenna had ever seen. It gleamed white in the filtered sunlight, made from the innermost wood of the Great Tree itself. It rose three stories at least with many windows open to the air of Highton that were as large as a person and in which green banners depicting Abrea's dragons fluttered in the breeze. She could make out balconies on at least two sides that must have offered astounding views of the rest of the city. Jenna's eyes began to follow bridges and paths as they led to and from the palace, spinning in place as she took in all of Highton's splendor. She ceased her movement when she came back around to face Sir Conor, who stood as stoic as an ancient statue, though a sense of understanding seemed to flow through his eyes.

"Come," he said simply, extending his hand further toward her.

She did not accept it, choosing instead to step gracefully from the swaying lift's small platform to the bridge, smoothly ducking under the handrail. Sir Conor dropped his hand to his side and led her north toward the palace that could only be King Rendor's. Highton's people stopped, looked, and sometimes pointed and whispered, for word of what she had done spread quickly, and this girl with the close shorn hair could only be the one they had just heard about. They whispered in each other's ears, knowing gazes washing over Jenna as Sir Conor led her to a pair of dark oak double doors with golden knockers. The Dragonknight did not knock, but instead opened one door, motioned her inside and then closed it behind them with a slight squeal of brass hinges and a thump that echoed into the hall beyond.

The place was dim, weak light from the windows Jenna spied outside barely penetrating the hall that was thirty feet in width and as far deep. The ceiling was almost lost in the gloom twenty feet overhead, and it was painted with gilded murals of dragons and their riders joining battle against great black serpents which could only be the dragons from Raucrud. As she gawked, she found tapestries draping the walls, depicting Abrea's past kings, fantastically heroic deeds, and Dragonknights of history. The quality, workmanship, and sheer artistry of these took her breath away, for some of them looked as real as if she stood watching Sir Jan and his dragon make their last stand. The story was well known – songs and tales told to children spoke of Sir Jan of the First Circle standing his ground against three Vulgeschi brutes to delay them long enough for the rest of the Brethren to arrive, saving the city of Soutton.

A rich rug of white fur, said to be made from a hundred of the northern bears and a gift from Isdal over two hundred years ago, stretched up the center of the Hall, flanked by several guards as it led to a tall throne of pure white wood, no doubt the same as the palace's construction. The trunk of the Great Tree made the wall behind the throne. Unadorned, its brown-gray bark struck a stark contrast against the rest of the hall, and Jenna spied an arched doorway cut into the tree itself, leading into its depths.

King Rendor sat expectantly on his throne, his longbow and great sword held by attendants that flanked either side of him. Conor firmly but gently took Jenna by the elbow, and the pair walked up the ten foot wide bear skin rug to come to a halt a mere six feet away from the king. Sir Conor dropped to one knee, Jenna following suit, and she hazarded a glance upward at the monarch. He was older than she realized from afar, perhaps in his fifties, at least old enough to have grandchildren if not great grandchildren. Crow's feet marked the outer corners of his eyes, no doubt from a lifetime of squinting into the sun from the back of a dragon, and his eyes contained a depth Jenna couldn't quite explain or understand, perhaps as if an unfathomable wealth of knowledge lay there.

"So, this is the girl who would be a Dragonknight?" Rendor intoned not unkindly. "Rise, so I may see you."

Jenna hesitated and only stood to her feet after Sir Conor moved first. She wasn't sure how to act in the presence of a king, except to exercise her manners as best she knew how. Rendor also stood and stepped forward to examine her, and she dropped her face a bit, averting her eyes though she wasn't sure why. The king's hand, its skin rough and calloused from a lifetime of using bows and swords, carefully lifted her chin upward so that he may peer at her. He should have been as tall as Conor, Jenna thought, but his back was faintly bent as wasn't uncommon with age.

"Such a pretty face to be ravaged by a brute's fists. You will heal, but I'm afraid you'll need some help with that nose," he said with a hint of sadness. He released her chin, circling around her as if he were appraising the quality of a steed. He had almost come around full circle when he lifted one of her hands and gently peeled her fingers open to reveal the palm. "You're strong for a girl of your age, very strong indeed. Your hands are worn. You've trained with weapons for years, I think. What am I to do with you?"

At this, Jenna's chin lifted pridefully for just a moment before she realized that he actually expected an answer from her, "Allow me to finish the Trials."

The king shook his head sorrowfully as he turned away, "I cannot. You know the law."

"The law is unfair. It's bullshit," she replied, instantly sheepish of her response.

But King Rendor turned back toward her, a slight smile almost completely obscured by his beard playing across his lips, "Such fire in this one, eh Sir Conor? What a glorious Dragonknight you would have made if you were but a boy."

"I'm better than any boy."

"Most to be sure. Your Trials prove as much, but –,"

"Then let me finish them," Jenna implored, and as a flash of rage crossed the king's face, she knew she'd pushed too hard having interrupted the highest voice in Abrea midsentence.

"It is unallowed!" Rendor thundered, his temper flaring such that Jenna flinched at the volume of his voice. Neither the guards nor Sir Conor moved a muscle, the professionals that they were, but the king's attendants shifted uncomfortably. The fire burned in his eyes for a long moment before he lowered them to the floor and loosed a deep cleansing sigh. "Leave us," he commanded without raising his eyes again.

Sir Conor, the guards, and attendants all filed out of the hall into the Great Tree's entrance behind the throne. Conor was the last to leave, and his heavy footsteps echoed as he thudded down a spiral staircase inside the tree itself. Rendor waited until he believed they were all out of earshot before he looked back at Jenna with a genuine smile.

"I have worked many years to control that temper. It's important for a king to be not so rash, though maybe others don't think so. But sometimes, usually around the obstinance I find in my grandchildren, it returns," Rendor explained, and his voice had lost the sense of air around it, as if the king spoke frankly to a good friend. "You have caused quite the hubbub. You know that, don't you?"

"I'm sorry," Jenna replied, contritely bowing her head. "I didn't mean t-."

"Oh, yes you did," Rendor chuckled. "What were you going to do? Win the Trials and then force us to accept you into the Brethren?"

Her silence was all the response he needed, and she suddenly felt like a chastised child who'd done something incredibly stupid.

"Jenna is your name? A young man named Thom told us. Don't be angry at him. He told Sir Tullus that he knew you from when you were children. That you were headstrong, rebellious, maybe a little bit mad. He asked that we release you to return to your home. Personally, I think the young man is lying to us, I think he knew the whole time that you were here competing in the Trials under the name of your father. Yes, I know Timbre was your father. I mourned him and his crimes against Abrea and the Brethren."

The hot anger that Jenna had felt her entire life when someone mentioned this returned, and her face flushed as if fire burned outward from it. She set her jaw and chin defiantly, but only held back a furious retort through intense force of will, and that the king had held his hand up to stay any response.

"Calm down. He was your father, and you loved him. I respect the faithful honor you pay him. I'd like to show you something, Little Dear, if you'd follow me."

Jenna's eyes narrowed at the words so often used toward her by Brasalla and her mother as Rendor turned without a second thought and strode purposefully toward the entrance into the Great Tree. After a

98

moment's hesitation, she followed him, as he surely knew she would, and passed through the large archway into a wooden hallway hollowed into the tree itself. It was perhaps five feet deep, and the wood of the outer portion was very much green and alive. When she emerged, she found the tunnel adjoining a narrow spiral stair, also carved right out of the tree, that led both up and down. The king had already turned left, climbing the steps, and Jenna quickened her pace to be two steps behind him. The steps ended at a closed door, dark oak banded with black iron, and Rendor produced an iron key from somewhere within his ring studded armor, which he inserted into a lock and turned to the left. A loud clang echoed through the tree as a bolt slid back, and Rendor opened the door.

A single room lay beyond the door, and as they entered, Rendor closed the door behind them. Jenna realized that the Great Tree had narrowed substantially as they had climbed, the door installed into the tree's outer layers. A square room encased the tree with balconies on each side, looking down upon Highton, but this wasn't what drew Jenna's attention. No tapestries hung here, and there was no rug across the wooden floor. Every square inch of the room's fifteen foot walls was covered in paintings, beautiful murals of dragons and battle. The ceiling was the bright blue of a cloudless sky with a glaring yellow orb that she was almost sure shined brightly down onto the room. The floor was of a grim desert, dusty dunes and cracked dry landscapes artfully displayed in a tableau of nothingness.

"I am the only one that comes here, but one day I will be gone. I hope the new king continues my tradition, as I have continued from past kings," Rendor said, and he pointed at certain murals and paintings as he spoke. "Please, look around you. The masterful images you see here were painted hundreds of years ago, and they serve to remind me of everything we have accomplished but also what we lost in so doing.

"Here you see the wars we fought with Isdal, pushing the aggressive northmen all the way back to their icy castles before their winters turned us back. There is King Raghva of Vulgesch felling the murderous assassins of Raucrud, starting a fifty year war between those two nations even as Vulgesch's dragons torched people's cities when they grew too large or too close to their caves. If you look about, you'll find other scenes of the world's dragons causing immense destruction, though we endured the least of it here in Abrea."

"Who is this?" Jenna asked before the portrait of a brown skinned man with a regal mane of white with a matching, flowing beard and mustache. He wore silks of white and blue with a long saber at his side.

"Ah, that is Phileppe of Azgua."

"Who is he?"

"As I am sure you know, it was King Maltos of Azgua and our own King Fathen who unlocked the mysteries of the Link," Rendor explained, showing her a glinting, golden ring on the ring finger of his left hand. "They gave us the knowledge and the power to imbue our talismans, so that we may learn to work with the beasts and keep them from destroying us. Soon, our Dragonknights and the Dragaval of Azgua flew over our armies, and our enemies fell quickly. It was Phileppe who betrayed the knowledge of the Link to the others."

"Why have him here?" Jenna asked genuinely as she looked over his round, brown face.

"As a reminder. Thanks to him, all the nations in Nahrea are equal. We cannot war amongst ourselves, or we'll spread Desolation across the world. Or perhaps worse – we lose Dragonknights, can't replace them quickly enough and the Link loses its power."

"The Link lets us control the dragons?" Jenna's brow furrowed as she asked the question.

"It…," Rendor paused as if searching for the right words, "melds the will of the Dragonknight with that of the dragon, I suppose is the best explanation."

"But what of the dragon's will?"

"It must be tempered, trained, no differently from a horse or a dog. They are the same – animals," Rendor explained, a higher pitch in his voice to indicate the simplicity of it all.

"But I don't understand. When I was little, I went out to Titan, my father's dragon, in the middle of the night. I touched him, and he looked at me. He was no mere beast. There was intelligence there. I could… *feel* it."

"My dear," Rendor replied, a hint of arrogance or condescension in his voice, "everyone feels that way the first time they come close to a dragon or look into its eyes. They are immortal as far as we know, so how could such a great creature be no brighter than a northern bear, a badger, or one of Vulgesch's mountain lions? It's a hard thing to swallow, and yet, I swear to you that it is absolutely true. They are no different from those creatures and ruled by all the same instincts. There are one hundred twenty five dragons in the world, and they're each able to destroy an entire city in hours. We stand on a depiction of their devastation."

Jenna looked down to her feet and circled a bit to take in the vast wasteland depicted with almost loving care on the floor. It looked so real, as if she actually stood in the Desolation, that great, vast desert of near endless death caused by the Dragon War. She began to understand why Rendor came here, began to feel the weighty responsibility that he must feel every day. She lifted her eyes back to the king's compassionate face, so kindly as he looked upon her.

"I still don't understand," she said, "why I can't be a Dragonknight? Nothing here explains that to me. I'm smarter than almost every boy I've ever met, I've trained hard with my longbow and my father's sword. I can do anything."

Rendor smiled at her for a moment, before a look of sadness, or perhaps sorrow, filled his face. "So much strength. I believe everything you just said, I've no doubt of it. To answer you, I'll tell you briefly about King Gundar of Vulgesch. Have you heard of him?"

As Jenna shook her head, he continued, "King Gundar reigned for thirty years, over half of that time during the Dragon War. He was a giant, some say eight feet tall, and he could fell mighty oaks with one heft of an ax, crush a man's skull with one hand. His wife, Queen Ullana was much his equal, at least as fierce, and he wanted nothing more than for her to fly alongside him into battle. When they attempted the Link, the dragon Gundar had chosen for her nuzzled her lovingly before melting her flesh with its fire, leaving nothing but her blackened bones behind.

"We learned that the Link simply does not take to your gender. It is nothing against you personally, Jenna, it just is. It isn't just tradition or law, it's necessity. It's fact, and for you, I'm so sorry. What a Dragonknight you would have made," Kind Rendor repeated the words he'd said in his hall below.

"However, now I have to decide what to do with you," he sighed. "I'm still not sure you fully understand the danger you put us all in, especially yourself. What if, somehow, you'd made it through the Trials, all the way to the Link, without being discovered. You would be dead, Little Dear, and how many with you when the dragon succumbed to its more animal instincts? You know I cannot allow that to pass unpunished."

"I'm sorry," Jenna mumbled feebly, tears welling up behind her eyes.

"Are you? Or is that just what you're supposed to say?" Rendor asked, and his sigh told her she wasn't meant to answer. "It doesn't matter. There will be those who want me to put you to death."

Jenna's eyes widened at this, and a track of tears broke from under the middle of her eyes and made their way down her cheeks. Could that be true? She hadn't stopped to consider that anyone would pass such a harsh judgement. After all, nothing really happened. All she did was knock out some boys that had no right to be considered a Dragonknight. Rendor reached up and tenderly pushed the tear away from her face, careful not to put too much pressure near her broken nose.

"I'm not going to do that. I'm no tyrant, and I don't believe in the traditions or draconian practices of some of the other nations. I will have a decision for you tomorrow morning, but for the rest of today and tonight, you'll rest well here in my humble home. Do not try to run or flee in the night; you will be watched closely. Do you understand?"

Jenna nodded dutifully, not trusting herself to speak as she worked to hold back sobs.

"Good, now let me fetch my physician to care for that nose," Rendor said with a long, appraising look down the end of his own nose at hers. "Such a pity. I hope it heals well."

Chapter 9

Rendor and the Dragonknights

King Rendor mused as he traversed downwards through the Great Tree and into the lower levels where the tree was almost eighty feet in diameter. He had come to a decision regarding the somewhat wayward daughter of Sir Timbre, himself a wayward Dragonknight, and he wasn't sure all of the Brethren were going to like it. On the other hand, he didn't really give a dragonshit whether they did or not. He liked the girl; she was courageous, gutsy, and showed adaptability, a feature that cannot be taught, and he genuinely hated to lose such blood in Abrea. It was those very qualities that made him uncertain which punishment she'd choose.

Rendor stepped off the spiral stair and into the Circles of the Brethren, the lowest room carved into the interior of the tree itself, before the stair continued down into the hollowed out catacombs. Dragonknights came to attention upon his entry, a martialed scuffing of boots and creaking of hardened leather armor as men leapt to their feet. He passed amongst them, saying nothing and looking at no one, headed for the raised dais in the center, and he thoughtfully cast his gaze around the room when he reached it. The Dragonknights of the First Circle – Tullus, Malum, Conor, and Westley – stood behind a circular table carved right out of the tree, each of them one of his commanders and each at a point of the compass rose. Some eight feet behind them, the twenty Dragonknights of the Second Circle sat upon lengthy benches, five each arrayed behind the man they hailed as their immediate lord. Of course, there were only nineteen at the moment, and a gap stood empty behind Sir Westley, a reminder of the lost Sir Garond. Rendor lowered his eyes for a moment, and the Dragonknights took their seats.

"Dragonknights, tomorrow we must see to the Link," King Rendor began, aware that they all knew this, and it was not the topic they wanted to hear the king's decision on. "We have only two days left to us, and releasing the dragon is not an option. We will continue as we have planned. The young squire from Sir Garond's house, Thom, has proven himself to be a capable warrior. We will choose him to replace Sir Garond in the Second Circle. I will announce it tomorrow morning to Highton, we shall have a grand feast in the afternoon, and the ceremony will commence at sundown. After that, he will be your responsibility, Sir Westley, but I believe he will serve us loyally."

Westley, a deathly silent man with broad shoulders and a tall forehead, nodded his understanding and obedience. He always wore a hood of black dyed wool as well as a wooden mask over the left side of his face, carved to be a mirror image of the right. He was the oldest of the Dragonknights, ten years even the king's senior, and he wore that hood and mask to cover horrific scars he received some years ago. He allowed no one to see what lay under them, for either their terror or his own embarrassment, but a wisp of errant blond hair attempted to escape the hood.

"Can we trust him?" asked Malum, his voice raised to echo across the Circles, and the question started a babble of discussion amongst the Brethren.

A voice behind Westley, the king wasn't sure whose, cut through the rising tide of voices, "He served Garond well and spent all of his time learning. He is a solid lad."

"Perhaps," Malum acceded, and he locked eyes with his king, though as a warning not a challenge, "but he knew the girl as a child. What is her name? Jenna? Surely, he knew that she was in Highton, and he hid her secret."

"We don't know that to be true," Conor shrugged, much to everyone's surprise, as he often let others do the talking in these councils.

"But it is *likely*, is it not?" Malum continued. "Can we trust someone who keeps secrets?"

"And what secrets do I keep for you, Malum?" asked Tullus, and laughter blurted from many of the Dragonknights at this jab.

Malum sat back in his chair sullenly, and instead changed topics. "So, what of the girl who would be a boy who would be a Dragonknight?"

The king assessed Sir Malum, and despite the defeated posture, he noted the mischievous light in the man's eyes. He was the shortest of the Dragonknights, and he had a reputation as a bit of an alley cat, something he enjoyed despite pretending otherwise. Rendor dreaded this part of the meeting, even though it had to come, and had he spoken, he would have cursed Sir Malum for pushing it this way so rapidly. The king raised his eyebrows while taking in a long, slow breath before answering the question, the eyes of every Dragonknight on him as they waited expectantly.

"As I am sure you all know by now, the girl, Jenna, is Sir Timbre's daughter. We are not here to discuss or debate his crimes. While the Brethren are free to engage in whatever merriment they desire, within limits Sir Malum," Rendor said with a lower tone and a nod to his Commander of the West, garnering many chuckles of amusement from the others, "the joys of hearth and home, wife and children are not allowed to us. The dangers to the Brethren and our solemn oaths forbid it.

"I brought up Sir Timbre because many of you knew him. He was courageous and yet kind. A fierce fighter, but he loved too easily. This girl is her father's daughter, through and through."

"Then she is a threat," hissed Westley in a way that dispelled the humor in the room like a frigid breeze, leaving discomfort instead. It was the edge to the words, the implication, but also that they issued from a mouth that sounded ill-shaped to speak.

"I have made a decision. Jenna will choose her own fate," Rendor explained, and he sighed as the room fell quiet as a tomb. "She will have the choice of banishment from Abrea for as long as she lives, or service as a Second Circle Protectress in the south near the border of Vulgesch."

The room erupted, as a dozen Dragonknights all went to speak at once, many shouting over each other in attempts to be heard. Rendor sighed again as the voices assaulted his ears and each other, an exhausted smile touching pursed lips. He heard some calling for her execution, others demanding banishment, and none seemed excited about the king's second option. He allowed them to continue, and he surveyed his First Circle. Tullus argued with Malum, while Malum ignored the comparatively giantish Dragonknight and hurled insults at Tullus' men. Westley sat still as a stone statue despite some of his own Dragonknights entrenched in the war of words, so much so that one might think him asleep but for the glinting of firelight in eyes that peered back without blinking. And Conor... Conor merely sat, a baleful fire burning in those blue eyes of his as he leaned back in consideration, his black mane hanging freely toward the floor.

Conor stood and approached his king, an uncommon thing within the Circles when Rendor stood upon the dais. He leaned over and whispered into his king's ear, "You know which she'll choose."

"She'll be happy with neither, but yes, I know. As do you, and it will be your task to keep an eye on her."

Sir Conor nodded and turned to step down from the dais. He roared with ferocity of a lion, "Enough!" and everyone in the chamber came to sudden silence. A duel between Dragonknights hadn't happened in over a decade, and no one would dare consider fighting Conor.

"I am King," Rendor said succinctly, "and the decision to offer such is mine. The matter is closed. Brethren of the Second Circle, leave us, please. The night is yours."

Conor took back his chair, resuming his stoic demeanor as the others looked to one another, shrugged, and filed out to the spiral stairs. They climbed upwards, as there was no exit in the base of the tree, and Rendor waited patiently with his Commanders as the other, mostly younger men, passed by. Tullus and Malum fumed toward each other. No doubt they'd work it out of their systems with drink or women later, while Westley continued his disconcerting, unblinking stare. What the man had lost in fighting ability and good looks from his trauma long ago, he'd gained twice fold in politicking and understanding. He said it was because he talked so little now that his ears had truly opened to what others said and thought. Making Jenna a Protectress had been his stroke of genius, and Rendor knew the moment he'd offered it up that she would take that option over banishment.

"I know they are allowed to speak their minds here, but must they do it so loudly?" Rendor wondered aloud once the others were gone, rubbing his eyes with the thumb and forefinger of one hand. He dropped it to his side and looked at Tullus and Malum pointedly in turn. "Am I to assume that either or both of you don't care for my decision here?"

Malum leaned back in his chair, his legs crossed at the ankles as he rubbed at his unshaven chin and lower lip with his right hand. His right leg bounced frenetically, perhaps in anxiousness like a child who expected he was about to get the belt, but it was Tullus who spoke up with his booming voice, "It is not our place to argue, my king. You asked our counsel on the matter, and we gave it. The final decision is yours, and we abide."

"Excellent."

"Highness, may I ask one question?" came Malum's voice. He had stopped his rubbing and bouncing, now sitting still with a finger held aloft as if he pointed at the ceiling. With King Rendor's nod, he continued, "Does not letting her live have risks?"

"Life has risks, Malum," Conor replied. "Perhaps you should learn to live for them instead of live in fear from them."

Anger flashed across Malum's countenance at the suggestion, but he contained it quickly before continuing, "I only mean that if she truly is her father's daughter, it seems unlikely that she will stop now. What if she realizes –?"

His question was cut short, and King Rendor turned his usually kind eyes, now hard as granite on Sir Conor and said, "We will have to count on our best and bravest to keep a close watch on her in the south."

Conor closed his eyes and bowed his head.

Chapter 10

On the Road to Soutton

A dark shadow blacked out the sun overhead, and Jenna looked upward to see the form of a forest dragon as it flew in front of the blinding yellow disc. The dragons of Abrea, thin of body and limb, were not like their massive, ponderous cousins to the south in Vulgesch who favored power and size over agility. They rose in the air naturally at speeds that the southern dragons had to expend immense effort to reach, and they maneuvered around the trees themselves, when they so desired, able to fly between them without so much as dislodging a single leaf. As she saw its form disappear behind the towering treetops, she thought for just a moment that she saw the powerful frame of Sir Conor upon its back, and then it came back into view, having wheeled hard about in tight turn. As swiftly as it reappeared, it vanished once more, and Jenna felt as if her future vanished with the dragon.

She rode with a party of three others, a Protectress from Soutton named Laina and two of Rendor's personal guards he assigned as escorts. Laina had bristled at the assignment of the two men, explaining to the king that she was the only escort that Jenna needed as they were in fact traveling through the heart of Abrea, and death punished any who attacked a Protectress. Rendor wouldn't hear of it, and Jenna wondered if the extra protection was meant for more than making sure the two women weren't accosted on the road.

Laina certainly appeared to need help from no one. The woman stood a mere five feet tall and wore a heavy padded gambeson and trousers common to squires of cavalry, which Jenna thought hid a well-muscled body. She kept her dark brown hair cut short like some men, and her matching eyes seemed to dart about, catching everything around her. She carried no sword with her longbow, but a pair of long daggers lay sheathed on her belt at each hip. Jenna had more than once spied the tiny handle of a throwing knife half hidden in her boots or armor, and this was confirmed on the first evening after they left Highton, when she produced one such knife seemingly from nowhere and cleanly skewered a rabbit some fifteen feet away. She cleaned and cooked the animal herself, dividing it amongst her traveling companions.

The first three days passed at an abysmally slow pace, the horses plodding step after step, mile after mile, and Jenna debated whether she had made the correct decision. It was three weeks to Soutton, and in three days, Laina had said hardly three words to her, though Jenna was keenly aware of the Protectress' observation. The woman's eyes judged her constantly. Admittedly, she had made no attempt to engage Laina in conversation; she didn't know where to start, and she had the distinct feeling that, while she had been selected for what many considered a great honor, the other woman looked at her as a criminal. *If this is life amongst the Protectresses*, Jenna thought, *I'm better off accepting banishment.* More than once she considered riding off in the night, though she had a weight in the pit of her stomach that told her she could not change her decision now.

The men for the most part kept to themselves, involving neither woman in their conversations, laughter, or dice games when they stopped for the evening.

At the end of that third day, Laina finally spoke more than a few words. She motioned at Jenna's bow and, without emotion or inflection, asked, "You can hunt?"

"Yes."

"Then, go find us some meat while I start a fire. It's several days to the next village."

"We have enough provisions. As a Protectress can you not ask for whatever we need when we arrive?"

Laina hardly blinked as she stared back with no indication that she'd even heard her charge's words. The woman, who Jenna thought must be a decade older than she, seemed almost to have turned to stone while the guards gazed on in mild interest. Finally, the woman replied with an edge of annoyance to her voice, "Yes, but we who can provide for ourselves need take nothing from others."

Jenna continued to lock eyes with her, but she saw no reason to argue or resist; the logic was simple and correct enough, as Jenna had been taught to hunt at an early age by her mother. She nodded in slight deference and looked away as she collected her bow and quiver from her horse's back. She felt Laina's eyes continue to bore holes into the back of her skull, and she wondered if the woman ever fucking blinked.

As Jenna slung her quiver over her shoulder, Laina stopped her again, "No. Leave them. You take one arrow."

"What? Why?" Jenna asked in confusion.

"Because I said so," Laina replied, and the edge in her voice had turned to razor sharp steel.

"But, why?" Jenna repeated, and she sounded almost like a petulant child even to her own ears.

"Because you are a Protectress now, and until Lady Ayn joins you to the Second Circle, I am your better. You follow my commands, and I command you to take one arrow, one arrow only, and find us some meat. If you fail, I will hunt, and you'll eat nothing tonight."

Jenna stood defiantly with her bow in one hand, the other planted on her hip as she appeared to consider this. Truthfully, nothing passed through her mind at all as her will contested that of the other woman's, and for about the fiftieth time in three days, Jenna decided that she'd made the wrong choice of the two options given to her by King Rendor. For a moment, she concluded that not only was she not going to go hunt with one arrow, but she would also climb atop her horse and ride off in a different direction. Isdal was the closest of the other kingdoms... Jenna sighed, tamping down her rebellious streak, and she shrugged off the quiver, allowing it to slide down her arm and fall to the ground. Bending down, she grasped one arrow by its fletching and withdrew it from the quiver to nock it into her bow before heading toward the edge of the forest road.

She vaguely noted that Laina's face, apparently carved straight from stone, changed in no way at all, whereas one of the guards chuckled softly as the other reached into a purse to pass over his lost wager.

Jenna passed between two elm trees and entered the forest carelessly, her feet crushing leaves underfoot that had already fallen as the season continued to turn. She hadn't noticed before how many of the leaves overhead had begun to change color, a mosaic of reds, oranges, yellows, and still some green painting the canopy. Perhaps they had changed so suddenly in the last few days as the air had gotten colder at night, or maybe she failed to notice because so many of the trees that comprised Highton were pines and other evergreens. She separated a pair of bushes and pushed her way through.

After a few minutes of sulking and crunching through the woods, she calmed herself enough to focus on the task at hand. She had been tasked with bringing back a kill, and her own resistance to the situation would not ease the burden at all. Only failure could come from stomping about and scaring off any potential game. Jenna breathed in the musky forest air several times to quiet her mind and calm her nerves, and she investigated where she stood with searching eyes. There was little to see in her immediate area – disturbances in a patch of grass and in a small pile of fallen leaves, likely from a squirrel or other such rodent.

She smiled, and Jenna considered killing such a small thing. In fact, as she stayed still and quiet, she took note of several squirrels running and jumping about, collecting the feasts that would sustain them through the winter months. She half drew back her bowstring. She was told to bring back meat, and it would be a shame if the only game she found was something so small that it couldn't even sate one stomach. That was it, that's what she would do!

Jenna took aim at a squirrel only twenty paces away which sat back on its haunches as it nibbled at something with its bushy tail almost blocking her shot. She must be careful – squirrels were often caught in traps, not shot with a bow, to avoid wasting such a miniscule amount of edible meat and organs. It must be a shot to the head, which would likely cleave the head completely off, leaving the body behind. She deliberately pulled the bowstring back to her ear and prepared to release the missile, but then Jenna hesitated at the last moment. The tiny creature turned suddenly in that twitchy motion that always seemed to be faster than the eye could see. A broken acorn held in its tiny fingers, the animal seemed to consider her for a second before dropping its prize and skittering to another about a foot away.

Jenna lowered the bow while easing the tension in her bowstring until she could comfortably hold both the bow and the shaft of the arrow where they met at her left hand. She hung her head and stared at her feet for a long moment. She was so stupid. What good would come of it? If she somehow missed her shot, she could ruin any sustenance the squirrel could provide. Or she might lose the arrow; a clean miss could result in it becoming embedded in the trunk of a tree or otherwise irrecoverable. Then her irreverent, sneering victory becomes a complete failure in what she now realized was her first test as a Protectress. The first of many. Once the epiphany struck her, she knew she dared not fail.

Thus attuned to the task, she cautiously, silently except to the wariest of ears skulked through the forest while watching for spoor - a tip of a shrub turned and broken awkwardly, displaced leaves, and flattened grass. She found a partial hoof print in a patch of bare ground, and this Jenna followed, her legs bent to keep herself small. The deer tarried at one point, and she spotted a dead tree, some of the bark having been stripped off some three to four feet off the ground. Bits of crushed and ground bark lay on the ground at the foot of the tree, and these still had the animal's saliva coating them.

A slight breeze blew into her face from straight ahead, bringing with it the familiar musk of a buck, and Jenna straightened her back to see over a row of hedges. A tiny stream, less than two feet across, babbled some thirty feet away, and there he stood, his head lowered as he drank. She judged him to be young, purely due to his smaller size and the antlers that had begun to grow outward, but he would make a far better meal than a squirrel. Jenna considered moving on for other opportunities, but the sun moved close to the horizon, bathing the forest in long shadows and gloom.

She pulled back the bowstring and aimed carefully for the back of the deer's skull, below his left ear. An easy kill shot at this range, the arrow would puncture his skull and pierce his brain, nicking an artery on its way through the thin flesh at that point. Even if he didn't die when the arrow struck, he would bleed to death in a minute or less. The arrow cut through the air with a whistle, but so close, the deer had no time to react. It crumpled immediately as the arrow struck home, legs flailing at first before slowing as the animal died. Jenna released a held breath, closed her eyes, and breathed calmly through her nose for a few moments.

Less than half of the sun still peered over the horizon when she returned to camp, though no one could see it for the forest trees. She slung the heavy animal about her shoulders. It had been quite a challenge to heft the deer, but Jenna refused to return to the camp for help. She didn't know if it would have been viewed by Laina as weakness, and she didn't care. She needed to return with her kill, and so she followed the smoke rising into the air from Laina's campfire. She staggered out of the woods, her right side covered in the beast's blood as it continued to ooze from its wound.

Laina stood from where she gazed into the fire, motioned at Rendor's men and said, "Take it, and set it there."

The two guards moved to intercept Jenna, one to each side of her, but she shrugged them away with a mumbled, "No." A flicker of a smile flashed across Laina's face, or was it a trick of the fire in the failing daylight? One man stepped backward in surprise, his hands lifted, while the other shrugged with indifference and returned to the fire. With ebbing strength, Jenna crossed the camp to the indicated place and crouched downward on shaking legs. Once low to the ground, Jenna released the deer and shrugged it off her shoulders to the cleared forest floor with a thump, and only her supreme sense of balance kept her from falling backward onto it. She stood exhausted.

"You know how to skin, clean, and butcher I should hope?" Laina asked as she approached Jenna and

116

the deer, and Jenna replied with a questioning nod. Laina continued with an outstretched hand that proffered a knife hilt, "Good. Get to work. We're hungry."

By the time Jenna completed the task, her three fellow travelers had eaten their fill and settled in for a comfortable evening, the warming fire proof against the chilling air. A fair amount of venison remained, and while she looked at it longingly, the lethargy in her limbs and the heaviness of her eyelids took precedence, silencing the growling of her stomach. After a few minutes, heedless of the blood and other stains on her clothes, she curled up on her bedroll and fell into a deep sleep.

She awoke early, shivering in the chilly air as the sky began to lighten from the first touch of the sun's rays. Of course, the forest trees blocked most of this from view, but any dweller in the forests of Abrea could explain that the early morning gloaming felt different. Songbirds and woodpeckers started their day, filling the trees with their songs, and the hooting of the owls had faded into the darkness. The fire had long died out, not even a smoldering ruin anymore as the coals turned cold hours before, and the cold of the night invaded the camp.

Jenna sat up slowly, imagining that she could both feel and hear her joints creak as she tried to stretch them, and her breath filled the air with great white plumes of fog. It was a typical autumn morning in this part of Abrea – cold in the early hours, but it would warm nicely as the sun finally rose. She glanced around their camp, noting that only one of the two guards stirred, his hand darting up to scratch an itch at the end of his nose before going still upon his chest. Laina lay on her side facing Jenna, and the Protectress opened one eye for a moment to peer at Jenna's upright form before rolling to her other side.

Jenna climbed to her feet, stretching her arms extensively while arching her back to work out the kinks of a cold night spent curled up in the fetal position, and she made her way into the slowly lightening woods to find a place to relieve herself. The muscles of her arms, shoulders, and legs ached with the exertions of her hunt. Some twenty feet away, she selected a spot obscured from the view of their camp by dense bushes, and she proceeded to stare unseeing out into the forest. As she finished and hiked up her trousers, looking downward to lace them tightly, noise accompanied by motion sounded just a short distance in front of her. In her still sleep addled state, she realized too late that she heard the impact of a rock amongst the brush as it rolled and bounced a foot or two to stop, as well as that the rock had sailed overhead from behind her.

Jenna had only thought to turn when something crashed against the back of her head. Purple and orange stars exploded in her vision, obscuring everything, while a tremendous roaring like the rushing waters of a powerful river flooded her ears. She staggered forward a step, fell to her knees as she fought the darkness that rushed from the periphery of her sight to fill it completely, and then dropped forward unconscious.

The first thing she knew was pain, an immense fiery torment that roused her from the blackness of oblivion to let Jenna know that she was still alive. It drew her out of that dark sea of nothingness and toward strange sounds her mind could not place or recognize. They grew in volume as her mind neared the surface, and when it broke through, a bright blur filled her bleary vision. She couldn't see anything, though she thought her eyes open, and the light pierced deeply into her brain, filling her head with intense agony. She clenched her eyes against it, hoping for a tiny amount of respite, but the throbbing torment only seemed to worsen as she grew more conscious.

Jenna opened her eyes again to find herself unable to make out her surroundings as shapes and colors continued to blend into one amalgamated mass of light, but she tried to blink it away. She opened and closed her eyes repeatedly, over and over, and every time she did so, her surroundings sharpened a bit more. Noises focused faster than her vision – the light rustling of a breeze, songs of birds, and the skittering of small animals – and she recognized the familiar sound of someone tearing at meat with teeth, chewing. Eventually, blurred lines and merged shapes regained enough of their form for her to know she was in the forest, sitting on the cold ground in a copse of trees. The chewing came from her left, and when she turned her head to look, a purple haze filled the periphery of her vision as pain exploded through her brain once more.

She must have let out a groan of some kind, for a voice spoke, "You're awake. That's good. I'm about done eating, and I wanted you to be awake."

Jenna closed her eyes against the anguish that threatened to knock her out again and felt her eyes roll upward into the back of her head towards darkness. The sensation gave a miniscule amount of relief and solace, and she wanted to lose herself in that. But she fought to bring herself back, to open her eyes again, hoping that she managed to bring a smoldering glare into the eyes of Brenton. He knelt on one knee as he mauled a familiar looking haunch of venison, and realizing she so stared at him, he tossed it to one side and wiped his mouth with the back of his hand.

"Thanks for that. I couldn't have asked for much more when I entered your camp last night. I'm surprised you didn't take shifts on watch, but I guess it's safe this deep in Abrea. Well, not so safe for you."

The ache in the back of her skull forgotten, Jenna tried to bark something back at him, only to realize she could only manage to utter a muffled sound. Her mind hadn't cleared enough to realize that a wad of linen or wool had been shoved into her mouth and a gag wound tightly about the back of her head. Maybe she had realized it, and she just didn't care, her aggressive nature coming to the surface.

"Shut up," he said as he stood and stretched his back.

Jenna sat with her spine against a tree and her hands tied behind her back, and from such a position, the red haired young man towered over her. His arms and chest bulged as he did so, and she had no doubt that he had no trouble slinging her over his shoulders to carry her here, wherever they exactly were. She looked about for a moment as he sighed in his stretch, and she realized he couldn't have taken her far. The forest had only really begun to lighten with the first rays of dawn; she couldn't have been out for more than an hour, and she doubted the ability of one so large as Brenton to move agilely through the forest while carrying a burden. She listened to the forest sounds and searched the nearby woods for any sign of Laina or the guards.

"They're not coming for you any time soon," Brenton admonished almost in a whisper, looking down at her intently as she met his eyes. "They were still asleep. For that matter, they probably won't look for you at all. Probably figured you ran away."

"Without my horse?" she tried to say, but it came out in a mumbled mess.

"I said shut up," he replied, and he kicked a splash of dirt into her eyes with the point of his boot. It burned terribly, and she shook her head and blinked over and over to try to clear it out. This caused a new bloom of agony in the back of her skull, and her eyes teared up as they tried to wash out the invading particles.

"Oh, cry. Yes, please. Cry," he whispered into her ear, and she managed to open one eye enough to see him right in her face. "You're going to cry a lot before I kill you."

Jenna pointlessly hurled an expletive at him, muffled and inarticulate due to the gag, but Brenton seemed to get the point. His mouth split wide in a toothy grin as drew a knife with one hand while aggressively cupping one of her breasts with the other. She tried to cringe and wriggle away, but the tree behind her provided nowhere to go. In her scrambling, Jenna realized her legs were free. She kicked up toward him, but, as limber as she was, she was situated so that she couldn't get enough momentum. Brenton laughed as batted her leg away, and to prove just how powerless she was in her predicament, he shifted and brought his full weight down on her thighs with the point of the knife grazing the soft flesh under her jaw.

"A girl Dragonknight," he sneered, his face an ugly amalgamation of round, over formed features, red stubble, and freckles. "I'll show you what a girl is for."

He leaned in and planted his mouth hard over hers, and Jenna felt his tongue probing around the gag. Jenna tried to turn her head away, but an iron grip took her hair close to the roots and forced her to face him. She writhed and squirmed, put all her strength into trying to kick him away, but his weight all but crushed her. His rank breath filled her nostrils, and as his saliva began to mix with hers on the gag, a sickness roiled in the pit of her stomach. She wanted nothing more than to vomit. It might end his attack, but she'd choke to death with the cloth obstructing her mouth. The growing bulge in the front of his trousers pushed her further to break away, but she couldn't match his strength or weight.

Fair fights are for suckers, Brasalla's words echoed in her mind.

Her hands tied behind her back and around the tree was one problem, but Brenton had neither bound her feet, nor tied the gag around the tree itself. That would have been smart, but it showed his disdain for his opponent, his lack of respect. He left himself open to attack because he thought her powerless against him, the same mistake he made during their duel.

Through incredible force of will, Jenna stopped fighting. She ended her feeble contortions, ceased her overpowered resistance, and after a few moments that felt like an eternity, Brenton also eased his own use of force. Her skin crawled as a hand explored under her tunic, but she valiantly controlled her reaction to it. She even leaned into his repulsive kiss and pressed back against the gag with her own tongue, hoping that if she showed interest, he would remove it.

He leaned back from her a few inches and said, "So, you do know what a girl is for."

Jenna acted, every nerve and sinew she had on fire with hatred for the red haired bastard and what he had done to her so far, to say nothing of his intentions. His face hovered just far enough from hers but not so far as to allow him time to react, and she whipped her forehead forward as hard as her neck could manage. The agony of where she'd been struck from behind erupted anew, but she ignored it as her forehead crashed into the point of his nose and then his upper lip and teeth. Something split the skin on her forehead, but cartilage bent and snapped under her assault; something behind his upper lip gave way.

Brenton reeled backward, half standing as he shouted, "You fucking bitch!" through fingers cupping the front of his face, blood running between them.

Jenna wasted no time, and she brought one of her legs up as hard as she could, her shin impacting the

122

underside of his manhood, as she had done with her fist once before as a child. Brenton crumpled as the wind blew out of his lungs, and he fell off to the ground on her left. She lashed her foot out again, and the knife went flying away as her boot struck his wrist. She struck again and again, and even her soft riding boots had an effect as Brenton rolled away to evade the assault, one of his hands down between his legs.

She raised her face to the forest canopy above her and shouted for all she was worth, though the gag still prevented most of the sound from escaping, and it even threatened to choke her by sliding further into her mouth and throat. But Jenna didn't care. She had walloped him a couple of times, and she only hoped they'd made enough commotion to draw Laina to them. But now she doubted if Brenton would hesitate long before killing her once he regained his composure. She falteringly made as much noise as she could manage with flailing legs amidst the detritus of the forest floor and her muffled voice.

"Shut up, bitch!" Brenton almost screamed at her, his voice noticeably higher than it had been, and she didn't even see the blow coming. It was an open handed slap that struck across her face, and it burned hot as lava across the bruiscs caused by his assault a few days previously. Her head cracked back against the tree trunk, and purple haze threatened to overwhelm her vision.

She lost track of time as she fought to remain awake. She knew she had to stay awake, and that something as small as blinking away the tears gathering in her eyes might force her to fall unconscious again. Everything seemed to move slowly, as if time had almost stretched out and stopped while she wavered and teetered on that edge over the other side of which was blissful darkness. Brenton seemed to lay curled up for hours, trying to regain his breath, and eventually moving to inspect his manhood away from her view.

As time returned to normal, he too returned and searched some bushes where he found his knife. He stood up to his full height and turned back toward her, waiving it so the short blade caught both the sunlight and her attention. There was no hint of a wicked smile this time, no indication of any intention except one as he said, "You know, I didn't have to kill you. We could've had a good time, and I might've let you go. But you had to ruin it. Stupid bitch." His speech had taken on a slight slur as if something in his mouth were broken, an aural match to the blood smeared across his nose, mouth, and chin.

Everything froze in a terrible moment of stasis as the blade splashed sunlight into Jenna's eyes and panic took hold. Brenton took one step toward her before a whistle pierced and drowned out the forest noise as an arrow cut through the air. It transfixed his wrist perfectly, his knife falling to the ground as his hand reflexively dropped it, and with the impact, he staggered a step as the arrow imbedded itself into a thin pine. Brenton clutched at his forearm with his free hand, screaming incoherently as blood rolled down his wrist to drip onto the ground. He took hold of the arrow by the fletching and roared in pain as he tried to pull it from the tree before he realized he could easily free himself by breaking off the arrow between his arm and the tree.

Just as this realization went through his head, Laina's voice shouted, "Don't move, or the next one is through your eye!"

Jenna shot a searching look to her right, and she saw the Protectress a mere ten yards or so away, her bowstring pulled back for another attack, and at this range, the longbow would propel the arrow clean through his eye and maybe burst the arrowhead out the back of Brenton's skull. Brenton saw this also, and he

124

ended his attempts to free himself, hanging his head and cradling his stricken arm. Jenna let out a long slow sigh as she drooped her head and shoulders in relief.

"Help her," Laina commanded.

A flurry of motion met Jenna's ears. She glanced up to see the king's guards, whose names she realized she didn't even know, as they popped out from behind some shrubs to hurry towards her. She started to snort and laugh uncontrollably, stricken with the thought that the two men almost seemed like groundhogs emerging from a hole in the ground to see what went on. Laina deliberately stepped closer, her arrowhead trained on Brenton, as the two men freed Jenna – one cautiously slid a dagger between the gag and her face, slicing through the fabric while the other severed the bond holding her hands behind the tree. She spat out a fist sized, fuzzy wool ball as she took one guard's canteen without asking permission, taking a long draught, the water running down her chin.

"Are you alright?" Laina asked, for a moment taking her hellish gaze from the red haired would be rapist and murderer.

"I think so," Jenna replied, handing the man back his canteen, and he helped her to her feet as she swiped a sleeve of her tunic across her mouth. "My head's going to hurt for days."

Jenna closed her eyes for a moment, knowing she was safe to do so, and she rubbed her eyes and face with open hands. She exhaled a deep, comforting sigh, a sort of cleansing breath, and when she opened her eyes, she narrowed them on her longsword. It hung on Laina's hip, the sheathe buckled to the woman's belt, and it was too long for her height as the bronze adorned point of the sheathe barely scraped the ground.

"I brought it for you," Laina explained, following Jenna's gaze. "You're going to need it to pass judgement."

"Judgement?"

"You know the law," Laina replied coldly. "You," she addressed Brenton, "what does the law say about an attack against a Protectress?"

Brenton paled visibly, and his entire body began to shake, starting with his knees and moving up his form. He almost seemed to be shivering, either from the cold air finally getting through the heat of his desired vengeance or pain and fear. His lower lip quivered fearfully as he answered as quietly as a child who had broken a dinner plate, "But, she isn't a Protect-"

"What is the law?!" Laina shouted, her intense raised voice disturbing a handful of sparrows nearby, who fluttered and flapped away. She lowered her bow, releasing the tension in the bowstring as she looked at Jenna. "What is the law?"

"To attack a Dragonknight, or a Protectress, is an attack upon the king himself," Jenna intoned, remembering her childhood lessons.

"And the penalty?"

"Death."

"But," Brenton blubbered, and panic and tears ran down his ruddy cheeks, quite the counterpoint to his massive size, "she is not even a Protectress. She's no one."

"Whether she has taken the oath or not, she is a Protectress of the Second Circle by order of King Rendor," Laina said without looking at him as she placed her arrow back in her quiver. She handed her longbow to one of the men and drew Jenna's longsword, the smoky Vulgeschi steel ringing with deadly beauty as it left its sheath. She held it out to Jenna and explained, "He is guilty, witnessed so by us three. As the one assaulted, I offer you the opportunity to mete judgement."

Jenna took her sword and held it awkwardly. It suddenly weighed heavily in her hand. Perhaps sheer

126

exhaustion from the ordeal was setting in, but maybe it was for some other reason she couldn't quite place. Laina turned from her, kicked a booted foot high into the air and then brought it down sharply as an axe cutting firewood onto Brenton's forearm. As he howled his misery, the arrow's shaft split and broke, and the big, young man dropped to his knees and cradled his wounded arm, the remains of the arrow still piercing through it. He looked upward, into the eyes of the woman he attacked, his own pleading for mercy. Jenna considered his face for a long moment and then raised her sword, her father's sword, to watch the play of the forest filtered sunlight across the blade and the channel that ran up the middle on either side. She fancied that the dark clouds in the steel, formed as the weapon was forged with dragonfire deep in the mountains of Vulgesch, billowed and moved just as the white clouds did in the sky.

"I am tired," Jenna announced, and she lowered the blade, turned, and began to walk away. But she stopped in front of Laina and almost whispered with tears forming in her eyes, "Thank you for coming for me."

"Oath or not, you are of the Sisterhood. Go rest, Sister."

As Jenna passed out of the copse of trees, following the trail back to their camp that Laina must have followed to save her, she heard Brenton's voice as he begged, "No, please! Please! I'm sorry!" An impossibly short, high pitched shrill sound came, followed by a thud and the sound of Brenton's body slumping into a collection of gaily colored forest leaves.

The days passed terrifically slow as they rode toward Soutton, but of course after what Jenna had just endured, anything would have seemed easier. Nothing happened, nothing at all. They passed various people on the road – hunters from nearby villages, merchants, and other travelers passing from place to place, from whom she hid her bruised and battered face. Most stepped aside as the small group passed, paying deference as Laina's armor and longbow marked her a Protectress. Nothing exciting or interesting occurred, and that suited Jenna just fine. Rendor's guards continued to stick to themselves, and on the fifth day, Laina released them to head back to Highton, much to their apparent relief.

"You must understand what it is to be a Protectress before you take the oath," Laina explained as they rode. She adopted a much kinder, friendlier attitude after Brenton. "I am sure you know some of it. Everyone does."

"I do. My teacher back home was once a Protectress," Jenna explained. "It seems simple."

"It is but tell me what you know."

"First and foremost, we protect the people of Abrea and enforce the king's laws. As a Sister of the Second Circle, I will serve a Lady of the First Circle, and she answers to King Rendor."

"Or to Sir Conor," Laina added, "as he is the right hand of the king in the south."

"Are we subordinate to the Dragonknights?" Jenna asked.

"Only to Sir Conor. He is of the First Circle and Lord of the South, but we do not follow the commands of those who serve under him."

Jenna looked over to her companion, "Who is Lady of the South?"

A rare smile touched Laina's lips, and a glow entered her eyes as she answered, "Lady Ayn."

"Tell me about her."

"She is…" Laina paused as if searching for words, "an amazing woman, beautiful and fierce. She can place an arrow in an eagle's eye at three hundred

128

yards. I warn you – she can be quick to anger, but in the end, she is even handed and fair. She is also quick to forgive, and she loves each one of us."

"Can she fight well?" Jenna asked, right away regretting what sounded like a stupid question.

But Laina answered eagerly, "Oh, yes! She is… strong. She can wield a sword as well as any man, and Sir Conor favors her as a dueling partner."

"Will we see Sir Conor often?"

"Why do you ask such?" Laina returned, casting a sideways look.

"I…" Jenna trailed off. Why had she asked that? What difference did it make? "I was just curious because he is Lord of the South. I would like to see him fight. Everyone in Abrea knows he's the greatest warrior in the kingdom, perhaps the world."

Laina returned her eyes straight ahead and raised one interested eyebrow as she responded, "From time to time, yes, depending on how often you're in Soutton."

Neither of them spoke again for an hour, and it was Laina who broke the silence, "That man who attacked you."

"Yeah. His name was Brenton."

"I… I'm sorry to talk about it so soon, but I hope you'll assuage my curiosity. Was he not who you defeated in the duel in Highton?"

"Yes," Jenna said, her tone clipped. "You knew about that?"

"I more than know about it. I saw it."

Jenna pulled up on her horse's reins, bringing it to a halt as Laina continued a few more steps before also stopping her mount and turning half around in the saddle to face her. Jenna swallowed a painful gulp and asked, "You were there?"

"I was," Laina nodded. "Lady Ayn had a dispatch for Sir Conor, and he was already in Highton. I stayed to watch the Trials. You fought… smartly. With guile."

Jenna wasn't sure how to react. She understood that Laina paid her a compliment, but the unease in knowing her companion, and probably everyone she would meet from now on and maybe the rest of her life, knew that she was *that* girl fought with her pride. And that knowledge, that discomfort, was winning. In the end, Jenna accepted the praise and started her horse forward again. Laina held her own mount in place until they were again side by side.

"You knew him from before, didn't you?" the woman asked after a few dozen paces.

"From my village. He left a few years ago."

Laina nodded and stated flatly, "The two of you had history."

"I, well," Jenna stuttered, "how did you know that?"

"It was obvious to those who saw, I mean, really saw," Laina said as if her words explained everything, but Jenna still looked on in confusion. "I knew the two of you knew each other before the first round; I saw it on both of your faces. There was unfinished business there."

"Well, it's finished now," Jenna replied with a tone that indicated she was done discussing the past, and they rode for a time in silence.

As the sun went down that evening, Laina continued to push them on their way south. Dusk arrived, and the gloaming took over the forests. Jenna saw pinpricks of warm firelight in the distance, and as the air grew colder by the moment, they approached the edges of a village. Small log and stone homes with thatched rooves met them at first, each with shepherd hook style posts outside holding small lanterns. The road took them straight into the center of the village, and the homes grew larger and more impressive, the rooves of shingled wood instead of thick mats of straw and leaves. Early in the evening, there were people about, dressed in the normal forest-wear of Abrea, and they smiled or greeted the two women in friendly manners as they passed.

They reached an intersection with another road that must have been ten yards in width and well-traveled as its dirt had been packed down long ago. At this intersection stood four buildings, two of which were wealthy, opulent homes of oak and granite. One of these carried a sigil on its door indicating it to belong to the village head or lead elder. Across the other side of the avenue stood a large smithy, from which still glowed warm flickering firelight and the clanging of metal even as the hour grew late, and a three storied inn that was the largest edifice in the village. Four iron protected stanchion torches burned at the corners of the intersection, providing some semblance of light and a modicum of warmth against the growing chill.

The inn had a sort of portico entrance, and inside stood a tall, round man as he attacked stone paving with a straw broom while muttering to himself. Laina handed the reins of her horse over to Jenna as she dropped off the mount to approach him, and he stepped out from the portico into the weak light. He wore a simple tunic and trousers with workaday boots, and a white apron, stained with unknown greases and fluids that wrapped around most of his body and hung to his knees. Short cut, salt and pepper hair wrapped around a mostly bald pate that reflected some of the torchlight.

"Good evening, Protectress," he greeted Laina affably as she approached.

"Innkeeper, I presume?" Laina asked, receiving a friendly smile and nod in response. "Is this the East-West road?"

"It is, Lady," he responded, pointing west, "Midton is less than a day's ride."

"Excellent. Thank you," Laina said with a polite nod, and she turned back toward Jenna and the horses.

"Uh, Lady?" he called, prompting her to turn back. "I am sure I can offer two Protectresses rooms for the night?"

Jenna's heart leapt at the thought of a real bed, indoors and someplace dry and warm as she hadn't slept in such a place since she left home (only about two weeks ago!), but her heart sank when Laina replied, "No thank you, good innkeeper. We have a long way to go."

"All the more reason to stop now," he prodded, "There isn't another good inn between here and Soutton, so I beg you stop and enjoy a comfortable night. Besides, I doubt you wish to continue much further in the dark. A horse might hurt himself if he can't see where he's stepping, or worse – get spooked by something in the woods like a bear or a wolf."

The realization struck Jenna of just how tired her body felt, and she yearned to call out to Laina, to beg her to take the innkeeper up on the offer. She had been traveling, first on foot and now on horseback, for two weeks with a couple of days for the grueling Trials in between, and she truthfully didn't know how much longer she could go without a good night's rest. She could see Laina's resolve waning, and Jenna wondered if a word from her would push the Protectress over the precipice or strengthen her resolve. In the end, she opted to remain quiet and barely restrained a joyful shout when her companion acquiesced.

"All right," Laina sighed, "but at least allow me to pay."

"I wouldn't hear of it, Protectress," replied the innkeeper, and he vanished into the portico, his voice echoing from within, "Wes get out here."

When he returned seconds later, Laina offered a compromise, "Then give us one room, please. We'll

132

share a bed, leave your other rooms for paying customers."

"Very well, very well," he replied, and a scruffy brown haired boy of about twelve joined his side. "I am your humble host Elian, and this is my son Wes. He will take your horses to the stables around back. Please come inside and warm yourselves."

Well-kept and clean, the inn's common room sat mostly empty and dim, light provided only by a burning fire and three or four lanterns. Several windows were already shuttered against the night, and a doorway on the other side led to a narrow hallway. A few patrons were sprinkled amongst the dozen or so tables spread throughout with two more sitting at a bar to the left, and Jenna got the distinct impression that these latter two were less travelers and more local drunks. At Laina's lead, the two women passed the bar, behind which she spotted a small kitchen, and took a table toward the back of the room near the fire.

Within minutes, Elian placed two steaming platters of seasoned potatoes and roasted pork in front of them, as well as a pair of plain but quite solid flagons filled to the brim with an almost golden liquid. He, of course, refused payment of any kind before he vanished back into the kitchen. Jenna took a tentative sip, and finding the spiced sweetness to her liking, tipped the tankard more fully. She enjoyed the warmth that spread as it washed down her throat and into her stomach.

"I didn't peg you as much of a drinker," Laina admitted.

Jenna placed the drink down to consider her food as she replied, "What do you mean?"

"That's honey mead," Laina explained, and seeing the complete lack of comprehension in Jenna's eyes, she added, "It's like wine."

"Oh. I, uh, didn't know. I've never tasted anything like it before. I've had wine a few times.

Sometimes merchants from the south would pass through, but it was very expensive."

"Yeah well, enjoy it, but go easy on it. You'll have a terrible headache tomorrow."

They ate in silence for a few minutes, Jenna noting Laina's lack of table manners or maybe she just didn't care. The woman eschewed the available fork or even her own knife, and picked the food up with her fingers, starting on the outside edge of the platter where it was coolest. She popped a potato or chunk of pork into her mouth and chewed loudly as her fingers darted back for another. Wiping greasy fingers right on the tunic under her leather jerkin, she belched several times. Obviously, her upbringing varied wildly from Jenna's.

Eager to avoid wincing at her companion's behavior, Jenna opted for conversation and asked, "Do we ride to Midton tomorrow?"

"I see no need," Laina shrugged, and she chewed open mouthed as she talked, causing Jenna to wonder if she made a mistake. "The North-South road is wider and maybe in better condition than the one we're on, but it's much more travelled. I like to avoid other people as much as possible."

I can't imagine why, Jenna thought, but she avoided blurting it aloud. After a moment of silent chewing, she said, "Tell me about Soutton."

"You'll see it for yourself soon enough."

"Tell me anyway," Jenna urged.

"Very well," Laina acquiesced, wiping her fingers on her trousers and running the back of her hand across her mouth. "It's… unlike any of Abrea's other cities."

Jenna recalled her memories of maps she'd seen, and she asked, "Because it's not in the forests?"

"That's right, it's in the plains and foothills between the southern edge of the forest and the mountains that mark the beginning of Vulgesch," Laina nodded, and she looked away, as if she visualized the city on the far side of the inn's common room. "Everything in Soutton is built with stone, not wood, quarried from the nearby hills. A reddish orange feldspar is plentiful for miles around, and it's favored by the people there. When the sun rises or sets and its rays hit Soutton, well, you've never seen such a thing, and you never will anywhere else."

"I've heard Soutton is big," Jenna prodded.

Laina looked back at her, and the first honest smile she'd ever shown to Jenna split her face as she said, "It's huge. Last I heard, over ten thousand people."

"Ten thousand!"

"Oh, yes. I'm sure you know it's the largest city in Abrea?"

"Uh, yeah, but that's incredible. Isn't that over double Highton?"

"It is," Laina confirmed, "and it needs to be. While we trade with Vulgesch, it's important that they view us as strong because the people there appreciate strength. Soutton displays our strength to them – you'll understand when you see it – and stone is much harder to burn than wood. I'm not going to tell you any more about it; you should see it for yourself."

"I can't wait," Jenna replied with raised eyebrows, and she meant it. Highton was the first of Abrea's cities she had ever been to, and she found it beautiful and amazing – the perfect representation of Abrea and of how its people lived harmoniously in the forests. The Trials alone had more contestants than her own village had people, and the throngs of observers from above in that amazing city suspended amongst the tallest trees of Abrea astounded her. But Soutton sounded marvelous and fascinating in a completely different way.

After a time, and a bit more mead than Jenna wanted to admit to, they had Elian show them to their room, which was up a narrow, bending stair to the inn's second level. He opened the door to a small, well cleaned room, dropped a brass key into Laina's empty palm and trundled back the way they had come. Inside was a wooden poster bed of basic make, complete with a wool filled mattress that was large enough for two and had clean linen and wool bedding. Jenna wondered if Elian had picked this room for that reason, or if all his rooms had such spacious sleeping accommodations. An empty basin, a pitcher of water and an empty but clean wooden bucket were on the left side of the room, opposite the bed, and a thick, but inexpensive rug covered the hardwood floor.

Laina wasted no time clomping into the room and Jenna shut the door behind them. She ran a hand over her face, closing her eyes as she did so, because the room had started to spin, and she wanted it to stop. She leaned back against the door for a moment, and when she opened her eyes, she saw that Laina had removed her leathers, her weapons, her belt, and even her clothes, stacking everything neatly to one side next to the bed. Jenna's face felt hot, flushed, she assumed from her first encounter with mead.

"You're red in the face," Laina chuckled as she slid into the bed. "Don't be embarrassed. Sometimes you will see your Sisters naked."

"It's not that," Jenna replied with a slight shake of her head.

"I told you to go easy on the mead. If you have a headache in the morning, don't say I didn't warn you," Laina chided as she pulled a down pillow under her head, punched it a few times to force it into the shape she wanted and then settled herself on her side, facing the door.

Jenna moved to the far side of the bed and followed Laina's example. She found the bed cold at first, but it eventually warmed from her body heat, and she relaxed as she stared at the ceiling. "Laina?"

"Yes?" the woman almost mumbled.

"Will the other Protectresses know who I am?" Jenna asked, and then she decided to add to the question, "I mean, what I did?"

"I don't know. Lady Ayn will of course. Sir Conor is already in Soutton."

"Already? Really?"

"Dragons are fast," Laina replied dismissively. "Sir Conor would have already explained everything to her by now."

"Do you think she will tell the others?"

"I don't know, but you can't expect it to be a secret forever."

"I know," Jenna whispered, and she wondered why she cared so suddenly. So, what if they heard that she had made a go at the Trials? She was fierce, strong, resilient, but for some reason, she now felt shame at what she had done, despite the fact that it was still unfair.

As she ruminated and stared at the featureless ceiling, her eyelids grew heavy, and Laina surprised her with a question when she'd thought the woman had gone to sleep, "Do you want me to not say anything about it to anyone?"

"I'd appreciate that," Jenna answered, and with nothing further to talk about, she drifted into a deep sleep.

Chapter 11

Soutton

Weeks of riding caused soreness in places Jenna didn't know she had, as well as many others she was painfully aware of. She had blisters in places not discussed in pleasant company, and her legs and arms felt unceasingly exhausted. For that matter, she feared that her legs had decided to stay bowed permanently, only returning to their normal shape when they dismounted to sleep. True to Elian's word, they did not find another village with an inn for the rest of the journey to Soutton, and that only added to the misery with the cold nights.

It was like an awakening, almost like being born Jenna thought, when they emerged from the forests and into the southern plains of Abrea. An emergence it was, for the giant pine, oak, and elm trees simply ended. As the road cut its way between tall grasses on either side, the sun shone brightly overhead out of a clear blue sky, and Jenna never imagined that the sky was so infinite, as every time in her entire life that she looked upward, she saw forest canopy with the occasional patch of sky or sunlight shining through. After a few hundred feet, she turned about in her saddle, and it amazed her that the forest ceased with no transition or warning, and it stretched to the east and west as far as the eye could see, a natural border that separated the forest cities of Abrea from the rest of the world, even Soutton.

"How far now?" Jenna asked.

"About a day's ride."

Within hours, the grassy plains gave way to cultivated plots and rows of crops. Jenna had seen ears of corn as a child, but she never knew the plants from which they came could grow so tall. She saw vast fields of golden wheat, ready for harvest, as well as people out working in the fields. Occasionally, they passed surprisingly large homes overlooking the far reaching farms, many of which had other buildings that Laina called barns for housing livestock, supplies, or harvested crops. At a distance, the farms looked like paintings, agrarian tableaus of a life alien to Jenna, and she was sure the life of a farmer would never appeal to her.

Despite the deepening autumn, the sun warmed everything around her pleasantly, and she shed her cloak, enthusiastically enjoying the feel of it on her face and arms. Soutton had a reputation for growing and trading massive quantities of crops with Vulgesch, as well as substantial distribution into the forests, and the truth of this bucolic existence settled upon her. Within the forests, they focused on tubers, mushrooms, and other vegetables, and the common villagers hunted and fished for much of their existence. But here, with few trees in sight to block a cordial sun beaming overhead, a farmer could harvest corn as many as three times a year, and the air tended to stay warmer the closer one got to Vulgesch.

As they continued south and the sun dropped into the afternoon sky, the farms became smaller but more plentiful, and outcroppings of other buildings began to appear as well – a small, open air market, a common use stable, and even a tiny tavern. The plains gave way to gently rolling hills, undulating kindly across the landscape and not slowing their progress at all. People – travelers, merchants, and homesteaders – became far more common as well, and few of them paid the two women any mind at all. Jenna assumed they were more used to seeing Protectresses here than in other parts of Abrea.

And then they crested a small rise, and Jenna's mouth purely dropped open as Laina halted to give her a good, long look at what was before them. Still some miles in the distance lay a city the likes of which Jenna had never seen, never even dreamed of. It reflected hues from bright orange to blood red in the late afternoon sun, a beacon of ruddy light that announced the existence of the massive city to the world. It spread across steeper foothills than the lands leading up to it, the majestic, gray mountains of Vulgesch serving as a contrasting backdrop for hundreds and hundreds of stone buildings. Jenna had trouble making out details at this distance, but even the smallest homes appeared larger than that in which she grew up. There were also massive rectangular edifices with crenelated walls and spires, and giant cylindrical towers reached to the sky, reflecting golden light off their pointed peaks.

And if all that wasn't enough to astound a girl who until a few weeks ago had never left her bumpkin village in the middle of Abrea, and it most certainly was, well into the air and west of the city flew four dragons. At this distance they appeared tiny, but this only served to underscore their incredibility, because Jenna wouldn't be able to spot even the largest of eagles at this distance. They maneuvered and danced around each other, their green and brown scales glinting in the sky, and now and again a lance of green breath would shoot from one toward another.

"Behold, Soutton," Laina announced grandly.

"What are they doing?" Jenna asked in an almost breathless whisper.

"Training," Laina answered, and she sounded almost bored. "If you look to the sky around Soutton, you'll often find Brethren of the Second Circle sparring with each other."

"This happens... often here?" Jenna gaped. Even from miles away, her heart pumped faster, and her blood quickened in her veins and arteries. She wanted nothing more than to ride out underneath that aerial battlefield, lay on her back and stare up at the majestic creatures and their riders.

"Almost every day. You'll get used to it."

"I doubt it."

"Come," Laina said curtly, and she nudged her horse forward down the other side of the hill. She motioned up ahead of them, "If you look ahead, see that small town? Our road merges with the North-South road there. We'll stay the night at my home. We'll rise early tomorrow, and I'll take you to Lady Ayn."

"You live here?"

"Well, I spend more time with the Sisters in Soutton, but yes, I was born here. Come."

Soutton glowed every bit as gloriously in the eastern, morning sun as it did the afternoon before, and up close, its marvels did not disappoint. As Laina had said, every building in the city was built out of stone, from the smallest house to opulent estates, from the enormous granary which was the largest building in the city to the towering spires. Homes, smiths, taverns, and merchant stalls abounded, and everywhere the noise of bustling civilization filled the air. Jenna had never seen, or smelled, anything like it, and she tried Laina's patience with her tendency to stop and gawk. They passed a structure in which dozens of children sat and listened to a middle aged man, and another edifice where robed men and women kneaded and rubbed the backs and bodies of others as if they were bread dough. Jenna saw smiths who only worked in iron or gold or silver or copper and merchants that sold panes of glass to be fitted into windows. She rode between a pair of merchants, both of whom sold stone, shouting at each other and prospective customers as to how theirs was superior to that of their rivals. Jenna's head spun with it all, but she loved the feeling.

"Do you see that?" Laina asked, pointing over a series of shops at the top of what almost looked like a small castle. "That's Elishia Place. It is the seat of our order here in the south, Lady Ayn's home, and our destination."

Jenna could hardly see any of it except for what looked like crenellated battlements, but her eyes focused more directly on a massive tower that rose into the sky from near the dead center of Soutton, dwarfing everything and everyone nearby. Perhaps standing a hundred feet tall and half that across, the feldspar blocks used in its construction had been arranged in such a way that the colored stones formed a sort of mosaic. The darker reddish brown stones formed a fifty foot tall figure, outlined by the lighter oranges, and that figure held aloft a giant hammer in one hand. Obscured by the nearby buildings, Jenna could make out the image of an anvil in front of that figure. Toward the tower's terminus, one level laid almost completely open to the air around it, a half dozen or so pillars holding the next level some thirty feet above it.

She gasped as it coalesced in her mind, and though she suspected the answer, she asked, "What is that tower?"

Laina smiled then responded, "Sir Conor's tower."

"He lives here?" she asked, sounding awestruck.

"He is Lord of the South."

"I…" Jenna faded off for a second, seeking the right words, "I haven't seen any place like this, before, but why is his tower…?"

"So huge? Conor is from Vulgesch, after all. Everything his people do is big, even their dragons."

"No," Jenna shook her head, "I mean, why does part of it have no walls?"

"Oh," Laina laughed, "that's where his dragon, Viir, lands and sleeps."

"The dragon sleeps *in* the tower?" Jenna incredulously asked to Laina's enthusiastic nodding. "How does the tower stay up under all that?"

"Sir Conor hired the best stonemasons from his homeland to build it. If anyone could engineer such a feat, I guess it would be them."

As they passed into an intersection, Jenna received a better view of the tower, and the miraculous triumph of engineering it represented truly bewildered her. She thought the tree city of Highton impressive, awe inspiring, and while the Great Tree itself stood over twice the height of Conor's tower, it did not dominate the city the way this did. She wondered if this was a reflection of the Dragonknight's arrogance, but he was considered the greatest warrior in Abrea and King Rendor's personal champion. Still, was any man worthy of such a testament of greatness?

"How much further?" she asked.

"Not very. We're close now."

The press of people began to thin as they closed on their destination. They neared the center of the city, and it seemed most of the business dealings and such occurred away from it. Jenna looked about and found their surroundings were rich estates with three and four story homes with their own gilded walls and gardens. Jenna could see Elishia Place more clearly now, and the street opened into a wide plaza, affording her a full view of a small castle. Its width measured at several hundred feet with a center keep that rose some forty or fifty feet into the air and was covered in narrow slit-like windows. A balcony hung from the front of the keep, and from this balcony dropped a golden banner emblazoned in black with a sword and arrow crossed over each other.

However, one feature made Elishia Place stand out from the entirety of Soutton, that it was totally constructed of unforgiving, gray stone, excluding the massive, iron banded double oaken door set into its front and the crenellations on its top that gleamed silver in the morning light.

Several men stood atop the castle at various places along its wall, as well as two that stood flanking its front door. They all wore heavy, chain mail armor, another thing Jenna had only ever heard of, and carried long pikes or halberds. Four fit women, two perhaps a little older than Jenna and two younger, exercised in the middle of the plaza with wooden training swords. All wore leather armor or padded gambesons with the sword and arrow symbol somehow marked upon it, and they stopped their training as soon as Jenna and Laina entered the square. They rode straight through the plaza and toward the castle's door, endeavoring to keep her eyes forward and ignore (or at least appear to ignore) the gazes that burned into her as they passed.

She couldn't help but notice the circular curve of Sir Conor's tower only a couple hundred yards to the west, not even as far as she could fire an arrow.

Jenna continued to follow Laina's lead, dismounting as they reached the enormous doors and their guards, and one of the younger Protectresses, a girl no more than fifteen, rushed forward to lead the horses away by the reins. As the guards opened the doors, the two women entered, and Jenna self-consciously noticed that the other three women from the plaza had filed in behind them. They stood in a ten foot square vestibule with racks to the left and right that probably once held weapons, but now sat empty. An arched doorway led into a grand room beyond, and as Jenna tried to angle for a view, Laina grabbed her attention.

"Lady Ayn waits for us through that doorway," she said.

144

"How does she know we're here?"

"I sent word ahead of our arrival this morning while you slept," Laina explained, and she turned to a tall woman with black hair, broad shoulders and sinews of iron, "I assume she requested everyone's presence, then?"

The black haired woman nodded and said in a deep, but melodious voice, "Yes. Except of course the two squads who are out."

"Who is out?" Laina queried.

"Kayleigh's squad is at the quarries to the southeast hunting something that has been killing workers, and Esther went to the coast to investigate rumors of pirate raids."

Laina only nodded as if this news was of no surprise or import, and she turned her face back to Jenna, "Mind your words, and speak only when spoken to."

Jenna's temper flared for a moment at the very idea that she had to be told such a thing, but she quickly poured cooler emotions on that fire. "I understand," she replied, ignoring the tiny amount of nausea that began to slowly build.

Laina took a position to Jenna's right and said, "All right, then, come on," and started through the doorway.

Jenna kept step with her escort, and her soft riding boots went from impacting stone to a plush burgundy rug that stretched some thirty feet in front of them. They walked into a grand hall, the walls of which were made of the same gray stone as the outside of Elishia Place. It had a high ceiling some twenty feet overhead made of golden oak, likely imported from the forests around Midton, and about a dozen ornately carved columns of red feldspar depicting powerful women warriors whose statues supported the upper floor. Six more columns stood unworked, nondescript rectangular slabs of rock that stretched from floor to ceiling, and over a dozen Protectresses waited amongst the columns, some bored while others looked on with interest. Several exits dispersed from the hall on either side and the far wall, but Jenna paid these, as well as the women straggling in from them, no mind.

The rug continued straight as an arrow to a set of four stone steps rising to a platform, at the top of which stood one of the most impressive figures Jenna had ever seen, resplendent in plate armor that gleamed in the sunlight that streamed into the hall through its many windows but also showed smoky, cloudlike designs in the steel like Jenna's own sword. With a confident stance and crossed arms, she embodied strength, confidence, and something oddly defiant as well. Her gray eyes stared down at Jenna as she approached, as hard and unflinching as the granite of Elishia Place itself, and her once dark brown hair showed lightening from being constantly caressed by the sun. Tiny crow's feet touched the corners around her eyes, and her mouth showed slight lines of both worry and laughter.

Stopping some five feet from the steps, Laina bowed her head and dropped to one knee, and Jenna copied her awkwardly as if the motion itself were unknown or alien to her. Laina said, "Lady Ayn, I have brought one named Jenna. She is to join the order by command of King Rendor."

"I know of her and his commands. Thank you, Laina, for your efforts," Lady Ayn replied, and her voice rang clear and powerfully through the hall with little apparent effort from the woman herself. She laughed very softly twice before adding, "You may look upon me, child. I'm not divine."

Jenna lifted her head at this, the monster of her intractability rearing its head before she realized that Lady Ayn was literally the third highest power in all of Abrea. She looked the woman right in her eyes, hoping that she had softened her reaction quickly enough. Lady Ayn gazed back unperturbed and unblinking, forcing upon Jenna a contest of wills that she could never win, and as Jenna blinked, she saw the right corner of Lady Ayn's mouth raise a little before a larger, caring but almost condescending smile formed on her face.

"You're a strong one, aren't you Jenna? And you don't like being called a child, do you?" she asked.

Jenna knew better than to answer such questions. Five years ago, she might have taken such bait, but instead, she kept quiet and tried not to offer a challenge with her very existence as she so often seemed to do.

"You may stand," Ayn told them as she approached, taking the steps very deliberately as if it were a show of her strength. She waived Laina and the other Protectresses to the side, and she circled the still form of Jenna. "So, you are the one Sir Conor told me about. You are the girl – I'm sorry – the woman that attempted the Trials, who challenged the way of things. How dare you? What arrogance! What insolence! What makes you so special that you believed you could do such a thing?"

Lady Ayn circled around behind Jenna as she berated her, and Jenna dared not move a singular muscle, though she doubted that she controlled the mix of emotions – contrition and regret, but also rebelliousness and stubbornness – that no doubt flashed across her face. If she had looked around the hall, she would have seen a mix of reactions from the Protectresses assembled around her. Many stood stoically, so disciplined that they were unable or unwilling to so openly display their thoughts, but others wore smug expressions with the knowledge that this upstart who thought she was somehow better than every other woman in Abrea was getting put in her place.

Lady Ayn came back into Jenna's view, emerging from her peripheral vision, paused for a

147

moment in her verbal onslaught, and added, "You have my admiration."

Startled at this sudden change of tone, Jenna's eyes shot over Lady Ayn, and warmth spread across her as she took in the woman's face. There was no guile, no sarcasm, or irony in the Protectress' expression, and again had Jenna looked around at the others, she would have seen those who were previously obedient and restrained now bore countenances of mirth and acceptance. Those who had enjoyed her reprimand seemed less agreeable to the turn.

"Give me your hand," Lady Ayn commanded, extending her own. When their hands met, Jenna discerned the numerous hard callouses on the woman's palm and fingers, and Ayn shifted the grip so that their thumbs intertwined. Their fingers wrapped around the top of each other's hands in the way that she'd seen men arm wrestle, a pointless obsession they all seemed to have starting as boys.

"Resist me," Ayn commanded again, and she immediately began pushing Jenna's arm downward. Jenna did as she was told, but the plate armor Ayn wore hid iron corded muscles that handily won the contest. Despite that and as she tended to do throughout her entire life to this point, Jenna refused to admit defeat. A glint of recognition blazed in Ayn's eyes, and the appreciative smile returned to her face.

"Enough of that," Lady Ayn announced, and she released Jenna's hand as she retreated back up the steps to the top of the platform. "Jenna of the Second Circle, you have come to us by order of King Rendor, and tomorrow at sunrise you will take the Oath to the Protectresses. Are you prepared to give yourself, your heart and, if necessary, your very life in service to me and King Rendor?"

Without hesitation, Jenna replied, "I am." Of course, she had little choice in the matter. King Rendor had made the options plain, and to change her mind now left only the other – banishment. Or worse. Still, something in her heart burned. This wasn't the life she was supposed to have! She felt, both at the bottom of her heart and the back of her mind, that her destiny lay elsewhere.

"Know now, that I have heard of your exploits at the Trials, as have all your fellow Protectresses. You've shown determination, independence, strength, and ability, but there is far more to being part of the Sisterhood. You must also learn humility, duty, and love of both your Sisters and Abrea. I think, for you, these will be the hardest lessons to learn. Laina!"

"Yes, Lady," Laina replied, stepping forward from the side; Jenna hadn't even realized the woman had left to melt back into the others.

"Sister Jenna's cell is prepared – number six in the west wing. Show her to it, and let her settle in."

"Yes, Lady."

"Then, take her to the stables, and have her learn from the stableboys how to muck stalls. After that, show her the latrines and how they are to be cleaned."

"Yes, Lady."

"You are dismissed," Lady Ayn said faintly, but with no lack of strength. Her voice then echoed throughout the hall, "Thank you, Sisters, for attending. You may remain to leisure for the rest of the day."

The empathy had fled from Lady Ayn's expression to be replaced with the sternness of a taskmaster, her rigid and now uncaring gray eyes boring holes right through Jenna's own. As she turned to be led by her traveling companion of the last few weeks to a door on the western side of the hall, she observed several of her now fellow Sisters, and immense trepidation threatened to cause her to trip over her own feet. Either that or it was the change in surface underfoot from the rug to stone. Several of them wore expressions of sorrowful compassion, as if they felt sympathy for what her life was about to become, and that frightened her. But even more terrifying were the many more that looked after her in a semblance of evil glee, a delighted satisfaction that her life was about to become unbearably hellish, and they would be the ones to visit those deprecations upon her.

Chapter 12

The Chores and the Oath

"I should have taken banishment," Jenna lamented to no one as she plopped down on her bed.

"Bed" was an extravagant, courteous word for a metal framed cot with canvas pulled taught across it. It dominated her tiny room, cell as Lady Ayn had put it, which at six feet in either dimension was not much larger than a closet. She had no window of any kind, only a small oil lantern for minimal light. Her door opened inward, but it could not open fully without striking the side of her cot which was set lengthwise on the opposite wall.

She spent two hours that day listening to a stable hand with eyes that looked in two different directions explain to her the science of properly cleaning a stall, after which she then stood and watched him for an hour. Then, he looked on as she cleaned a stall with his intense supervision, and he explained everything she did wrong as she did it, forcing her to do it the correct way. At last Jenna was given the opportunity to show all she had learned, cleaning a stall by herself with no help or oversight as the stable hand stared at an hourglass to time her, but he had his other eye on a blank wall, so she wasn't sure to which the of the two he really paid attention. His criticism of the quality of her work seared her pride.

She fared better at the latrines, which as it turned out, were nothing but a row of holes covered by wooden lids into which piss and shit simply fell into a trough of running water to be carried away. There were two sets, one in both the western and eastern wings of the castle, and they had several windows or arrow slits that opened into outdoor gardens, likely to help with the smell and airflow. They looked relatively clean except for an obvious accident where someone didn't make it in time. Jenna was still cleaning this as the spears of sunlight coming through the slits had grown long and narrow. Calls echoed through the halls and signaled the start of the evening meal, and she resolved to come back afterward, since she hadn't eaten since breakfast.

An over six foot tall, well-muscled Protectress with long black hair and bright blue eyes named Dominica prevented her from doing so. "Perhaps you aren't used to this in your little, backwoods village, but we don't leave our jobs incomplete here. Finish up, clean yourself up, then come eat." Dominica disappeared for maybe twenty minutes, magically materializing the moment Jenna decided the latrine was finally clean. The woman studied Jenna's work and found several missed spots, though Jenna found nothing when she peered at the indicated places. Dominica kept her there for at least another hour while the sun disappeared below the horizon, and a young girl came through to light torches and oil lanterns in all the common areas of Elishia Place. By the time Jenna satisfied Dominica with the quality of her work, the hall stood empty as the kitchens had cleared supper away, and she was too tired to go searching for even something as easy as an apple.

Besides, she smelled. Dominica had been kind enough to show her the bathrooms so she could clean up. There were two in each wing, but the marble tubs in each were occupied by Protectresses. Jenna considered that for a moment; at any given time there had to be at least two dozen women in the castle, Protectresses alone, not even including others who worked various tasks. Either they didn't bathe very often, or there weren't enough facilities for everyone. At least, there wasn't enough for her. She waited an hour in the west wing near her cell, only to check the east wing and find that all four tubs occupied by new women who hadn't been there before. After a few instances of this, she gave up and went back to her room.

As Jenna dropped down onto the middle of the canvas cot, it gave readily and then threatened to eject her off as the tension bottomed out and rebounded back upward. Finally, it slowed its oscillations, but it caused her to lean back most uncomfortably against the cold stone wall, so she gripped the edge of the frame. Then, she realized her hands hurt, so she instead moved her rear to the unforgiving metal rail that made the edge of the cot as she slumped her shoulders, sighed deeply, and hung her head.

"This is horseshit," Jenna mumbled. She looked at the backs of her hands, finding her skin dried and cracking from the day's exposure to soap and a lot of water, and she turned them over to view her palms. Callouses from years of training seemed to have protected them better, and she curled her fingers inward to inspect her nails. Several of them had dark lines encrusting them, and she grimaced as she lifted her right hand close to her nose to smell it. Jenna chuckled soundlessly – it really was horseshit!

"Did I miss a joke?" a voice called, and Jenna looked up to see Laina's head poking through a gap between the door and doorjamb.

"No," Jenna shook her head glumly. She had forgotten to close the door behind her.

Laina slipped through the opening sideways with superb nimbleness, and she held a gray, wool blanket, clean and folded in her arms. She nodded to it and explained, "I brought you this, in case you get cold."

"Thanks," Jenna replied emotionlessly, and she neither moved nor looked up at her former travelling companion.

Laina's nose wrinkled a bit as she set it on the cot beside Jenna, saying, "You, uh, may want to bathe before going to sleep. While away from Elishia Place, you may have to go weeks without that opportunity, I think it would be wise since you take the oath tomorrow morning."

"I tried," Jenna replied with a shrug, "for hours the bathrooms were full."

Laina sighed as she sat beside Jenna on the edge of the cot, and something Jenna never expected occurred. She suddenly felt Laina's arm around her shoulders, a gesture of warmth and friendship she hadn't surmised the woman capable of as she said, "Do you remember when we were first on the road, and I made you hunt with one arrow? And then you came back with a deer, and I made you skin and clean it?"

"Yeah."

"I was testing you."

"I know."

"And the Sisters are going to test you. They want to see how tough you are."

"I know," Jenna repeated, still with no sense of feeling.

"Jenna." Laina saying her name caught her attention, and she turned her head toward Laina to see the woman looking at her from mere inches away. She tightened her arm about Jenna's shoulders for an instant before saying, "You're tough. I knew it when you brought that young buck back, and you proved it again... the next morning. You never gave in to that bastard. What was his name, Brenton? You kept fighting until the end."

"Until you saved me," Jenna mumbled dejectedly. Banishment would have been better; at least,

154

she'd be in control of where she went and what she did. Then a thought occurred to her. "You saw it all, didn't you?"

Laina drew a deep breath through her nose, steeling herself to admit something she wasn't entirely proud of, and she replied, "Most of it."

"And you, what, let me handle it? Another test?" Jenna asked. Something all too familiar started to rise in her chest, anger and indignance, and she shrugged Laina's arm from around her. "Get off me."

Laina inhaled sharply to respond, but she thought better of it. She dropped her arm from Jenna's shoulders and stood to move back toward the ajar door. She paused in the opening for a moment, and Jenna watched as she turned and said, "I'm sorry for that, but yes, I wanted to see what you were made of. I wouldn't have let him hurt you, no matter what. You're my Sister, Jenna, but you have to understand, the next few weeks, maybe even a month or two, are going to be hard. The Sisters aren't going to make anything easy for you, because they want to see what you're made of, too."

"Please leave," Jenna said frigidly, not moving her gaze from the cold, stone floor.

"I will wake you just before dawn," Laina replied, ignoring Jenna's anger. "Do you want me to wake you up earlier so you can bathe?"

"I said leave," Jenna growled. After Laina pulled the door closed behind her, Jenna rolled onto her left side and faced the wall. With legs pulled up to her chest and her arms wrapped around them, she wept alone.

Jenna forced herself up early as soon as her brain registered the first sounds of movement beyond her cell. She uneasily pushed into a sitting position, the ridiculously uncomfortable and unstable cot threatening

155

to either upend her onto the floor or have her fall backward into it, and she held onto the frame for dear life as a seasick traveler on their first cruise might. She stood up, every muscle and joint protesting and aching as she did so, not from the hard and menial labor of the previous day but rather from the phenomenally spartan accommodations.

Truth be told, Jenna wasn't sure she slept at all. Once she'd gained control of her emotions and stopped berating herself for being a stupid girl who'd done stupid things to land herself in this stupid place, she closed her eyes in acceptance, but sleep didn't come readily. Sleeping in the wilderness came easy to her, as she had slept in the woods many times, and in the end, sleeping outdoors was much the same wherever one did it. But sleeping within these cold, stone walls and on such a luxurious surface as well? No, she tossed and turned most of the night, never finding comfort even after she'd folded up the blanket and placed it underneath her body for some degree of cushion, using her arms as pillows. Even when she drifted off, she never really made it to that alternate realm of dreams and deep slumber, but rather wandered aimlessly in that half asleep restive state where every unfamiliar sound brought one to complete wakefulness.

She opened her door into the hallway beyond, glancing at the nearby window slits. A muted, subdued glow, the first sign that the sun neared the edge of the world, cast a blue light across the hall, and it penetrated only a few feet, weak as it was. She gauged the time, and deciding she had enough, she stumbled out of her cell to go bathe, closing it behind her. The bathrooms were mercifully empty, and she approached the tubs, great basins of marble set into a raised wooden platform with steps. Each basin had a spout at one end with a tiny metal wheel attached. Jenna heard about the engineering feat of running water but had never seen it before. Tentatively, she tried to turn the knob to the right, and finding it unmoving, she tried to the left. Water poured from the spout into the tub, and she located a piece of cork to plug the hole in the bottom, her skin prickling at the cold water. Jenna assumed some contrivance nearby would allow for hot water, but she had neither the time nor energy to look, dropping her clothes to the floor and plunging into the near full tub as if diving into a cold lake for a morning swim.

Gooseflesh rose on her skin almost instantly, and she fought the urge to exclaim or cry out at the chill of the water. She huddled in the frigid tub, shivering as her skin touched the smooth marble underneath her. After a few minutes, Jenna found the cold soothing, even comforting to her throbbing muscles, and she closed her eyes, relaxing for a time in the hushed calm of the empty room. With a start, she opened her eyes, having fallen asleep in the tranquilizing water, and with a sigh, she sat forward, reached for a worn cake of what she assumed to be tallow soap and worked at removing many days' worth of travel grime and other even more unmentionable stains from her body.

She almost groaned when the door opened, hoping for a few more minutes of blessed solitude, and Laina's head appeared in the gap. Her gaze alighted on Jenna, and she pushed the door a little further open before entering. She carried folded clothing under one arm while her other hand was slung over a shoulder, trailing something behind her Jenna couldn't see.

"Good, you're up," Laina announced as she entered the bathroom, leaning against the door to close it. When Jenna said nothing, she approached as she said, "I doubted anyone helped you or told you where to look, so I brought you fresh clothes. Hopefully, they fit alright, but also this."

Unslinging her right hand from over her shoulder, Laina brought a blackened leather cuirass into view, plain and unadorned but for the golden symbol of a crossed arrow and sword. The emblem of Lady Ayn and her Protectresses laid over the wearer's heart, which was not uniform from what Jenna had seen. It appeared that all the Protectresses bore than symbol on their armor, but the location varied, causing Jenna to wonder why Laina had chosen this particular cuirass.

"It's easy enough to put on," Laina explained, "Just slide it over your head and adjust the straps on the sides to fit. You want it snug. It won't stop a good sword, but it doesn't restrict you much, at least, not once you get used to it."

Jenna said nothing at first, questions running through her head as different emotions did the same in her heart and gut. After a moment of silence, she went with, "Why?"

"Why what?"

"Why are you being kind to me?"

"Because someone has to. Because I like you. Because I think you'll be a damn fine Protectress," Laina explained, and she sat down on the steps leading up to the platform, turning to face Jenna. "For what it's worth, I am sorry. I thought about it last night. You're right to be mad that I let that bastard go as far as he did. I should have just led the men in and taken him."

Jenna leaned back in the tub and planted her eyes on the ceiling, replying, "I suppose it doesn't really matter."

"No, it matters. You have the right to be angry with me. I want to be your friend, and you're going to need a friend for a little while."

"I've never needed anyone," Jenna rebuked stubbornly, and even as she said it, she knew it wasn't true. She had always followed her own path, done what her heart told her to do, but people had always been there for her when she needed them – Mother, Brasalla, even King Rendor.

158

"Maybe not, but you will here. You're about to be a sworn Protectress, and there's going to be some hazing for a while. Maybe a month or two."

"What does that mean? Hazing."

"The others will treat you badly. You'll have more menial chores than you know what to do with, and you won't finish with one before another is assigned. And you have to study and train, too."

"Seems unfair," Jenna mused with a slight shake of her head, and she took in a deep breath.

"It is, but you'll get through it. Like I said, the others just want to see how tough you are, and..." Laina paused for a moment, "you may get it worse than others have before you."

"Because they know what I did," Jenna concluded, and the sudden desire to simply run away tried to overtake her. She fought it down into the pit of her stomach and held it there.

"I listened to them last night. Some of them believe you think you're better than them."

Jenna almost squealed, her voice rising indignantly as she met Laina's eyes again, "I don't think that."

"I know, but you'll have to prove it."

"How do I do that?"

"Do everything that's demanded of you and do it your damned best. Now, come on. Let me find you a towel. Your lips are turning blue, and we don't have much time."

A mere half hour later, Jenna stood alone in the middle of the hall in very much the same position she had the previous day, her hair still sopping wet and looking almost black. She never liked the feel of armor and never trained with it with Brasalla, but the leather was supple and easy to maneuver compared even to other leathers she had seen. It had been easy enough to get into, and though Laina helped her this time, she was

159

sure she could don and adjust it herself with minimal practice. Her sword hung on her left hip, and she held her bow in her right hand as instructed by Laina, though it felt entirely abnormal. She always drew the bowstring with her right, holding the bow itself in her left.

Some two dozen women flanked her, lined shoulder to shoulder at the edges of the long carpet that led to the steps and the dais. They all wore armor of varying sorts – leather, brigandine, or thick padded cloths, but Jenna noted that Dominica wore a heavy chain coat that dropped to her mid-thigh. Several wore helms of various styles such as open faced steel or leather caps. All of them bore Lady Ayn's emblem somewhere on their armor, and as she stood between their martial rows, Jenna noted the lack of conformity of their armor, unlike what she saw among King Rendor's guards or the occasional soldier.

In the hall's wings behind the Protectresses, feasting tables, chairs, and benches had been placed, and a number of steaming platters had already been set out. The glorious scents of bacon, sausage, and other things permeated the air, and Jenna's stomach began to growl to her embarrassment. She hadn't eaten in a full day, and the smell of cooked food reminded her of that fact while causing a slight lightheaded nausea at the same time. A low buzz of movement and voices hung in the hall as Protectresses spoke in hushed conversations and laborers traveled back and forth from the kitchens.

All fell into reverent silence, watching expectantly when the door at the back of the stone dais opened and Lady Ayn strode out purposefully, her armor ringing as she approached the top step. Clad from neck to foot in Vulgeschi steel, her emblem in shining gold filigree on her chest, she carried a matching, visored helm under her left arm. The wire wrapped hilt of an enormous two handed sword extended from her back, the blade no doubt also forged in the southern kingdom, and Jenna noted the crosspiece, stylized as a sword and arrow crossed. She could imagine no other woman more impressive, and despite her usual dismissiveness of things others considered impressive, even she found herself awestruck at the Protectress of the First Circle, Lady of the South. Everyone present sensed her strength as a reverent silence dominated the hall.

Moving with the silent grace of a cat, another form came through that back door, and Jenna tried not to stare at Sir Conor as he took a place at the back of the dais. He said nothing, and Lady Ayn acted as if he were not even there, while his intense blue eyes bored holes right through Jenna. He was no less impressive than Lady Ayn herself, as he wore only his steel ringed leather cuirass and a matching fauld, the bronzed iron thews and sinews of his arms and legs crossed over each other almost casually.

"Sisters," her voice carried throughout the room, booming as if shouted even though she expended no great effort, "The Protectresses have served Abrea and her King for a thousand years, defending our borders and enforcing the law, and we in the south have earned our renown as the best of the Sisterhood. We have the best fighters, the best archers, and the best trackers. You Sisters of the Second Circle who serve me work and study harder than any others. I demand it of you, and I am honored that you always rise to the high expectations I set.

"Today, a young woman of only twenty stands before us in Elishia Place, among immortalizations of great southern Protectresses of the past, to be made one of us, a Sister, a Protectress of the Second Circle. She has much to learn, and we will teach her all that we know. She will be held to the same standards as all of you, and she will serve as your Sister. Is there anyone present who sees cause for her to not serve among you?" Lady Ayn asked as she surveyed the women flanking the

161

runner, and Jenna longed to turn and look, to see the different expressions on the other women's faces.

"She has endured no Trials," one strong voice called from behind and to Jenna's left, and she recognized it as Dominica's of course, no doubt the ringleader of those who would haze her.

"Not so," Lady Ayn disagreed, "She participated in the Trials at Highton to become a Dragonknight."

"Then she broke the law, and we're to be punished by having a criminal serve among us?" Dominica challenged, and a few voices chorused semi-verbal agreement.

Lady Ayn's eyes flashed angrily as they fixed on a point beyond Jenna's left shoulder, and her voice projected powerfully with a razor's edge that hadn't been present before, "By the order of King Rendor himself, Jenna is to be made a Protectress, and Sir Conor of the First Circle is here to see that it is done. Do you Sister Dominica, or any other Sister, wish to defy such an order?"

The question echoed throughout the hall, and once it died, silence reigned absolute. No one answered that question, spoke, or moved an inch. Jenna unwittingly held her breath, and the soft exhales of several others around her expressed that she was not alone. Finally, Lady Ayn nodded with the knowledge that none would argue further, and she reached over her shoulder to draw the six foot sword from the sheath on her back. The steel blade rang clearly, and she held the sword toward Jenna, the point of its deadly Vulgeschi steel less than a foot from her face.

Lady Ayn pulled the weapon back and to her right, her body coiled to bring an horrific, decapitating blow any moment as she spoke, "Jenna, you are here to be made a Protectress. Do you understand the meaning of this title?"

Laina had schooled Jenna as to how and when to respond during their journey south, and at the pause, she replied in a raised voice, "I do, Lady."

"You understand it means to spend your life in servitude to your fellow Sisters and to me?"

"I do, Lady."

"You will forsake all else – love, family, and even joy if need be – in service to the Sisterhood? You will follow my commands, no matter the cost to you?"

"I will, Lady."

"You will protect and honor your Sisters, myself as Lady of the First Circle, King Rendor, and above all else, Abrea, even if it means your death in so doing?"

"I will, Lady."

Ayn's muscles unraveled and straightened as she slowly brought her sword back around, genuine warmth glowing from her smile. "Then welcome, Sister Jenna, Protectress of the Second Circle."

A cheer went up from the women around Jenna with applause from those setting up their breakfast, and although she was certain that some of the voices were halfhearted at best, and Dominica's was not among even those, she couldn't help but return the smile. This was not what she always thought herself destined for, but something about this acceptance while standing below the fiercest warrior woman she'd ever met, even so briefly, swept her up into the moment of it. As Lady Ayn sheathed her weapon, Jenna dropped to one knee and bowed her head.

"Let's eat!" Lady Ayn called, and another cheer sounded, this one fully enthusiastic.

Jenna sought Laina out and found her friend just to her right. She let Laina lead her to one of the tables, a number of the other Protectresses congratulating her as they made their way to an empty bench and a long table laden with food.

"See?" Laina said. "There are those of us who won't make this hard for you."

"All that with the sword," Jenna asked, "she wouldn't really kill someone who answered no, would she?"

"Of course not. It's to make the point. Though, in your case…" Laina trailed off thoughtfully as she tore off a hunk of bread while scooping a sizeable helping of shredded, browned potatoes onto a silver plate. Jenna's hands shook as her hands shot from dish to dish, filling her own plate with a host of different options. Having not eaten in a day, she couldn't decide on anything in particular and opted for a little of all of it – bacon, fresh bread, thick slices of cheese, and cuts of bacon. "Easy," Laina warned, "you don't want to be sick. You still have a hard day's work in front of you."

To anyone watching, it appeared that Jenna ignored her friend's words, but the truth was that she could think of nothing else but piling food in front of her. Once she was certain that she was ready to attack the array before her, a voice asserted from behind her, "Thank you, Sister, for such generous helpings. Please find your own place to sit and help yourself." Jenna half turned, knowing who she would find standing right behind her. She looked at Laina, who merely sighed and shrugged with her eyebrows.

Jenna stood from her place on the bench, stepped away from it and replied with a friendly, if forced, smile, "Of course, Sister," but she paused for a long moment, standing less than a foot from the tall Dominica.

Jenna nodded and stepped aside to allow the other Protectress to take her place. She turned to find that another half dozen other Protectresses had filled in most of the benches on either side of the table, and she noted with certainty they were part of Dominica's cadre. A place had been left open directly across from Dominica and between two of her Sister goons, and in the scant seconds it took Jenna to round the table to that side, all the choice options had been moved to plates. She had only moldy breadcrusts, runny eggs, and pork fat left to choose from, and the women on either side of were less than generous in the elbow room they allowed.

"I'm sorry, it seems there's almost nothing left. Maybe the other side has more," Dominica offered with a thumb pointed over her left shoulder at the other table on the far side of the hall, and her leer showed no contrition despite the apology.

"No, this suits me well enough," Jenna replied thoughtlessly, much to the approving glance of Laina.

The woman to her right, named Maddie she thought, suddenly banged her elbow into Jenna's, proclaiming, "What table manners! You have to share the space, Sister!"

"My apologies," Jenna replied, pulling her arms as close into her sides as she could manage.

"So, what backwoods village do you come from that your manners are so poor?" Dominica prodded. "You are from the woods, right? We here in southern Abrea are so much more civilized."

"She's probably not from a village," said a black haired, bronze skinned woman. "Even the villages teach their children the basics. It's not her fault. Her mother is probably one of those wandering forest whores."

Jenna slammed a knife down onto her plate, and the buzz of conversation across the hall suddenly stopped in response. All eyes looked her way, including those of Lady Ayn and Sir Conor who ate privately at a small, round table that had appeared when no one was looking. Catching a disapproving glance from Laina, Jenna pulled in a deep breath, grinned, and said, "How clumsy of me."

As conversation continued, the black haired Protectress pushed further, "Do you know who your father is, Jenna? I mean, if you don't, it's not really your fault."

Jenna forced a smile as she answered, "I... I'm sorry, Sister, I don't know your name."

"Damaris."

"Damaris, yes I know who my father was."

"I know who your father was, too," Dominica's voice almost growled, and when Jenna looked at the woman across from her, she saw a vicious grin.

"Oh? Do tell!" exclaimed Maddie.

"Oh, I'll let Jenna tell you. Who was your father, Sister?" Dominica, her eyes narrowed, and it seemed as if everyone in the hall listened intently, despite their own conversations.

"His name was Timbre," Jenna answered.

"Sir Timbre, was he not? And what was he?"

"He was a Dragonknight," Jenna replied with a slight turn of her head, her voice remaining low.

"No, he was a traitor," Dominica corrected her, and Jenna's fists tightened, her knuckles turning white around her fork and knife as her heart began to burn white hot in her chest. "He betrayed the Brethren, did he not? He betrayed his king and his Oath."

"He wasn't a traitor."

Dominica laughed wickedly at that, and there was no mirth in it. "How can you say that? He betrayed everything he swore to obey. He took a wife and had a child, in secret at that. He knew it was wrong, but he did it anyway," she paused dramatically in what seemed to be a rehearsed speech before continuing, "Just like his daughter who thought she could fool the world and be a Dragonknight. How long before the daughter betrays her Sisters?"

Jenna slammed her fists to the table and shot to her feet, and again the entire hall fell silent as everyone's gaze fell on her. Jenna's eyes searched the assembly for a few seconds, noting that Lady Ayn was

166

also on her feet, and Sir Conor simply watched, his face impassive and unreadable. Jenna returned her gaze to the Protectress on the other side of the table and finding the woman smirking maliciously, she wanted nothing more than to punch Dominica right in the teeth. Instead, she again took a deep breath and exhaled it out slowly.

"Thank you so much, Sisters," Jenna said between clenched teeth with a slight bow from the waist, "for the warm welcome. I think it's time I see to the horses."

Chapter 13

The Father's Sword

Hunger continued to grind Jenna's will throughout the morning as she went about cleaning the next set of stalls in the stable. Laina had been kind enough to seek her out with a few saved morsels and an apple from the kitchen, which Jenna greedily devoured in minutes. Laina went about whatever her day entailed while Jenna continued her chores. It seemed that anything the Sisterhood needed her to do had something to do with piss and shit. Regardless, she endured.

When she returned to her room after the third day, she found three thick, leatherbound tomes awaiting her with instructions from Lady Ayn that she was to get to know their contents intimately within the space of a week. Dominica, always a thorn in her side, stopped by to ask, "Do they teach you to read in the woods, or do you need someone to read them to you?" Jenna said nothing back as she cracked the first giant book, leaned against the cold stone wall, and read by faint lamplight of the history of the Protectresses as laid out by the most boring of narrators. She caught her eyes closing on several occasions, shaking her head and blinking her eyes over and over to drive the drowsiness away, an arduous task with the abundance of names and dates being hurled her way. Jenna soon realized she would remember none of it if she didn't find a way to take notes, so the next day she asked Laina where to acquire such.

The hazing continued, though most of the Sisters let her be. It was Dominica and her followers, six or seven spineless toadies as Jenna had come to see them, that continued to exact needless revenge upon her for whatever reason. They delighted in demanding menial tasks of her, even more so when she took time to read. "Jenna! Take this sack of clothing to the laundry!" "Get me some bread and cheese." "Clean the dirt off my boots." It was often shit. No sooner was she off on one task before another person demanded her immediate attention, delaying completion of the first command and earning the ire of that Protectress. More often than not, Jenna fought back violent impulses; her pride yearned for her to stand up for herself, but Laina would remind her that it wasn't the way.

After a week and almost no time to herself for anything but a few hours of sleep each night (that was all she could manage with academic tasks being foisted upon her), she finally graduated from latrine and stable duty to arms and armor maintenance. While no less physically demanding, these chores were more familiar to her, and Jenna excelled and even enjoyed them to an extent. She learned years ago, thanks to Brasalla, the sharpening of blades, oiling armor, and repairing bowstrings and arrow fletching. Jenna spent hours each day doing so, and she began to wonder if Dominica and her sisters were damaging the gear on purpose to create more work for her. She wouldn't put it past them, but she chose to say nothing, as she was expected to do.

Every night, Jenna returned to her cell with aching and exhausted muscles, but a long, restful night's sleep was never on her list of duties. She stayed up late into the night to read. As the weak yellow glow from other lamps scantly emanating from underneath the doors of nearby larger and more comfortable rooms went out, hers stayed lit until the moon was well into the night sky. She read about all the women that came before Lady Ayn, the honorable Protectresses of the First Circle who led heroines into battle against bandit

169

kings, pirates, and once even a Drakkritt of Vulgesch. Though that last story had been a wonderful tale of honor and bravery, it seemed so pointless to Jenna, as fifty Protectresses had no chance at victory against one of the southern kingdom's Dragonknights. It was all to show that they would do as ordered by their king, no matter the cost.

Mornings came and with them stiff muscles and soreness throughout her limbs. Jenna often awoke with her hands, well calloused from years of training with Brasalla, clenched into tight fists, forcing her to pry them open to return the blood flow and stretch the muscles. The first time she extended her arms and legs to their full length, a white hot brand shot through her sinews, and she often wished she never came to this place. Even still, she rubbed the sleep away from her eyes and commanded aching muscles to rise and go to work.

She usually took her breakfast away from the hall and ate amongst the swords and other weapons of the armory, for they never caused her grief. The solace of eating a filling morning meal away from the jeers of her "sisters" helped Jenna center her mind and will on the day to come. If she was lucky, Dominica and the others would not seek her out for yet another ridiculous task, and she could focus on the real work that needed to be done. She was no smith, but Brasalla and her mother both had taught her the basic keeping of weapons.

She often skipped the midday meal, choosing to work through it or spending it on the massive amounts of reading the stacks of history that continued to grow no matter how many volumes she completed. When the day ended and the Sisters met for supper, Jenna snatched a few morsels from the hall and retired to her room – all the better to avoid any troubles and to get a start on more reading. She hungrily downed strips of roasted pork, bread, and cheese, and she carefully wiped her

170

greasy fingers on a linen napkin so as not to damage the voluminous tome. As usual, she ignored the footsteps and conversations of the Sisters as they passed her room, as Jenna had learned that showing any interest would garner her unwanted attention.

"It's really a well-made sword," said a voice from beyond her open door, raised so that it was meant to be heard.

Jenna looked up to see the all too familiar bane of her recent existence, Dominica, as she stood in the hallway with at least two other Sisters, and she held a naked blade by its hilt in her right hand, a longsword with razor sharp edges. The torchlight in the hallway caught the weapon as she turned the blade over to look at each side in turn, smoky clouds in the steel making it plain and obvious to everyone where the sword was forged. Though more common in southern Abrea due to its proximity to Vulgesch, steel forged by the dragons of that land was still heavily admired.

Jenna's eyes shot to the corner of her tiny room, where her sword had leaned since the day of her arrival at Elishia Place and found it missing. Her eyes narrowed for a moment on the empty shagreen scabbard that still stood rigidly in the corner, though the tip had slid out a few inches, as if it lost its own sense of pride now that the sword was gone. Her eyes shot back to Dominica, to the sword in her hand and then Dominica's face, and Jenna jumped to her feet, standing less than a few feet away from her tormentor.

With a slight growling hint of menace, Jenna stated in a low voice, "That's mine."

"As you know, Sisters, Vulgeschi steel is nigh unbreakable," Dominica continued as if she neither heard nor saw Jenna, and in fact, she hadn't looked her way in the slightest.

"I saw Sir Conor break his broadsword once," a Sister's voice said from behind the wall where Jenna couldn't see, and she didn't like her odds should she need to try and take the weapon back – four against one.

"Yes," Dominica replied in a catlike hiss full of malice, "I know the great Sir Conor can do anything."

"Well, he hit the Drakkritt's shield so hard, both were destroyed," the disembodied voice explained.

"The duel against Ser Tolar," Dominica nodded. "I understand Ser Tolar almost killed Conor. I'd have liked to have seen that."

"Careful, Sister, Sir Conor *is* Lord of the South," called a voice from down the hall, and Laina stepped into view, her gaze stopping on the sword in recognition.

"I said that's mine," Jenna repeated, force and volume filling her voice, and it had the desired effect as all eyes turned towards her.

"Who needs a sword for cleaning up shit or making arrows?" Dominica asked, and she turned to carefully hand it off to one of the cronies behind her. She stepped forward, filling the doorway. "If you want it, you have to get through me, Little Dear," she challenged, the common affectation of love for a child turned to a sneer of contempt.

Jenna's eyes darted across the others' faces, even the hidden Sister who had come into view, and saw both humor and hostility in them, excepting of course Laina, who remained stoic and calm though a hint of caution showed in her eyes. With her nerves on fire, Jenna resisted her first impulse to try and bull rush through the larger Dominica, realizing that she would have no chance against three others, and she couldn't count on Laina to help. She wouldn't intervene in what she called hazing.

"I'm not going to fight you," Jenna replied, needing all her willpower to calm herself.

"Then, I thank you for the sword."

"It doesn't belong to you."

"Prove it. Sisters, you remember when I bought that sword, don't you?" Dominica turned her head to look back over her right shoulder as she spoke, and her henchwomen met the question with choruses of affirmation.

Jenna acted then as she did so often, without concern for repercussions as she brought her right hand up to slap her palm against Dominica's left ear. The taller Protectress grunted in surprise, and her own hand shot up to cover the ear as if doing so would muffle the sudden ringing that filled it and her head. Jenna followed up with a left handed punch to the jaw. Jenna grudgingly admitted that others far exceeded her in fisticuffs, but surprise was her goal, not power or permanent damage. Dominica reeled backward into the hallway, falling against one of her Sisters, though not collapsing to the ground.

Jenna pushed forward with her momentum and the element of surprise, bowling bodily into Dominica, knocking her back onto her ass, while lunging for the wrist of the Sister who held her sword. An iron grip enveloped her right ankle, and Jenna fell as if she ran through a tripwire, the knee of her right leg colliding with Dominica's shoulder as they crumpled into a tangled mass. On the way down, a burning, slicing pain shot up the upper flank of Jenna's left arm; somehow the point of her own sword had been lowered toward her, and it cut through the sleeve of her tunic as well as flesh. Shouts of surprise and calls of alarm accompanied the sudden action, as none of them expected the focus of their depredations to react so aggressively.

"Get her off me!" shouted Dominica, and a set of rough hands tried to get a grip on Jenna's flailing limps. "You're going to pay for that. Oh, are you –"

"Lady Ayn!" a voice rang out in surprise, Laina's perhaps, and within minutes, Dominica and Jenna were both righted and standing side by side as the

173

woman marched toward them from around a corner. Jenna had the sudden feeling that she had been caught by her mother while sneaking pastries, and a surreptitious glance at the other Sisters confirmed similar feelings among them.

"What is this about?" Lady Ayn demanded, her voice clear and strong though not raised.

"We... we were admiring Jenna's sword," Dominica explained.

"Is that so? I thought I saw you two fighting."

"An accident."

"Accident?"

Jenna blurted, "I tripped."

"Tripped?"

"Yes and fell into Sister Dominica."

"We both fell," Dominica agreed with a quick nod.

Lady Ayn's piercing eyes stared at Jenna for several seconds, shifted to Dominica and then back again. The gaze then followed down Jenna's left arm, taking in the blood soaking the rent sleeve of her tunic and beginning to drip on the floor. She said only, "You're hurt, Sister Jenna."

Jenna lifted her left arm, appraising it as a bird might its wing, and saw that the sword's point had only nicked her, carving a shallow, superficial cut three or four inches down her upper arm. Nothing that wouldn't heal, but seeing the exceptionally minor wound caused it to hurt tremendously. She used Dominica's word, saying, "It was an accident."

"Accident," Lady Ayn softly, again shifting her gaze from one Sister to the next before finally landing it on Laina. "Anything to add, Sister Laina?"

Laina paused, locking gazes with Ayn for a moment before shaking her head with innocently raised eyebrows, "No, Lady."

174

Lady Ayn sighed and said, "Very well. About your business, then. Sister Laina, perhaps you would help Sister Jenna bind that wound, and please clean the blood up before it stains the stonework."

With that, Lady Ayn continued down the hallway and turned another corner to go out of sight. Laina led Jenna back into her room as Dominica took back the longsword and the other Sisters dispersed to flee the scene. Jenna, however, ignored both her bleeding arm and her friend's demands that she sit down, turning to face Dominica only a few feet away, just as she had only a few minutes before.

"Give me my sword," Jenna demanded.

Dominica glared at her, measuring her own will against Jenna's as both women's hearts thudded in their ears. She then looked at the blade, to Laina who had adopted a tired expression, and then back to Jenna, finding the younger, smaller woman's face and will to be hard as granite. She extended her arm toward Jenna and released the sword's hilt, and it fell to the floor, filling the small cell and the hallway beyond with the ringing clang of the world's hardest steel striking stone.

"Who would want a traitor's sword anyway?" Dominica shot, and she stormed away.

Chapter 14

Lady Ayn and Sir Conor

Jenna attended supper with the other Protectresses, something she generally avoided between the work demanded of her and the amount of studying required. Usually, she would be in her room reading while the others ate. She thought this a waste, but it had the added benefit of some quiet time away from those who would trouble her. On this particular evening, her near starvation got the better of her (when she bathed, she noticed how thin she was getting between the constant work and lack of regular eating, but it had the added benefit of well-defined muscles in her arms, legs, and even abdomen), and she set out for the hall to dine with the other Sisters. Thankfully, Dominica seemed reticent to engage her at all, her retinue sitting quietly with her to one side. Jenna began slicing meat off a joint of mutton, as well as partaking of other dishes; there seemed to be a quiet anticipation in the hall.

"I knew you wouldn't miss this tonight," a voice whispered in her ear, and Jenna turned to see Laina who had come in behind her.

"Miss what?"

"The entertainment."

"What are you talking about?" Jenna asked, her stomach ached as she grew weary of the vague language, the secret that she should intrinsically know something about.

"Just wait," Laina said with a broad smile. "I guess you hadn't heard. Don't worry, you're gonna love it."

Jenna turned back to her meal, paying no mind to anyone else in the hall, even as Laina sat down beside her. As she slowly sated her hunger, she began to look at and watch the other Protectresses, and she noticed that they tended to glance up towards Lady Ayn's platform, sometimes every few seconds. As her hunger subsided, her senses, well-tuned as they were for hunting, began to pick up on an eagerness, an expectancy among her fellow Sisters as they too ate, watched, and waited.

With a whine of metal hinges, the door at the back of the platform opened, and into the hall stalked Sir Conor. Wearing his ring inlaid leather cuirass and a matching fauld that ended above the knee, he strode purposefully to the steps with a sheathed sword in his hand and surveyed the room. Jenna's pulse quickened. She heard that he was seen often in Elishia Place, but it had only been ten days since she had taken her Oath. And here he was yet again, with an announcement, perhaps? Orders to the Protectresses from the King? Where was Lady Ayn?

Jenna had only to wait seconds for that last question to be answered, as the steel clad Protectress of the First Circle entered through the same door, closing it behind her. As she did so, Sir Conor whirled toward her and pulled an ample bladed, unwieldly broadsword from its sheath, discarding the latter off to his left. Ayn reached over her shoulder to draw her own weapon, and while holding the great sword with but one hand, she unbuckled the thin leather strap across her chest that held the sheath to her back. It fell to the ground behind her, and Lady Ayn took the six foot sword in both hands.

Almost all the Protectresses in the hall had either turned about in their place to watch or even stood from their benches. Some, their meal forgotten, came around the table and approached within a few feet of the steps, wanting to be as close to the scene as possible. This caused others to come join them, wanting an unobscured view, and Jenna glanced at the hall's main entrance as a half dozen men entered. They too wore leather armor with sigils indicating their allegiance, and they strode right up the middle of the hall, standing anxiously at the bottom of the steps. Dragonknights! Jenna glanced over to Laina, who looked back with searching eyes and a broad grin, and then she shot Jenna a quick raise of two eyebrows before climbing to her feet, standing on the bench so her view wouldn't be blocked.

Jenna found herself doing the same as the two warriors, a Dragonknight and a Protectress, took guarded, readied positions with their weapons, and they rotated about an unseen axis to afford everyone gathered a better view of both. Her heart thudded in her chest as she drank in the spectacle. Truly, these two must be the greatest warriors in Abrea – Lady Ayn, beautiful and resplendent in full plate armor forged in Vulgesch, and Sir Conor, King Rendor's personal champion, a statuesque portrayal of strength and vitality. The Dragonknight stood impassively, his mouth a tight line and every corded muscle ready for action. His eyes squinted noticeably, a brief recognition as an almost mischievous smirk crossed Lady Ayn's face.

Steel death shot forward with Lady Ayn's sudden thrust, but Conor was ready for it, deflecting her blade to his right with a downward stroke of his own. He followed the parry with a backhanded upward swing, an overall weak blow, but it caused Ayn to jump backward to avoid it with agility Jenna hadn't expected from someone in such heavy armor. Conor launched into his own attack, a furious fusillade of overhead blows that his opponent had no choice but to block and parry herself. The deafening ring and clash of steel filled the hall, a brilliant ringing that drowned out the gasps and wagers of the onlookers.

Lady Ayn gave ground before the onslaught as she sought an opportunity to strike back, but Conor moved faster than eyes could follow, his steel flashing in the hall's torchlight. He pushed until he pushed her back against the stone wall on the backside of the raised platform. Jenna gasped, and a hand flew to cover her mouth as the crowd let out a chorus of disbelief as Conor aimed a furious strike right at Lady Ayn's head. She ducked just in time, the broadsword clipping a few strands of her hair as the blade struck the stone behind her, showering both of them with shards of rock and dust.

Jenna stood utterly transfixed by the scene, knowing that Conor had come within Lady Ayn's ability to defend herself with her own giant sword. She saw no way the Protectress could win now, but she doubted yielding was in the woman's nature. Jenna thought as a Protectress she should want Lady Ayn to win, but Sir Conor was so captivating to watch even in his brutality. He attacked with such smooth grace and crippling power Jenna could imagine no foe standing up to him for long. His lightning blue eyes glinted with the lust for battle.

Having ducked to avoid his stroke, Lady Ayn uncoiled her legs like a giant mechanical spring, pounding the shoulder of her plate armor right into the stomach of her attacker. Conor's ringed leather cuirass and thick muscles were no match for the pure strength of steel, and he let loose a gusty breath as she knocked him backward four or five steps. He dropped to one knee, stunned, and he barely raised his sword horizontally to the floor and above his head in time as Lady Ayn's enormous two handed blow, meant to cleave the man in twain vertically, crashed into the blade. Even with arms any blacksmith would envy, Conor gave under the attack, his sword pointing downward as the edges of both blades scraped and grinded against each other, showering the fighters with sparks.

Had both weapons not been forged by dragonfire, they surely would have shattered from the impact, blinding both combatants with steel splinters.

With the celerity of a striking viper, Conor turned his blade to cause Ayn's edge to slide further down its smooth width, and he brought his own sword around in two handed blow that would chop an enemy in half at the waist. Off balance as she was, Ayn could do nothing to defend herself, and the sword crashed against her plate hauberk with such a terrific force that those closest to the battle sought to cover their ears. Awed moaning and choked breathing accompanied this attack as Lady Ayn wheeled backward from the intensity of the blow as she regained her balance, and her armor showed little more than a scratch on its surface.

The battle ebbed and flowed for countless seconds, perhaps even minutes or hours. Shouts of exultation flew from the crowd as Lady Ayn took command, and Dragonknights' fists pumped when Sir Conor riposted and took back the initiative. Jenna, standing on the wooden bench, dared not look away, so engrossed in the titanic duel just like all those around her, but as the steel cacophony continued, Lady Ayn's strokes, parries, and ripostes grew increasingly sluggish. The enormity of her blade, combined with being clad head to toe in steel, began to wear on the Protectress, whereas her opponent fought tirelessly. It became clear she could not defeat him.

And Lady Ayn knew it, too, as she growled in a low, dangerous tone, "Just finish it already."

"Then yield," Conor replied grimly.

"Fucking make me."

Lady Ayn returned with a barrage of attacks with her sword that, to the untrained bystander, looked terrific and deadly, but those in the hall knew otherwise. It was her last valiant attempt. Sir Conor evaded the attacks agilely with a thin smile, and his blue eyes that at the beginning of the duel raged with the joy of battle, now seemed ice cold with the grim assurance of victory. He parried one more attack from his left, took Lady Ayn's armored wrist in an iron grip, and pounded the chest of her hauberk with his sword's hilt while simultaneously hooking a foot behind her right knee.

Lady Ayn went down with the crashing of steel on the stone floor, Conor releasing her wrist as soon as her tipping momentum guaranteed she would go down on the floor. Only through either force of will or strong, well trained muscles did she manage to keep from slamming the back of her head on the floor underneath her. Still, the clatter filled the hall, and her sword had dropped away from her hands to fall several feet away. Her vision cleared after a moment, and Sir Conor towered over her, the point of his own blade mere inches from her face.

"Yield," he said to the cheers of Dragonknights and the dismay of Protectresses, and Lady Ayn closed her eyes in assent and drew in a deep, calming breath.

As Conor stepped back, he offered Lady Ayn an arm to help heave her to her feet, and both retrieved their sheaths to replace their weapons. The hall was alive with chatter as the spectators talked amongst themselves, and there were quite a number of small silver coins changing hands along with excited statements. One tall figure stormed away from the hall toward the front entrance of Elishia Place.

"What's her problem?" Jenna asked Laina as she stared after Dominica.

Laina sighed, "She's angry, as usual, probably going to drink. She views this whole exercise, and Lady Ayn's loss, as her fault. It hurts her pride and honor. Like a lot of people here in Soutton, she's part Vulgeschi. You know how they are."

Jenna nodded absently, though she didn't quite understand what Laina meant by the last part. She turned back to her friend and asked, "Why is it her fault?"

"Well, it's a long story."

"I have time," Jenna encouraged.

After a few seconds, the crowd had begun to disperse with a few Protectresses heading out after Dominica, while others left to go about their evening as commoners entered to begin cleaning away the meal. Lady Ayn disappeared back the way she came, discomfort plain in her slow stride, while a few other Protectresses had paired up with Dragonknights to head toward various rooms, sharing salacious grins and expectant glances.

"What are they up to?" Jenna murmured, not wanting to draw undue attention.

Laina laughed at her friend's reticence, "They're going to work off some tension."

"I thought," Jenna said haltingly, "it was against the Oath for either of us, I mean Dragonknights and Protectresses, to have…"

Laina loosed a deep guffaw and wrapped a friendly arm around her friend's waist, leading her toward her room as she explained, "It's against the Oath to take a husband or a wife, or even a lover some would argue. But that's not what they're doing. A good roll in the hay is neither of those things."

"Um, wow."

"Oh," Laina stopped, suddenly much more serious, "I'm sorry, no village lad back home you had a good romp or two with, then? Well, you should try it sometime."

Blue eyes followed her unseen from a corner of the hall as Jenna and Laina turned a corner on the way to their rooms while the latter told the story of how Lady Ayn and Sir Conor's duels came about.

Chapter 15

The First Mission

"Sister Jenna, Lady Ayn needs you right away," the young girl informed her with her head only stuck through the doorway into the armory. Ten years old, Cassie had been running errands for the Protectresses for four years, messenger of Elishia Place being the most common of those. The little blond haired girl (uncommon this far South) had no desire to join the Sisterhood herself, but rather just enjoyed being around them. Jenna found that odd.

"What is it, Cassie? Do you know?" Jenna asked as she fitted several swords she'd sharpened back into their racks.

"I don't, but something's going on."

Placing the last weapon in the place from which she'd taken it an hour before, she turned and said, "All right, let's go."

Minutes later she emerged into Elishia Place's hall to find a dozen Sisters seated at either side of one of the dining tables, including Lady Ayn. She looked drawn and haggard with angry purple rings under her eyes, likely still exhausted from her previous evening's duel with Sir Conor, and she had foregone her plate armor for this meeting in favor of far more comfortable robes of silver silk. Though the robes had their own glimmer and reflection of light, they transformed Lady Ayn from a noble warrior, Protectress of the First Circle, to a noblewoman of station, and Jenna wasn't sure which presentation made the woman more beautiful even with her wearied exterior.

Lady Ayn turned at the sounds of Jenna and Cassie's footsteps and said, "Very good. Thank you, Sister Jenna, for breaking from your tasks in the armory. Please have a seat, we have an important matter to discuss. Cassie, Little Dear, you may go."

Jenna smiled at the young girl as she curtsied in her plain, woolen dress and scampered off to elsewhere, and she found a place to sit at the table. She looked at those around her, eleven Sisters in all including both her best friend Laina as well as her nemesis Dominica and her cadre. The visage of the latter forced Jenna to reassess her opinion of Lady Ayn's level of exhaustion, because that would mean that Dominica positively hated the daytime, any noise above a whisper and, perhaps, her own existence. Obviously, the woman had stayed out late and drank more than she should have after Lady Ayn's defeat, and Jenna averted her gaze before Dominica recognized the staring.

"Sisters," Lady Ayn began, drawing everyone's attention, "we have a problem in the west. As you know, Sister Esther took a squad two weeks ago to meet Master Rall of Portton about rumors of pirates. We've heard nothing from her or her squad."

"You're concerned?" Dominica grumbled. "Sister Esther is a seasoned veteran. I'm sure she can handle a few sea dogs. Besides, who would dare attack us? All know the penalty for assaulting any one of us."

Jenna straightened her back and even reared backward as if she had been struck by an unseen blow. She felt suddenly ill, realizing that Brenton had attacked her less than a month ago, and yet it seemed like years or even another lifetime. She was sure Laina would have reported the attack and her passing judgement to Lady Ayn, as the guards likely did when they returned to Highton, but Jenna realized that no one had mentioned it to her at all. No questions were asked, not even for verification of Laina's version of events, and Jenna now wondered if the Protectresses meted out such justice so regularly that they felt nothing for it. How many of them knew about Brenton? Did Dominica?

"I agree," Lady Ayn nodded solemnly, "or I did agree, but now I'm concerned. I'm sending two squads after Esther. Obviously, that's why I called you and your squad, Dominica.

"Sister Laina, you will take command of the others. In eight years, you've never led a squad; your time is due. Understand, the mission is under Sister Dominica, but you lead your squad at her command. Am I clear?"

"Yes, Lady," Laina nodded deferentially, "and thank you."

"I'll thank you to find your Sisters," Lady Ayn returned.

Dominica asked, "What is the mission, Lady?"

"To find Sister Esther and her squad. I admit it's likely nothing is wrong at all, that she may have forgotten to send a report."

"Sister Esther has never forgotten anything," interjected the colossal Protectress that greeted Jenna and Laina when the first arrived at Elishia Place. Everyone called her Gargantua, which seemed insulting if that wasn't her name, and her deep, contralto voice always wavered with a sense of melody as she spoke. "I served under her command at the Calgerd Mines. She is the best of us, begging your pardon, Lady."

"Not necessary," Ayn replied with a dismissive way, "I agree with you, which is why you're going. Find Esther and her squad, and make sure they're all right. If they're not, find out what happened to them."

"If we need assistance," Dominica said, haltingly with an unasked question in her voice.

"You'll have only what you take with you," Lady Ayn explained. "If the situation is something you can't handle, return to Soutton immediately so we can plan. If we have lost an entire squad, I do not want to lose two more. The Dragonknights will be of no help to us as their Convocation in the Desolation is in three days. Portton is four days hard ride. I already have horses and provisions ready, so grab your gear and leave at once."

There had been no time for discussion, for questions or answers, or perhaps Laina and Dominica left no time for such as they handed out specific orders to individual Sisters. The twelve Protectresses left Elishia Place within minutes of Lady Ayn's command, as she had a dozen horses loaded and ready to go. They only had enough time to retrieve their personal weapons and armor, if they had any, and meet outside the castle in the plaza. They took their time in the city, but once they reached the outskirts of Soutton, away from congested streets full of hundreds of people, they began a hard gallop away and to the west. None of them spoke to each other as they rode with the two captains at the lead of the small contingent, and Jenna realized how much she appreciated being away from Elishia Place and the constant chores and menial tasks pushed onto her by the other Sisters.

Though, literally watching Dominica's back as they crossed miles of lazily rolling plains, Jenna believed there was yet more of it to come. No doubt Dominica would leave every distasteful task available to her, though she hadn't said a word since leaving Soutton. Perhaps she was having trouble recovering from her night of drunken debauchery? After last night's tale, Jenna admitted a grudging respect for the Protectress, beyond the obvious deference she would have to show her leader.

Three years before, Dominica led a squad into the badlands east of Soutton toward the Desolation in search of a band of brigands responsible for raiding villages and farmsteads away from the city. In a show of guile Jenna wouldn't have expected from the woman, Dominica set a trap for the brigands by arranging a small caravan of wagons setting out for the unoccupied lands further east – a half dozen determined men looking to start new lives with their notably unarmed wives – and she made certain that the news spread ahead of them as they passed. Two days after passing through the last village, the brigands sprung their own ambush, falling right into Dominica's trap.

Her Protectresses produced bows and swords, surprising the bandits, though after a brief pause, they caught their wits to attack the small band of women. Unfortunately, Dominica gained no honor, no glory from her plan as a Dragonknight named Sir Quent swooped into the fray, his majestic green mount dissolving those furthest from the wagons with its acidic breath. Others it snatched up with massive claws as it dipped through the air to attack, dropping them again once the dragon had risen hundreds of feet in the air. The ambushers scattered in all directions, about half their number dead within the first minute of the dragon's attack, but either Dominica's mounted squad or Sir Quent and his dragon hunted them down one at a time.

When the chase ended and the squad returned to the wagons, Sir Quent had landed the dragon nearby, speaking with both the commoners and several of the Protectresses. His golden hair, high cheekbones and sharp jawline announced his northern heritage, and he gratefully absorbed the attention that was being lavished on him. When Dominica saw this, fury drove her nose to nose with the Dragonknight, her finger stabbing into his chest.

"What are you doing here?" she demanded. "Do you have any idea what you just did? You could've ruined my entire operation!"

Sir Quent merely shrugged it away and replied with an audacious grin, "I saw people I've sworn to protect under attack by ruffians. I did my duty. You're welcome."

The words held no humility, and the sheer haughtiness behind them pushed Dominica into a rage, "We didn't need your help! I am Sister Dominica of the Second Circle, and this was my mission, under my command! You Dragonknights –"

Sir Quent's words cut her off, "What, *Sister*? Us Dragonknights *what*?"

The dragon, sensing its rider's ire or perhaps responding to some mental command of his, had lifted its great, green scaled head menacingly behind him. Its mouth opened, revealing white teeth, each over a foot in razor sharp length, and the acrid, irritating smell of its breath assaulted the noses of everyone present, though Sir Quent either didn't notice or didn't care. He stood with his hands on his hips as he awaited her answer.

The display certainly calmed Dominica, or at least brought back her sense of caution, as she more evenly replied, "Your aid was unneeded, sir. Everything was in hand. You have taken the honor of victory from me."

Sir Quent chuckled humorlessly as he said, "No, I don't think so. You can still report to your master of your success."

"Lady Ayn commands me, but she isn't my master. That term is for men," Dominica bristled, and her mother's pigheaded Vulgeschi pride filled her gut and heart. "Regardless, I cannot take credit for this with your interference. It wouldn't be right."

"The deed is done, your task complete. What difference does it make?" Quent asked with a shrug, and he turned to climb up one of the dragon's massive paws for his saddle.

But Dominica could not let the matter lay. Her pride demanded it, and she lurched forward, yanking ahold of the Dragonknight's shoulder to pull him back toward her.

"Unacceptable!" she shouted, even as the dragon opened its mouth, displaying rows of deadly teeth that caused the other Protectresses to shrink backward.

But Quent, annoyingly unperturbed, replied, "If that's how it is, then find me in Soutton when you return. An honor duel it is, then."

"No, I demand it now!"

"You're in no position to demand anything from me," Sir Quent answered with a slight bob of his head toward the leering dragon. "I will meet you in Elishia Place upon your return, and we will duel before Lady Ayn, Sir Conor, and anyone else who wishes to see."

He turned away again to climb up into his seat upon the dragon's back, and he shouted down, "If you choose to let it go, I am fine with that. Consider what you'll do when I take all of your honor from you." With that, the dragon launched itself into the air with a rush of wind and dust.

Dominica was not one to let his actions or statements go, and she challenged him to such a duel upon arriving home at Soutton, though the rumor was that Lady Ayn willingly accepted that the mission was complete, regardless of how. Sister Dominica soundly defeated Sir Quent in the test of arms at Elishia Place, and apparently Sir Conor felt his honor tarnished by the outcome. On the spot, he demanded she face him in single combat, at which point Lady Ayn stepped forward to deny the demand. As Sir Conor answered only to King Rendor, he then challenged Lady Ayn for refusing to allow Dominica to face him. Lady Ayn relented, and a colossal duel ensued, which she lost at length. However, it turned into a custom of sorts as Lady Ayn continued to invite Sir Conor back for rematches, which she, unfortunately, never won. Over the last few years, the two provided incredible sport and entertainment for both Protectresses and Dragonknights, and the stain on certain persons' honor had been forgotten about. More or less.

As the sun went down on the first day, Jenna found herself riding beside her friend and captain while she mentally relived the battle between Lady Ayn and Conor, and she asked idly, "Are they lovers?"

"Who?" Laina returned with stitched eyebrows.

"Lady Ayn and –"

"And Sir Conor?" Laina completed the thought, her eyebrows raising in surprise as Jenna turned to face her. "No, I don't think so, but they may have blown off some steam once or twice. Why?"

"Just curious," Jenna answered with a half shrug and a slight shake of her head back and forth. Why had she asked, anyway? She glanced at Laina and found the woman looked back with a very slight, almost curious smile and a light in her eyes, and Jenna swore she felt her face flush as it so often did. "No, it's just, there seemed to be some... I don't know... some passion between them."

"Uh huh," Laina nodded before urging her horse forward near Dominica's. "How much longer should we go tonight, Sister?"

From her place, Jenna couldn't hear Dominica's response, but a surly tone accompanied it as she kicked her horse faster. The woman's mood had not improved since the morning, and she continued to push them onward throughout the dusk as the sun sank into the horizon's gaping maw. The air grew colder, and before long, the breath of both riders and horses came in gusty white plumes. The sky stayed clear, and they stopped only for a brief rest as they waited for the moon to rise and cast a blue-white glow across the landscape. Dominica pushed them onward into the night.

190

"Have you ever been to Portton?" Jenna asked Laina around the fire when they finally stopped for the night.

"No."

"I was born there," Gargantua offered from across the fire.

"What's it like?" Jenna prodded.

"You'll see soon enough. We're up and moving before dawn, so go to sleep. Or at least hold it down," Dominica barked from behind them where she lay in her bedroll. She rolled onto her side to face away from the campfire.

"So, tell us about it," Jenna urged, her whisper just audible over the fire.

"It's, uh, nothing as grand as Soutton," Gargantua started, softly, but her voice still carried a depth that made it feel loud. "About half as many people live there. It's actually a bunch of villages that all grew into one another to make one long, narrow city. It's about trade and commerce there."

"What does that mean?" asked another Protectress.

"Everything's for sale there," Gargantua explained, and then she added for emphasis, "Everything."

"Go to sleep!" shouted Dominica, and the women around the fire looked at each other, shrugged, and then turned to their own bedrolls.

"Does it always look like that?"

"No," Gargantua answered with a shake of her head, black hair waving in the sunlight, "something is wrong."

Jenna wasn't sure who asked the question, but the thought hovered in everyone's mind. Three and a half days of hard travel brought them to a hilltop, looking out toward the Unending Ocean on the west coast of Abrea. The rippling waters seemed to extinguish the sun itself as it set, slowly disappearing as it appeared to drink deeply from them. Jenna hadn't seen the ocean before – it struck her how she hadn't seen much of anything until the last few months – but she'd heard or read of the water as being blue on sunny days or gray when it stormed with foamy white caps atop crashing waves. But these waters glowed orange and red with light of the sun, as if the great orb's rays illuminated them from below their surface, and something about this glorious sight held her in place as a chill wind swept across them.

But it was the sight of the city called Portton that elicited the query, not the rapturous sea. It stretched up and down the coast to the north and south for miles, for as far as they could see from their hill as the day's light vanished. Everything about the city seemed so haphazard as if none of it fit together properly. Dozens of piers extended out into the water with a variety of seagoing vessels moored at them, from tiny fishing boats to ocean crossing galleys. Some of these docks had clusters of thatch roofed huts surrounding them, while others adjoined to giant rectangular edifices no doubt as large as Elishia Place or King Rendor's palace, though they were not castles as plain as they looked even at this distance. Meager homes of mudbrick stood next to wealthy estates of stone blocks with their own high walls, and unlike Soutton, no farmsteads or other villages spread out along Portton's outskirts. A gray black cloud of smoke hung lazily over the city, being fed by a dozen fires that varied in size as they burned throughout the city.

"It was attacked. Recently," Dominica flatly announced what they all deduced. "The city's still on fire."

"Where is Esther and her squad?" Laina mused as she stood up in her stirrups as if by gaining a few inches of height she would be able to pick out the Protectress and her Sisters from the city in the distance.

"Only one way to find out," Dominica replied, and she commanded her horse to move forward.

"Wait, Sister," Laina called after her, and Dominica turned with an angry glare. "I mean no disrespect. We don't know what's happened here or if it's still happening. Perhaps we should wait? Approach under the cover of darkness?"

Dominica opened her mouth to retort, but she was cut off by another Sister, "It makes sense, Captain. There was talk of pirates. If they sacked the city, they may still be here. For all we know, they could be watching us now with a glass."

The anger and hubris on Dominica's face faltered for a moment as she saw the wisdom, and she nodded and said, "Fair. We'll pull back. If someone down there is watching us, they'll see that. We'll move north a bit and then approach the city when its dark."

They waited until the moon had risen, a silvery crescent shining coldly on the city below, and they rode in at a gentle pace, hoping the darkness would muffle the sounds of their horses as well as obscure any onlookers' view of them. They saw no one dallying about even as they entered the city's outskirts. It seemed that the city dwellers locked themselves in at night, their closed doors and shuttered windows proof against the cold, salty wind that blew across Portton and carried some of the hanging smoke away with it.

They kept a sharp eye around them, and more than once, Jenna spied an inquiring face as it peered out at them from an upper story window. A creeping sensation rose up her spine, sending a chill through her that might otherwise have been dismissed as the chilly night air of late autumn, and it struck her that the folk of

Portton weren't locking themselves inside in fear of the cold. She urged her mount forward to pull alongside Laina, who also shifted her eyes quickly from building to building, window to window.

"Something's wrong here," Jenna whispered.

"I know. A city of this size is busy even at night. The people are afraid of something."

"Silence," urged Dominica from the front of their band, "and be ready."

They rode past dozens of modest homes, soft orange light glowing from the cracks around their windows and doors, followed by stalls and shops of smiths, tanners, carpenters, stone masons, and other services often found in large cities. The businesses were closed tight, with no sign of anyone inside or nearby, their workers and owners likely having fled to nearby homes. Stanchions holding lanterns or torches stood forgotten and unlit. The small band had but the light of the moon and the tiny lances of light from inside homes by which to see, though further into the city, the ever present glow of large fires dispelled the gloom. The sense they had of being watched would not abate despite seeing not one resident of the city, and the Protectresses at the forefront and on the flanks rested palms on sword hilts, while those toward the middle of the group had arrows nocked into bows, their strings ready to be drawn at a moment's notice.

Dominica threw her hand into the air, calling them to a halt, and Jenna stood in her stirrups to get a better view of the street ahead as a dark form scurried toward them, stopping in the shadowy gloom between buildings. The figure, a man to be sure by the breadth of his shoulders, realized he'd been spotted and darted toward an alley. Dominica handed her reins to Gargantua, and in a phenomenal show of dexterity, vaulted from her horse and landed on her feet to cut off the man's escape.

194

"Stop!" she commanded, and the man backed against one of the nearby buildings, his hooded head turning this way and that in search of escape.

"No, please," a desperate voice cried from under the hood, and Jenna may have imagined she saw two pin pricks of light reflected by equally desperate eyes.

She held her hands out to him and calmingly said, "We're Protectresses from Soutton. We're here to find some of our Sisters," though the words had no effect on him.

"We're not supposed to be out at night," he stammered. "I need to go."

"By whose orders?" Dominica asked, but he suddenly scampered into the alleyway, overturning a stack of empty crates behind him to delay her just long enough. The sudden commotion set a lone dog barking somewhere down another alley. As he disappeared into the gloom, Dominica turned to face her command with hands placed on her hips in annoyance, and her eyes settled on Gargantua as she queried, "Any reason they shouldn't be out at night?"

"No," the woman replied, "Much of Portton never sleeps, especially the brothels."

Dominica nodded as she approached, climbed into her saddle, and took the reins back from the woman. "If there is some new command or ordinance against it, then we should move on. Can you lead us to Master Rall's home from here."

"Of course, Captain."

"Then, take lead," Dominica replied with a slight nod of her head up the street, and they fell in behind her.

They encountered more of the same – shuttered homes, silent businesses, and the occasional darting figure hiding in the shadows, though these they chose not to intercept. They rode toward a wide intersection, a reddish-orange radiance driving away the darkness as warmth flooded the air, and upon turning the corner, they found a once huge structure burnt to the ground as planks and beams toward its center still glowed with active flames, black and gray ash coating the streets and buildings around it. Several similar structures stood nearby, and the lapping of gentle ocean waves could be heard beyond the weak firelight.

"This was a merchant warehouse," Gargantua explained, "a series of docks are just over that way."

"Why would it have burned down?" Jenna asked bewildered, and as her eyes searched the destruction, she saw remnants of rugs and silks, shards of pottery that had likely shattered when their wooden shelves succumbed to the blaze, and charred remains of wooden crates. Nothing was salvageable.

Gargantua shrugged, but she pointed at the warehouses nearby as she replied, "Look. The others have been soaked with water to keep the flames from spreading to them."

"They protected the others, but didn't try to save this one?" Dominica asked no one in particular. "Very well, how far is it now?"

"Another mile north at most, no more."

They passed by another series of wood built warehouses, which Gargantua explained were used by merchants for the proximity to the docks to unload goods from ships or hold those that were outbound. Within a few minutes, the street widened into an open air market, circular and at least two hundred feet in width with wooden stalls surrounding the perimeter. Dozens more filled the center of the market, although they stood empty and silent, despite the light emanating from scores of lanterns hung on crisscrossing cables overhead. A sickly sweet stench hung in the air, not to be dispelled by the ocean breeze.

"Why is this place lit?" Dominica asked aloud what Jenna and others wondered.

"Many of these markets are open day and night," Gargantua answered.

"Yes, but if no one's supposed to be out, why is it lit now?"

Jenna's eyes searched the lanterns above, and then she gasped as her eyes found the source of the deathly scent in the air. All eyes turned to her as she pointed upward toward the middle of the market and said, "Look!"

As her Sisters followed her gaze, their eyes came to rest on the form of a woman hanging from one of the cables stretched across the center of the market. Manacles encased her wrists and the chain between them suspended her in midair, resting as it was on the cable itself. She had been dead for some time, the flesh drooping and sagging as it had rotted and pulled away from her bones, aided by the eager pecking of seaside scavenger birds. Several of these alighted on the cable above her or on the head and shoulders of the corpse itself, vicious beaks seeking out morsels yet unclaimed by their other airborne brethren. The corpse hung naked, stripped of all armor or even clothing. A shortsword and an arrow pierced the body through the breasts and were crossed in a brazen mockery of Lady Ayn's symbol.

"Who is it? Is it Esther?"

"Too hard to tell," Dominica mouthed grimly, her voice inaudible. She then directed two of the Sisters, "Get her down from there."

"Who would dare do this?" Laina asked rhetorically, as they had no answers to any questions they may pose.

One of the Sisters produced a heavy, steel treble hook and worked at tying a rope to its end while another dismounted and searched her saddle bags. Less than a minute later, the first tossed the hook upward, hanging it on the cable overhead on her first attempt and chasing away several gulls that perched nearby. She held the rope taught while the other Sister scurried up the rope with the agility of a forest squirrel, several lockpicks held between white pressed lips. A moment later, Gargantua appeared at the rope and gripped it to climb.

"Sister Eddena has it," sternly said the Sister holding the rope.

"How will she bring her down, or does she plan on just letting our Sister fall fifty feet to the ground?" Gargantua argued, and receiving an agreeable nod, she climbed the rope hand over hand, with less agility but more raw strength than Sister Eddena, who had left the rope and dangled from the cable as she studied the manacles around their dead Sister's wrists.

When Gargantua reached the top, the looped one arm over the cable, reaching the other out to pull the manacles so they slid across the cable toward her, and she grimaced as they cut into the decayed, purpled flesh of the corpse's wrists. The sickly miasma of rot hung thickly so close to the body, and she steeled her stomach as she prepared to throw the corpse over a strong shoulder once it was free.

Just then, all stopped as a long rectangle of lamplight stretched across the market, emanating from a doorway that opened nearby. A buxom shadow appeared in the doorway, its curvaceous figure and the ethereal silks wrapping it obscuring most of the light, and it rushed into the square, the line marked face and gray streaked mane of a middle aged woman materializing out of the shadow as she approached.

"Stop! You mustn't!" she urged in a roaring whisper, her rushing movements eerily soundless.

Dominica stepped squarely up to the woman, stopping her dead in her tracks, and firmly replied, "She is our Sister."

"I know, but –"

"Then you know the punishment for this crime," interrupted Dominica. "Do you know who did this?"

"Of course."

"And you did nothing to stop it?" the Protectress demanded.

"Please, Sister Protectress," the woman pleaded in a hushed tone, "bring your Sisters inside so I can explain everything. Portton has new masters right now. We mustn't draw their ire or give them reason to suspect your presence. Please, come with me."

The Protectresses held their breath for a long moment, even Eddena and Gargantua in their elevated and precarious positions, as they waited for Dominica to make a decision. Most of them failed to realize until this instant that a handful of persons had disgorged from the building the woman had emerged from. Four young women and a man, certainly none of them over twenty five shifted nervously in the weak lamplight from within, all of them dressed in minimal or transparent garments of silk or linen, excluding the man who wore nothing but a loincloth, a muscular torso on display. Hints of cloying scents, perfumes derived from various flowers across Abrea or even some far off lands vaguely wafted through the market, a testament to how liberally they must be applied. Soft, sultry music from flutes and harps beckoned to them enticingly from behind them.

"You run a brothel?" Dominica asked the middle aged woman.

"Yes, yes, please come in. I'll explain everything inside," she replied, shifting her eyes across the empty market as she searched for any who may be watching.

"All right," Dominica relented, and she motioned for her two Sisters to come down.

"Quickly, take them around back, show them where to stable their horses," the madam called back behind her, and as she turned back to Dominica, she said, "Make sure your Sisters leave nothing to identify you as Protectresses with the horses. Come inside, and we'll talk where it's safe."

Chapter 16

Portton

A stone hearth as tall as a person and even wider held a fire that raged to keep the cold of the autumn night and ocean winds beyond the brothel's walls and doors. This boded well for its occupants, as they all lay languidly across couches and divans throughout the common room, their various stages of undress or minimalist clothing giving them no protection from either the cold or roving eyes. Though Jenna supposed the latter wasn't much of a concern; it was important that such roving eyes find something to feast upon if one were trying to sell their owners a brief repose with the wares of the flesh. Such thoughts aside, the room which occupied almost the entire first floor of the brothel was comfortable and inviting. She had never been in such a place before (Soutton had them, though she hadn't had any opportunity or desire to investigate one), and Jenna endeavored not to stare at any of the workers, specifically the man-whores and their various bulges that they seemed to exaggerate now that they were surrounded by potential female clientele.

"Their ships came in from the west, south, and north all at once," Madam Rahni explained, and her voice had an almost musical lilt to it, captivating in its own right.

In the dank gloaming in the marketplace outside, she'd appeared to be a woman of her late thirties or even early forties, but now that she spoke in a well-lit room with all the Protectresses gathered round, Jenna was certain the woman applied heavy amounts of cosmetics to cover the deep lines of an aged woman probably sixty years old. Such vanity felt odd to Jenna, as elder women were revered, or at least respected, in the forest villages for their wisdom and knowledge, whereas this woman with her dark olive skin, black hair (now gray and white stricken), and contrasting blue eyes common to the islanders of Azgua preferred to cover and hide the physical effects of aging. Even still, Rahni maintained a voluptuous form; no doubt she was well sought after in her own day before attaining her current position.

"There'd been some trouble with pirates," she continued, "but most of us paid little mind. There are always pirates on the sea."

"Much as there are always bandits on land," Dominica mused.

"I suppose so," Rahni nodded, "It was pirates who brought me here when I was a girl. But anyway, there was talk of organization, of a pirate prince, if you can believe such a thing, and the attacks on both incoming and outgoing galleys increased. The captains began sailing in pairs or even threes for safety. One claimed to have even seen an attack close to dusk, a galley from Vulgesch burning on the horizon as it sank."

"When did Sister Esther and her squad arrive?" Laina queried, pushing the story to the part they all wanted to hear.

"About, uh, two weeks ago, I think," Rahni replied, her eyes rolling upward as if to search her brain for the answer. "They rode in and interviewed Master Rall and a good many sea captains. I think your Sister Esther was planning on taking her Protectresses out to sea."

"To set a trap," Dominica nodded her agreement with the plan, which to Jenna seemed very little different than Dominica's own when facing bandits years ago.

"She didn't have the chance," Rahni sadly intoned, looking down at the aged, wine stained rug

202

beneath their feet. "At night, three huge frigates came in to dock all at once. The sailors aboard them swept down and slayed the dockmasters and anyone in their way. Portton has never been attacked like that; we were unprepared. The Sisters fought bravely, but they all fell protecting Master Rall and his family, at least we think."

Silence reigned amongst the women crowded around Rahni, somber eyes staring at the floor or ceiling. Only the cracking and popping of the fire made a sound, as even the prostitutes refused to break the mood upon realizing the Protectresses had no interest in purchasing what they had to offer at the moment. A thud broke the stillness as Gargantua slammed a fist against a wooden beam nearby.

"How many?" she asked.

"I… I don't know," Rahni almost stuttered. Her face adopted a calm as she seemed to look into the distance, recalling what she remembered of ships of the sea, "I think… ships of that size usually have crews of about a hundred men each, but it seemed that there were far more than that. They took the city so fast. The city watch fell in minutes. All we could do is lock our doors and hope they didn't come for us, which eventually they did."

As she said the last words, she fought back tears that welled up in her eyes. Several of her employees also held back the need to weep, single tears making lone tracks down their faces, and they turned away to maintain their pride and dignity. One man crossed his arms and laid his head upon them, leaning against the wall, while two women wordlessly covered their faces and left the room to go upstairs.

"At least they paid for their pleasures," Rahni snarled.

"Spies," Gargantua concluded, drawing everyone's attention. "They had spies, their own people, and a lot of them, here just waiting. It's Portton. No one pays attention to unfamiliar faces."

"It makes sense," Laina agreed. "They knew to attack before Sister Esther and her squad set sail. They decided to take the city and rid themselves of the Protectresses at the same time."

"How would they have known about the Protectresses and their plan?' Jenna put forth. "And attacking the city? Killing the Protectresses? It doesn't make sense. King Rendor will kill them all for that."

Rahni replied, "If he can find them. A frigate with the wind is almost as fast as a dragon. They plan to be gone the day after tomorrow, and they'll have enough head start to escape."

"How do you know their plans?" Dominica asked with a dangerous, narrow gaze.

"For the same reason the pirates knew of the Protectresses and their trap," Rahni shrugged. "There are many loose lips in Portton, and *everything* is for sale."

At this, Dominica's gaze shot over to Gargantua who loosed a deep sigh and leaned on the same beam she'd just pounded her fist against as she crossed her arms. "All right," the captain said with a deep inhalation, "so we haven't much time. Tell us about them."

"What do you want to know?" Rahni returned, daintily wiping away a few errant tears from long eyelashes with a curled finger.

"A man we ran across said no one is supposed to be outside at night."

"By command of Prince Ghenake," she nodded.

"Ghenake," mused Laina, "sounds like Raucruish."

"His... appetites are surely in line with that foul land," Rahni agreed. "He and his captains have taken Master Rall's estate for their own, at least until they leave. No one is to leave their homes at night, and only during the day if on business for *Hulgre Fratencav*. That is what they call themselves. They all have a black tattoo on the underside of their wrist."

"Definitely from Raucrud," said Laina with pursed lips. "I think it means Black Brotherhood."

Jenna started slightly as her eyes searched her friend's face. "You know Raucruish?"

"*Drutin*. A bit."

"Are you two done?" Dominica asked, annoyance at the interruption obvious as she looked between the two Protectresses and seeing that neither had anything else to say on the matter, she turned back toward the madam. "How many are there, do you know? How many around Ghenake at Master Rall's estate?"

"I don't, but we can find out easily enough. My house is the closest to them, so they... requisition entertainment from me every night. My whores will know."

"Good," she nodded, "I need you to find that out for me. Besides this Ghenake, how many captains, other officers, and just pirates in general. How are they armed and armored. You know Master Rall's place well?"

Rahni's blue eyes lit up, a playful glint passing through them along with a brief upturn of her lips before she brought it under control with a clearing of her throat. "Absolutely. I've... been there many times."

"Good, then you can draw me a map of the estate, and your employees can mark who tends to be where."

Gargantua pushed off from the post to come stand behind Dominica, asking, "Planning an assault, Captain?"

At this, Dominica stood from her seated position and turned to face the even larger woman, "I think if we cut the head off the snake, the rest of the body will slither away to die elsewhere."

"Bold," Gargantua approved, "but do we attack at night? A headlong rush under cover of darkness?"

"I wouldn't advise it," Rahni argued, drawing everyone's attention again as she explained, "They have at least three or four men with bows in the main house's upper level. If they raise an alarm before you get inside, it could be bad."

"Stealth," Gargantua bristled, "I am more suited to splitting skulls in a straight fight."

"No doubt," Dominica smiled warmly with a hand on the Sister's shoulder, "but Lady Rahni is right."

So much about this exchange caught Jenna off guard. While Gargantua had not given her a hard time during her chores, she hadn't been particularly friendly, either. The woman obviously had her own tasks about Elishia Place and went about them with an almost stoic attention, but Jenna never experienced anything from Dominica except contempt and belittling insults. She almost hated the woman, and at times hated Laina even for explaining that she had no choice but to accept the abuse. The idea that Dominica was capable of genuine friendship never occurred to her, and now that it did, Jenna somehow hated Dominica both more and less at the same time – more because the woman hadn't even shown her basic kindness much less goodwill, but less because it proved she had true feelings.

Dominica turned back toward the rest and looked over Rahni's shoulder as she started a rough sketch of the estate, starting with the outer wall, "So we need a way to get inside and strike before they know what's going on."

Rahni paused in her work and smiled up at her, "I have a way. Let us talk behind closed doors."

They marched through vacant, dark city streets, heads lowered so that the hooded cloaks would hide their features in the gloom from any who might watch from behind shuttered windows and closed doors. Cold blew in from the sea and the north, adding a sense of necessity to the heavy wool the Protectresses wore to hide their identities as they approached the ten foot stone wall that wrapped a sizeable estate. *Hulgre Fratencav* planned to sail away from Portton tomorrow morning, leaving behind a city that had been sacked of both wealth and pride, ripe to be sacked again the next time the king and his Dragonknights would be nowhere close to defend it as they were otherwise occupied.

Madam Rahni led the procession, along with three of her other whores. It was against her better judgment, but Dominica understood the importance of the pirates seeing someone they recognized. If they peered too closely at some of the "whores" who wore heavy winter cloaks to protect themselves from the chill in the air, they may realize it was a ruse, and Dominica didn't want that to happen until it was too late. Prince Ghenake had demanded that Rahni dispatch everyone in her employ to the master's estate no doubt requiring the same of other brothels in the area, promising one final, incredible night of joyous debauchery, so Dominica and her squad of Protectresses replaced six of the prostitutes.

The plan was simple. A six foot, iron gate stood at the front of the house, guarded by several pirates, though they would probably be drunk by nightfall. Rahni would lead her charges to the gate, and the pirates, seeing the friendly female faces they expected, would gladly let them inside, no doubt with leering gazes and voiced innuendos. Every Protectress studied the rough map Rahni had drawn for them, committing it to memory, along with the expected locations of Ghenake and his three captains in the opulent bedrooms on the upper level of the manor house. Three first mates and some thirty other pirates were about the estate, including no less than three archers on the upper level. Some of them might have crossbows as well, a disquieting thought for the weapon's pure punching power at close range. Once inside, the real prostitutes, as well as Rahni, would disperse amongst the pirates, drawing the attention away from the Protectresses and hoping to engage the interests of the first mates. With any luck, four of the Protectresses would be able to make their way upstairs to find Ghenake and his captains while the other two locked the front door to the manor house so that no pirates outside the house could rush in to help when the fight broke out.

Meanwhile, Laina led her squad through the alleys to the back of the walled estate, where a small but solid wooden gate allowed a second exit, and it would be up to them to get through or over it. Hopefully, they could do so quickly and silently to lie in wait in the gardens with drawn bowstrings. Only they had bows, as Dominica and her squad would have enough trouble concealing their swords and daggers, and the captain hoped that Laina's squad, which consisted of the best archers at her command after shifting a few Sisters between squads, could pick off at least a half dozen of the pirates before engaging in the melee.

In the end, it was a good plan, a solid plan, but Dominica and her more veteran Sisters understood that few plans survived first contact with the enemy. When the fighting began, either at her word or the Protectresses having been discovered by the pirates, a high pitched whistle would shrilly split the air of the estate – the signal for Laina and her squad to attack with haste. All Protectresses were to fight their way to the manor's upper level to cut off the escape of Ghenake and his ships' captains.

Jenna found skulking through a city's alleys to be little different from skulking through the forest near her home. Instead of thick oak trees to hide behind, one darted into darkened doorways. Rather than slink behind rows of bushes or giant logs, the remains of ancient trees long since fallen, she hid behind piles of rubbish or stacks of empty, discarded wooden crates. Though, the stench of rotten meat, urine, and excrement replaced the ruddy, earthy scents of soil and green growing things. Jenna and her Sisters also wore hooded, dark cloaks, acquired over the course of the day from local seamstresses and tailors, the better to help them blend into the dark of the tight places between rows of buildings. And they too hid the hilts and guards of sheathed swords and the metal buckles of leather harnesses, lest an inopportune gleam reflect light toward the wrong eyes in the night and raise an alarm. They carried their bows in one hand so either they could be discarded in favor of a sword or the free hand could reach for an arrow drawn from a back slung quiver.

As the six women moved stealthily toward Master Rall's estate, Jenna felt somehow trapped in a dream, a surreal existence from which there was no breaking free. Everything, all the way back to those days in Highton a few months ago, suddenly seemed to have transpired in only distant memory, as if none of it had really happened, and yet here she was – a member of a group of warriors about to attack a manor house full of pirates? And more than that. She would be joining battle. This was not training or sparring, nor even a test or Trial. Arrows would streak and steel whistle through the air, and the screams of the dying would call out in the night while blood flowed.

Her heart rushed, pounding so fast as to remind her of a bunny's she had once caught as a child. She jumped from the brush, surprising the white furred animal, grabbing its ears and hind legs in one fluid motion as she'd been taught, but she had no intention of bringing that particular bunny home to be supper. She peered into its deep, ocean blue eyes and cuddled her head against its coarse white hair, her ear pressed to its long body. The creature's heart thudded at a lightning pace, faster than even a small child's during a thunderstorm, and she released it to watch it bound into the bush. Jenna discovered that her breath shot in and out just as fast, and she fought to control it.

Her attention returned to the dark alley as the Sisters came to a sudden halt, and a hand laid gently on her shoulder. The cacophony in her ears of roaring blood driven by her rushing heart vanished, replaced by a stark silence, and Jenna looked over to see Laina to her right with a steadying hand on Jenna's shoulder. Though Jenna could see little in the gloom, as little moonlight penetrated it so early in the evening, the worry was plain on Laina's face and in her eyes.

"Are you all right?" Laina whispered.

Jenna took in a long, slow breath and ignored the instant dizziness that came along with near hyperventilation. After a moment, she nodded and replied, "I think so."

"Don't think. Just do. We're here."

Two ten foot stone walls intersected at a right angle a few feet away from the lead Protectress, and three buildings peeked out from behind them. Two were only rooves, expensively shingled with rows of overlapping gray-black slate, gleaming irregularly in the moonlight. These would be the guest and servant houses, but the third, the manor house itself, showed more than just its roof. The stuccoed edifice rose above the estate's privacy wall, reflecting the flickering orange of fires and torches that couldn't quite be seen from their vantage point. A railed balcony wrapped the sides and rear of the house, a feature Jenna recalled from the map, allowing those above to look down into the gardens behind the house. Marble columns rose every ten feet or so to help support the roof, and sconces were mounted to these, each holding a torch at a steep angle from the column to prevent the flames from touching any part of the house and to help dispel both the darkness and the cold. The manor house was at least a hundred feet away from them, and Jenna spotted the shadow of a bowman moving boredly about the balcony. She could skewer him neatly at so short a range.

Laina lifted a hand, beckoning them to come together, and in a hushed tone she told them, "Stay low and quiet, hug the wall. The gate should be some thirty feet down. Once we're through, we sneak into the gardens and wait."

The women all nodded or mumbled their assent, and Laina turned as they set about the work. If the Sisters had been specters, there would have been more sign of their passing, but as it was, they approached a wooden gate set into the stone wall with no one in Portton the wiser. A soft snore filled the narrow alley as they closed in, and they found a man slumped against the wall, fast asleep. Jenna could see little in the shadows, but he was almost naked, shirtless and his trousers pulled down around his knees. He smelled more strongly of fresh urine than the rest of the alley, and a broad mouthed, bronze flagon was still clamped in his left hand, though he had already drunk or spilled the contents.

"Check him," Laina whispered as she laid one hand on the sturdily made, wooden gate, and its hinges whined softly as it swung inward. The arched entry stood only about four feet tall and a little more than half that wide, and Laina hunched to peer through into the gardens.

"He has the mark," reported Sister Eddena, her voice hoarse and hushed, and Jenna watched her Sister pull a plain but razor sharp dagger from the snoring man's belt.

Laina pulled herself back into the alley and replied, "We're in luck, Sisters, that he chose to drink too heavily too early. The gardens are on the other side, and there's plenty of cover. Stay low behind the hedges, bushes, and benches, and make ready.

"Kill him," Laina commanded with a jut of her chin at the drunken pirate, and as she disappeared through the tiny arch, her words ethereally whispered, "Come on."

Jenna opened her mouth to object, but Laina vanished so abruptly, there would have been no one to argue with. She looked to her left to find Eddena slitting the man's throat with his own dagger, the competent movements speaking of ruthless efficiency. His eyes shot open for a moment. He gasped in astonishment, but only a slight rustle of air entered his widely split neck even as his blood gushed outward over his chest, belly, and crotch. Eddena stepped back; Jenna assumed it was to avoid the gout of red, but in fact it was to wipe the dagger on the pirate's lowered trousers, staining his clothes with his own blood. Jenna stood aghast in silence for a moment before Laina's hand turned her back toward the gate, the captain having come back for her.

"Damn it, what are you doing?" Laina demanded.

"We just killed him."

"And if we hadn't, he might have woken up to kill us from behind," Laina argued, and then she added, "It's your first time, I know, but this is the job. Stay close to me. Don't think, just do."

Jenna gulped in a breath of cold air, steeled herself and nodded, blinking several times as she did so. Her entire life, she'd wanted to be a Dragonknight, one of those great protectors of the realm wheeling through the sky on the backs of beasts with enormous leathery wings. It never occurred to her that those same men

212

were highly trained killers, able to deal death at a moment's notice, and quite often they were demanded to do just that. Out of her own hubris, Jenna was virtually drafted into the Protectresses, a Sister of an elite order that maintained so much peace and order when the Dragonknights could not be spared. If she never thought of the Dragonknights as killers, the idea felt even more alien when applied to the Sisters, despite this being the second man Jenna witnessed being slain by one.

With a slight hesitation and an urged, "Go on," from Eddena, Jenna followed her friend and captain through the open gate, crouching as she did so. On the other side, she followed Laina's example and kept near the ground as her eyes searched the gardens. Flowers of many colors – reds, oranges, yellows, and even blues and purples – met her eyes, though the dark night subdued the wonder of them. An eight foot wide, circular marble fountain of half-naked mermaids frolicking amid a tall, massive statue of a man occupied the center, and four foot long stone benches with legs and feet carved to mimic those of dragons had been arranged around it at each point of the compass. Hiding places abounded behind manicured hedgerows – veritable three foot walls of green – as well as the handful of short orange trees and other wonderfully carved statues placed randomly throughout the garden, and the three Protectresses inside already penetrated as far as twenty feet in and to the left of the fountain, bows at the ready.

Laina, Jenna, and Eddena fanned out to the right, using the gloom and the conveniently placed foliage to hide them from the four men sitting slovenly on the benches around the fountain. They had two women with them, members of the oldest profession, and Jenna squinted in the uneven firelight to be sure they weren't Rahni's girls. The pirates had called in other entertainment, some of which had already arrived. The two women, in varying stages of undress, laughed musically at the attentions and jibes of the men, and though Jenna couldn't hear exactly what was said, she recognized forced laughter issued from people who didn't really want to be in their present situation.

Her stomach roiled, and a restlessness built in her shoulders as the need to do something grew. Jenna nocked an arrow and slowly pulled the bowstring back, drawing a bead on a filthy looking, bearded pirate. She could put an arrow through his open mouth, draw, and down one of his friends before they even figured out what was going on. She could probably manage dropping a third before they determined from where she was firing, and in the dark, she could almost drop and skirt the bushes to another position without them knowing.

"No, wait for the signal!" called Laina's faint voice, and Jenna looked maybe ten feet to her left to see the other woman's hard glare. She was right, of course; one didn't draw back a bowstring unless one intended to fire. One wrong move, one twitch of a muscle, an unexpected, startling sound, or any number of other possibilities, and the arrow was loosed, possibly not even hitting the intended target and certainly betraying the ambush.

A door of near white wood with contrasting bands of black iron opened at the rear of the house's ground floor, and a giant bastard, close to seven feet tall and perhaps even as broad stood framed by bright, cheerful light. Music fought to squeeze around his huge form as it filled the doorway, the lilting tunes of pipes accompanied a harp and drum freeing itself to drift across the garden. The strongman shouted into the gardens, his voice gravelly and the words slurred into each other from drink, "If two's not enough, there's more inside, boys! Madam Rahni's whores are here!"

The whoops and hollers of two of the men oddly mirrored the feeling in Jenna's heart, though surely not for the same reason. The question of timing had been a huge concern. If Laina's squad had trouble getting through the rear gate, they may not have been able to support Dominica when the time came. Laina suggested they could leave early to make sure they had time to make it into the garden, but that would have had them leaving the brothel during the last rays of daylight. That combined with possibly spending quite a while in the garden itself provided too much opportunity for Laina and her squad to be discovered, and that would have ruined the entire plan anyway.

And then a high pitched, shrill whistle, issued from between Dominica's fingers split the night, carrying well over the sounds of music and merriment.

"Shit!" Laina coarsely swore, knowing that Dominica could not have had enough time to get the Sisters in position upstairs, and shouts echoed from inside the manor. "Take 'em!"

The Protectresses stood, drew their bowstrings, and fired in one fluid motion, identical movements from several women, all trained to do what they must. Two arrows *thunked* wetly into the chest of one of the remaining pirates by the fountain, the sound disturbingly similar to Jenna as when they struck a deer. The arrows marginally missed the woman hanging on his arm, eliciting a panicked scream from her, and a third arrow barely missed his partner's clean shaven head, taking his right ear as it went by and ricocheted off a statue. Laina's own arrow hit the same man in the neck, and he went down with both hands trying to stop the flow of so much blood as he gargled his life away. Eddena planted an arrow into the back of one of the pirates headed for the house, and only the leather jerkin he wore protected him from a fatal wound, though he fell out of sight into some flowers.

"Bloody fuck!" shouted the giant, and he slammed the door shut as several arrows imbedded into the white wood rather than his chest. The remaining pirate pounded on that door, calling for his compatriot to open it as Laina and two other Sisters pounded arrows into his back. He fell against the door, his body and face sliding with an almost comic, painful sluggishness down its wooden front. A form with an arrow protruding from its back stumbled up out of the flowers, tilting precipitously as it pulled itself to its feet by way of a statue. Eddena hit him again in the chest, and he disappeared once more.

Jenna advanced, her bowstring still pulled taught with her first arrow, an arrow she hadn't fired yet. It all happened so fast; within a few scant seconds four men lay dead or dying, and she hadn't even shot her bow. She couldn't even decide who to fire at before they had been struck by another's arrow.

The Protectresses advanced with purposeful speed, bows at the ready but with no targets to fire upon. The two women, only just out of their teen years by the look of them, screamed near the fountain, adding a confusing cacophony to the urgent sounds of shouts and steel from inside the manor house. Laina shouted at them, "Shut up! Go! Out the back!" as she passed them by. Two men charged at them from around the house's left side, from either the guest or servant house, with swords drawn and murderous intent plain on their faces. Their bodies stumbled and fell less than ten feet into the garden as Laina and her Sisters neared the door that had been shut against them.

Jenna trailed behind them, her arrow still at the ready as she looked for a target. Her Sisters might have thought her covering their advance, but actually, she'd hesitated at every opportunity to fire. The first arrow she pulled from her quiver, the first arrow she ever intended to use on a man, still awaited her action. A motion from the balcony above caught her eye, and Jenna noted the shadowy outline of a man looking down on her Sisters from above. Without a moment of thought, she adjusted her aim upward and loosed her arrow. It streaked through the night air and impacted the shape dead center, and it stumbled drunkenly before tumbling over the railing. It was a man, screaming as he fell below onto the paving stones of the garden's path. He landed upside down, on his neck and shoulders, the former of which bent unnaturally with a sickening crack. A loaded crossbow fell into a bush less than a foot away from the body.

Laina looked back at Jenna, who was already drawing another arrow and fitting it into her bow and gave her a thankful nod. *Don't think. Just do*, Jenna repeated to herself, and the words were filled with all the sense in the world. She kept her bow at the ready while two Sisters moved the corpse away from the door, and Laina pulled against the wrought iron handle. The door neither budged, nor even groaned at all against her effort, and she proclaimed, "He barred it from the inside!"

"Shit!" shouted one Sister, another asking, "Around front?"

"Not if the front door is locked!" snapped Laina.

Eddena and another strained against the door without success, and she reported, "This is white ironwood. It'll take a strong axe and a week to break through."

Jenna stood with her bow still trained on the balcony above them, and the idea struck her. "The balcony! Up and over!"

All eyes turned to her under furrowed brows, and the realization passed across all their faces at once. Laina's face lit up with a giant smile as she cheered, "That's it, Sisters! Up and over!"

The women discarded their bows as they stepped out from under the balcony; if they lived through this, they would collect them later, and if they died, well, it didn't much matter then. They took stock of the distance, some twelve feet to the balcony and another three to the top of the rail – not an insurmountable distance at all.

"I wish Gargantua were here," Laina mused as she made her calculations.

"I got it. Come on," Eddena replied, dropping to one knee with her hands clasped together to make a step.

Laina backed into the garden eight or ten feet and then took several long strides forward. With perfect timing, Laina landed her left foot into Eddena's linked hands, and the former pushed off into an upward leap while the latter uncoiled all her muscles into an upward push. Jenna's bow dipped for a moment as she gazed in awe as Laina flew into the air with outstretched arms. Her hands grasped the top of the balcony's railing, her body banging forcefully into its spindles, and Laina held on through an impressive feat of strength. Within moments, she'd yanked herself upward, planted her feet between the spindles of the railing and swung over to the other side with a drawn sword.

"Come on!" Eddena called out to the next Protectress, and the process was repeated. As the second warrior hung and began to clamber over, two forms rushed at Laina, one from each side of the balcony as it ran along the sides of the house. She met one with a clash of steel while Jenna launched an arrow into the shoulder of the other, turning him about to face her as his sword clattered to the floor. Thrust and parried steel rung out, adding to the rising clamor from inside as the second Protectress made it over the rail and buried a dagger to the hilt between the ribs of Laina's combatant. Jenna sank another arrow into her target, and he bumbled backward, tripping over his own feet until his

218

back met the wall behind him. He slumped downward when a third arrow pierced his breastbone.

The third Protectress made it up and over, though Eddena's power under their airborne leaps had begun to wane. Tossing people required much more concentrated power than one might realize, and the fourth Protectress barely got one hand on top of the railing, her other flopping like a fish out of water as she fumbled to find something to grasp. Laina turned to help as a voice boomed from inside, "Assassins on the balcony! Look to the rear!"

With renewed vigor, Eddena crouched back into her one knee position, cupped her hands, and yelled, "Come on!"

"I'll lift you!" Jenna replied, and she dropped her bow as she stepped forward.

"No, you're lighter than me, and I don't know if I can fight after this," Eddena returned, causing Jenna to pause as battle was again joined up top. Eddena glanced up, and then motioned with both hands in the universally signal known as come here. "No time! Come on!"

Jenna released the buckle on her quiver to let it fall next to her bow and charged the fifteen feet or so toward her Sister. She had never been a particularly fast runner, but her lighter weight let her reach her top speed faster than most. Having never done anything remotely like this before, she stuttered her step once before landing her right foot into Eddena's hands; otherwise, she would have missed completely, sending them both into a pile of arms and legs. Her Sister thrust upwards underneath her, and Jenna soared into the air before banging her ribs hard against the lower part of the railing's spindles. Her hands missed the top rail, but she managed to grip the wooden spindles as she fought to catch her breath, her weight pulling her back toward the ground.

The other Protectresses offered no help as swords rang, throats grunted from the rigors of combat, and men loosed dying screams. Jenna looked down to see Eddena had retrieved her own bow and searched for targets she could skewer without risk of hitting one of her Sisters. With a squeal of iron hinges and the slam of iron banded wood against the stucco, the rear door on the ground floor opened again, and Eddena lowered her aim and fired, her hand immediately grasping another arrow.

Realizing her legs dangled in the view of anyone coming through that door, Jenna kicked one foot up as high as she could and contorted her body to get it even more leverage. She managed to hook it onto the balcony's lip between two spindles and pulled the other up just as an axe passed through the open space where her legs had once been. She worked to pull herself up the rails, straightening her legs to give herself purchase, and Jenna looked down to see the giant from before, holding a similarly sized axe aloft to cleave her where she hung.

His body lurched forward as something impacted his back, and he turned as a second arrow punched into the bulk of his massive stomach. Knowing she could do nothing to help unless she jumped down, Jenna worked to pull herself into a standing position as Eddena, backing up as she did so, launched arrow after arrow into the faltering but still oncoming form of the enormous pirate. Looking like a pincushion used by a fifty foot tall seamstress, he closed to within ten feet where his lengthy arms and five foot axe could cleave Eddena, and the Protectress discarded the bow once more to draw her sword. As she did so, the giant's massive arms finally fell to his sides, and he slowly tipped forward rigidly to fall dead on his chest, snapping arrow shafts or driving them deeper as he did so.

Jenna breathed a sigh of relief as she vaulted over the top rail to survey the carnage on the balcony. She didn't take the time to count, but there were eight or ten dead or dying men, incredible amounts of dark red blood splashed about the walls and pooling around them. One Protectress lay slumped on her side, a stroke having nearly severed her head from her neck, and Jenna felt guiltily thankful that it wasn't Laina. The balcony wrapped around the sides of the house where it led into the interior, doors leading inside on the upper level, and flights of stairs led down as well.

"Go," Eddena called as she retrieved her bow and readied another arrow, "I'll cover the back!"

Jenna nodded and turned, following the balcony and the sounds of battle. She turned the corner and reached the rest of her squad as they dispatched two more pirates, both women, at an intersection. Spacious wooden steps went straight down presumably into the main room, and from the sound of things below, Dominica and her squad had never made it up the steps to find Ghenake and his captains. A corridor stretched to the right and then met another that went in both directions with several doors in sight. Another high pitched whistle echoed up the stairs from below.

Laina commanded, "Down!"

Laina led her Protectresses into a melee, a screeching discordance of metal on metal as combatants fought viciously. Jenna was the last to reach the main room, and she almost stumbled as she surveyed the carnage before her. Over a dozen men lay strewn about the floor, as well as a half dozen women, some crawling and pulling themselves away from the fight with severed limbs or entrails dragging behind them. Others lay unmoving with fatal wounds as they wailed in agony, and then there were the dead. Her quick scan of the butchery showed her that two of her Sisters were down, at least one prostitute, and it appeared by the tattoos on their wrists that three of the other dead and dying women were with the pirates. The rest of the whores, two men among them, bunched into a front corner near the barred exit, several of them wailing in useless despair.

Dominica and Gargantua fought back to back against four men with swords and clubs, their strength waning in the prolonged fight, blood seeping from several minor wounds. Two other Sisters had their backs to the walls as they traded blows with their foemen. Laina and the Sisters joined the battle ferociously, without concern for their own safety, cutting down pirates from behind before they could react to the new threat.

Four more buccaneers emerged from the stairs on the far side of the blood covered hall, their seaboots splashing and squishing in the pooling, let blood. Two women brandishing wickedly curved sabers fell into the fray, throwing themselves with a flurry of blows at Dominica and Laina who had just defeated their own duelists. Two others carried loaded crossbows, stopping near the stairs to find targets for their quarrels.

Jenna barreled at these, and the first saw her coming only too late. Instead of drawing a bead and firing his weapon, he lifted it up to intercept her blade that slashed down from above. The Vulgesch forged blade hacked clean through the weapons limb and crashed into the foregrip, where the bowman's hand still rested. He screamed as he lost fingers, and the crossbow string twanged having suddenly lost tension, hurling the bolt end over end somewhere into the fray. Jenna recovered swiftly and thrust the blade into his naked torso once and then twice, the sword rending his guts as well as flesh and muscle.

She yanked her sword free and hopped past the falling body as the second crossbow shot off a bolt into Dominica, who had just dispatched yet another

222

opponent. But the pirate, aware of Jenna's approaching attack, rushed the shot, and the Protectress spun away and to the floor as the missile struck her hard in the shoulder. He turned and hurled his weapon at Jenna, who dropped low to avoid it, and then he ran out of sight back into the stairwell. A quick look around showed the melee was over, at least in the manor's main hall, as Laina helped the wounded captain to her feet. Someone pounded on the door leading to the estate's front yard, likely several other pirates trying to join the now ended combat.

Stupid, Jenna thought, *they could just go around.*

"It's not bad," Dominica breathed, referring to the bolt protruding from her shoulder despite the numerous other bleeding wounds she carried.

Laina inspected it and agreed, "Your leather stopped most of it. Went through the thin part, hit the bone."

Jenna winced as Dominica gripped the shaft and summarily ripped it out, asking, "Where are the others?"

"Eddena is out back with her bow, and I sent two Sisters to find Ghenake," Laina reported. "I'm sorry it took us so long –"

Dominica interrupted, "Upstairs, let's go."

"What about?" Gargantua asked, ending her query with a broadsword pointed at the barred door.

"They should know it's over," Laina shrugged with rolled eyes.

"Explain it to them," Dominica said with a nod, eliciting a vicious, mirthful grin from Gargantua.

Laina and Gargantua faced and eliminated several pirates from outside the manor with terrible efficiency, cutting them down as they burst through the door just as it was unbarred. Two others, upon seeing the carnage and quick deaths of their cohorts, threw down their arms and surrendered, while the rest of the Protectresses fanned out above and below. Two cleared the rest of the lower level – consisting only of the kitchens and two small rooms – and unbarred the door leading out to Eddena, who had surrounded herself with the corpses of those who thought to slip out the back of the estate, likely with the intent of blending in to normal life somewhere in the city or even elsewhere in Abrea.

Dominica led Jenna and the rest back up the stairs to search the bedrooms of the manor. The house had become eerily silent, neither friend nor foe deigning to make any noise. They found the double doors to the largest bedroom, certainly Master Rall's and the one surely assumed by the pirate leader Ghenake, standing wide open and no one inside. Jenna had never seen so large a bedroom for one person, as it consumed close to half the manor's upper level with an enormous, black varnished wooden poster bed with accents of smoky, Vulgeschi steel and its silken canopy no doubt from Raucrud. Several matching bureaus stood against walls, and a half dozen chests, massive and worn, lay strewn about haphazardly and some of them open. Plush, expensive imported rugs from Isdal and Azgua carpeted almost every square inch of the floor.

"Spread out. Find them," Dominica urged.

Exiting the bedroom, Jenna broke left down the hallway to investigate a branch they had bypassed while the other two Sisters went in the other direction toward the rear of the upper level. The hallway ended with an open door to the right, and as Jenna peeked her head around the corner, she saw a woman, a Protectress, laying on her side next to a small but comfortable looking bed. A lone candle lit the room reflecting in a silver mirror to spread its minimal light around and cast jaunting flickers. She darted in to kneel next to her fallen Sister, and Jenna placed a hand on her shoulder, feeling the flesh had already begun to cool. Despite the weak candlelight, her eyes took in the gutting slash across the woman's belly and the ropey intestines that

224

had begun to spill from her before she fell. Jenna realized she knelt in a pool of blood.

The clatter and clangs of steel and battle joined met her ears, and Jenna jumped to her feet. As she turned, the door slammed shut with an echoing bang, a shadowy form emerging from behind it. Jenna cursed herself for a fool as a middling height man, several inches shorter than six feet but still taller than herself, materialized from the gloom. He wore silk breeches, black or purple she couldn't be sure in the feeble candlelight with a matching sleeveless tunic or shirt that seemed to almost flutter and billow as he moved despite the stillness of the air. He had long, curly, almost greasy black hair and an olive complexion turned deep bronze from long hours in the sun. He wore several gaudy and golden earrings in each ear, and more gold glinted off his hands, one of which clutched a wickedly curved scimitar common in Raucrud. His other hand held a common dagger. Jenna brandished her sword, but he showed no care for it at all.

"You should just let me go, little girl," he threatened in an exotic accent the likes of which she hadn't heard before, his tone dangerously low. With the pommel of the dagger in his left hand and without taking dark eyes off his prey, he pushed a thin bolt across the door, which would only delay a determined invader by a few seconds, and he added, "Or better yet. Help Ghenake escape, and I will make you a queen of the seas, bathe you in gold coins and adorn you with jewels and silks."

"Until you bore of me. I'll pass on that offer, pirate filth," Jenna replied with a hard edge and a confidence that she didn't feel.

Ghenake shrugged and attacked with blinding speed.

Chapter 17

The Pirate Prince Ghenake

Every time the swords struck each other, the ringing of steel carried on the subtle wind currents of the warm summer day. Training for one to two hours per day, three days a week for the last two years had wrought lean sinews in Jenna's arms and legs. While other girls her age mooned and obsessed over boys as they grew to notice certain differences between the genders, Jenna crossed swords with the one armed teacher of the village's children. She was the only one among them Brasalla took the time to mentor in swordsmanship and, to a lesser extent because she left it to Jenna's mother, archery, and Jenna swelled with silent pride even as the other girls jeered at her. Two years of training to help her gain strength and then learn the basic forms of fencing had led to sparring with real swords, though with dull edges and blunted points. Brasalla had several of these weapons in her cottage, as well as a number of wooden practice swords and other such weapons, to avoid any real wounds besides bruises and damaged pride. The one armed woman had taught Jenna so much, and yet every time a new lesson was unveiled, Jenna found herself bested once again. She had never once defeated the former Protectress, despite the woman having but one arm, or even landed a single point. But still she fought, knowing that one day...

Brasalla attacked with a downward stroke meant to slash down and across Jenna's body starting at her right shoulder, and Jenna recognized her opportunity when it presented itself. Bringing her own sword around, she parried the blade to her left, and scraping steel on steel, thrust her blade forward in such a way that it would skewer her opponent, if not for the spherical mound of steel that made the weapon's point. But her sword met nothing, and in her hurry to take advantage of Brasalla's careless attack, Jenna stood suddenly off balance as her arms extended well forward. Brasalla's weight came to bear on her parried blade, forcing the point of Jenna's sword down to the ground as she could contest neither the woman's weight nor strength, to say nothing of leverage.

"You overextended your thrust, Little Dear. You're dead, I'm afraid."

"I know. Damn it all," Jenna swore.

With a disapproving glare, Brasalla eased her weight and lifted her sword from Jenna's, allowing the girl to recover her blade, and she said, "If I were your mother, I'd likely tell you to watch your language."

"Then, it's a good thing you're not, huh?" Jenna shot back, but the tone held more playfulness than challenge.

"I suppose."

"Just once, I want to kill you. Just once," Jenna complained.

Brasalla chided, "Don't do that."

"What?"

"Whine," Brasalla explained. "It's unbecoming of you. You're strong and brave, and you're growing into a beautiful woman. Such bellyaching is unacceptable, especially among the Protectresses."

Jenna's eyes narrowed, and she answered, "I don't want to be a Protectress."

"Is there something wrong with being a Protectress? Something wrong with being a trusted defender of Abrea and our way of life?"

"No," Jenna replied quickly, noting her teacher's solemn tone and emotionless face. She chose her next words carefully so as not to give further offense, "It's just not what I want to do."

"You cannot do what you want to do, Little Dear," Brasalla calmly reminded the girl, and it was now Jenna's turn to grow silent. "Anyway, do you know what your mistake was?"

Jenna sighed, puffing a snort of air out of her nostrils in annoyance as she clenched her jaw and turned her head from side to side, looking at nothing. After a moment, she answered, "I assumed."

"Assumed what?" Brasalla asked with raised eyebrows.

"I assumed that you, a trained warrior, someone who has killed people far more skilled than me, made a basic mistake."

Brasalla prodded, "And?"

"And I tried to capitalize on it."

"As you well should've, but that wasn't the fatal mistake."

"No?" Jenna asked, looking up at her mentor, and her face betrayed a mix of impatience at the drawing out of the lesson and aggravation at her own ineptitude.

"You did the right thing, but you're right in that you assumed. Never assume your enemy has made a mistake but be ready to take advantage of it if they did."

The impatience turned to more annoyance as Jenna worked to unravel the riddle in her mind. "How does that work?"

"Even the best trained warriors make mistakes," Brasalla explained, indicating her missing arm with a pointed look, "and you must take advantage when they do. You parried my poor attack perfectly, but you were so certain of victory that you telegraphed your thrust badly."

"What does that mean?"

"I knew the attack was coming because I was testing you, but most trained warriors would have seen it

228

coming, too. You pulled your sword arm back just a few inches to give more force to your thrust."

Jenna breathed in a slight hiss of air between her teeth as understanding dawned on her. "So," she reasoned, "by doing that, you saw the attack coming and had more time to react to avoid it."

"Exactly! We're fighting with swords, not clubs or staves or some other weapon that we have to bash each other's brains in with. Your father's sword came from Vulgesch. It is so strong, can hold such an edge that it can easily punch through most armor, except maybe Vulgeschi plate. Fight with grace, finesse, dexterity, not force."

"I..." Jenna began, but she suddenly wasn't sure what she wanted to say, so she nodded and replied, "I understand."

"Maybe a little, but I think you'll understand more in time. There's one more thing I'd like you to consider, just keep it in mind. As a woman and not particularly tall, people, definitely men will underestimate you. Take advantage of that. Lure them in and do something they don't expect. Remember what I told you before – fair fights are for suckers."

Jenna nodded idly at this, her eyes downcast as she mulled it over. Without warning, she shot her left foot out, hooking her soft leather boot right behind Brasalla's right knee while giving the woman a sudden push with both hands. Caught unaware, Brasalla's legs bent as she tumbled backward and landed hard on her back, only the thick grass behind her cottage slightly cushioning her impact. Even so, she felt the wind knocked from her lungs as she struck the ground.

"You mean like that?" Jenna asked with an amply proud grin. She pointed her practice sword at her mentor and said one word, "Yield."

"You little shit," Brasalla spouted as she struggled up to one elbow, and then she noticed the tip of the sword, blunted with a sphere of steel as it hovered only a half foot away from her. Laughter took the woman for a moment, and she tipped her head backward, answering, "Yeah, something like that. Here, Little Dear, help an old woman up."

Ghenake's scimitar slashed in the wan light, and Jenna avoided the first swipe without trouble. Another came, also avoided with minimal movement, followed by a third which caused her to lean backward about a foot. She followed this with a thrust at the pirate's midsection, which he deflected effortlessly with his dagger. The curved blade came at her again, aimed at her neck, and she blocked with her sword held vertically, point towards the floor, quickly whipping it back in a slash that met only air. Ghenake chortled, low and menacing, and the realization that she was hopelessly overmatched struck Jenna like a lightning bolt. Worse, Ghenake knew that too.

He launched a flurry of attacks with the curved blade, and Jenna could only manage to keep up with their speed. The shape of his weapon allowed him to slash with much greater ease, minimal wrist movements as opposed to the obvious motion of his entire arm. More than that, Jenna could anticipate the destination of a straight blade by the movements of the upper arm, but her opponent barely had to move as such. The scimitar came at her with such blinding speed, and she endeavored to keep her distance from it rather than parry. When she had no choice but to parry the curved blade, Jenna expected the ten inch blade of the dagger to skewer her at any moment, but Ghenake kept the weapon in reserve, rather than ending the battle.

Jenna had nowhere else to run. In a handful of seconds, she had backed away from his attacks to have a wall only two feet behind her back, and a tiny table ate up half of that space. The bed occupied the center of the room, and she dove to her right to somersault across it as Ghenake slashed. At the last moment, he shifted his wrist to alter the path of the blade, and Jenna felt the air part near her head as it came near. She recovered onto her feet on the other side of the bed, some five feet away from the pirate, as strands of her hair billowed down to join a thick lock that lay among the disheveled bedding.

Jenna noticed the thuds sounding in the hall past the door, leather boots banging footsteps on carpeted wood flooring. They weren't close by, but they grew louder as she listened. Her eyes darted to the door, as did Ghenake's, and they both calculated how much time it would take for her to reach the door and slide the bolt back. Jenna thought for certain they came to the same result – he would cut her down from behind well before she could flee the bedroom into her oncoming Sisters.

"You won't make it out of here alive," Jenna warned, her sword ringing as clearly as a bell as she deflected the scimitar.

Ghenake shrugged, "Neither will you, and I have lived, little girl. Have you?"

She doubted his sincerity as he renewed his attack in earnest, steel flashing across the width of the bed, and this time the dagger darted here and there. The short, straight blade was easier to track, as Ghenake's shoulder betrayed its imminent attack, though he struck with the speed of a viper. She narrowly avoided the blade once, twice, before it nicked her arm and drew blood that ran in a narrow line down her triceps. Keeping pace with his assault, Jenna's arms began to tire. She dared not try to fight him much longer.

Someone pounded on the door, and Laina's muffled voice called, "Jenna, are you in there?"

"Help!" she cried, and the door groaned with a deep thump as someone threw themselves against it.

Ghenake hurriedly brought his scimitar around in a blow meant to decapitate her. She ducked a few inches to avoid it, but the pirate's dagger was already in motion, on course to punch between her ribs on her right side. Expecting the attack, Jenna maneuvered her longsword to intercept his wrist. The angle was sloppy, the move poorly executed, but it worked as her sword met Ghenake's left wrist, hacking through tendons and sinews. The blade met bone, and the pirate howled as blood sprayed with a severed artery, and his dagger dropped, bounced off the end of the bed and clattered to the floor.

"You bitch!" he screamed in fury.

And Jenna broke for the door as another, harder whump impacted it from the hall, dropping her sword in the lunge away. Ghenake bounded after her, screaming obscenities in both of their languages. She had mere inches on him as they both rounded the bed for the door, and his left hand useless, he reached out with his right to take a full fist of her hair. Before his fingers could close, Jenna dropped back and to her right, feeling a few strands yanked from her scalp. She ignored the pain, dropping to the floor and rotating on her right foot, gaining momentum as she went. Her left leg swung around and took Ghenake right behind both knees, and as he crumpled backward her hand found the hilt of the bloodied dagger. She lifted upward as hard as she could as he fell, and the blade plunged to the hilt into his back. Something hot, thicker than water and nearly black in the shadowed, weak light of the flickering candle drenched the hilt, her hand and even her forearm. Ghenake weakly grasped her throat with his right hand, but with the awkward angle combined with his lifeblood flowing out the wound in his back, the pressure of that grip slackened. For good measure, Jenna wrenched the blade with a sharp twist, causing a gurgling, coughing groan to emit from the pirate's throat as his hand lost purchase on her neck. She yanked the dagger from his back, and Ghenake died in a growing pool of his own rapidly cooling blood.

The door burst inward, with a bending of steel and rending of the slide bolt, sending several pieces of metal flying somewhere into the gloom. Gargantua and Laina came through at once, swords drawn as the bedroom flooded with friendly torchlight from the hallway.

"Jenna, are you all right?" Laina queried, genuine concern showing in both her eyes and voice as she came to kneel next to Jenna.

Watching with unblinking eyes as Gargantua checked perfunctorily on the other dead Protectress, Jenna nodded, "I think so."

"This is him, isn't it? Ghenake?"

Jenna nodded again, and she blinked her eyes twice, trying to clear a sudden fog that seemed to settle in over her. Something felt... wrong. Gooseflesh rose on her exposed arms, and she began to shiver. Her hands shook, though not from any sense of cold, and Jenna's hand flew to cover her mouth as she turned away from her friend. The coppery, acrid scent smothering her hand was enough, and Jenna scrambled to the far side of the bed, barely making it away before she vomited. The waves struck her, and just as soon as she thought she was done, as the terrible need to empty her stomach subsided, another crest approached. She heaved again and again, and somewhere during that eternity, she felt a gentle hand on her shoulder, heard Laina's calm words, "It's okay. It'll pass."

Cloth tore from somewhere nearby, and as soon as she gulped and gasped for air, certain nothing else was to come, someone forced it into Jenna's hands. She wiped the drool, bile, and vomit from her chin as well as some splatters on other parts of her body before discarding the wool in a vile ball. Laina helped her stand uneasily, knees shaking like a newborn foal's, and she sat down on the end of the bed, busying herself with attempting to wipe the sticky blood from her hand and arm onto the damaged bedclothes. Laina sat next to her as Gargantua lifted the body of their dead Sister, passing Dominica as the captain entered the bedroom.

"That's him," Laina announced. "Jenna killed him."

Dominica kicked the man's naked foot while declaring something about his sexual appetites involving pigs, and she took in the sight and smells of the room. "Are you all right, Sister?"

Jenna didn't want to look up. She felt ashamed, somehow guilty at getting sick just moments ago. What would the others think? How could they trust a Sister who didn't have the stomach for what they're about?

"She got sick," Laina explained, and Jenna turned her face toward her friend, a sting of betrayal touching her heart.

A hand lay on her shoulder, strong but not heavy or overpowering. It felt... caring, gentle. Jenna looked up to see Dominica looking down on her with an unfamiliar light shining in her eyes. It was something like love.

Dominica bent down to bring her eyes level with Jenna's and said, "Don't worry about it, Sister. It happened to all of us the first time or two. Shit, Laina pissed herself in her first sword fight."

"Shut up, Sister," Laina shot back, but a sheepish smile adorned her face.

"You saved my life tonight, Sister," Dominica continued, her unblinking eyes staring into Jenna's, "and I will never forget that. You're worthy of the Protectresses, and I'm proud to call you Sister."

Jenna had nothing to say in response, didn't know what to say. Tears welled up in her eyes, and though she fought them, they began to pour forth and

234

down her cheeks. Her Captain leaned forward and took her in an embrace, two Sister warriors, their hearts open and lending each other strength and solace. One of Laina's hands found one of hers and gave it a gentle squeeze.

Dominica released first and backed up a step to stand at her full height. She spoke with the authority of a leader, but the soft approach of a friend, "Take a minute or two, but we still have much to do. There's more of them around in the city, trying to hide, and we have to find Master Rall, if he's alive."

Jenna nodded twice, trying to wipe the trails of her tears away on her forearms, and Dominica moved to leave the room. As she reached the doorway, her figure blocking the light much like the moon eclipsing the sun, Jenna called after her, "Thank you, Sister."

Dominica stopped for just a moment, half turned to nod, and strode out of the room.

Chapter 18

A Return Home

An icy wind blew in from the north, from across the great forests of Abrea, and it bit clear through leather armor, the woolen layers over it, and the linen worn beneath as the Protectresses looked at Soutton from the height of a frozen hill some two miles or so away. The weather rarely grew so cold this far south, so close to Vulgesch and its volcanic mountains, and when it did, the local populace was hardly prepared for it. The people stayed in their homes, only venturing forth to retrieve more firewood or check on their livestock before rushing with all speed back indoors and the small comfort of their fires.

Snow had started to fall halfway between Portton and Soutton, thick and fluffy white flakes lazing to the ground around them while they camped in the night. When they awoke for the morning, only their fire had kept the snow at bay, making the ground where they slept soft and wet, almost muddy. Away from the fire, three or four inches collected overnight, followed by two or three more as they journeyed home. Before the flakes ceased to fall, the storm offered one last vigorous puff of the stuff as gigantic flakes, some as large as two inches across, fell furiously and unexpectedly. It almost blinded them as they trudged their horses through it, and the snowfall ended as abruptly as its last breath began. An iron gray sky continued to dominate the white covered plains and hills below to cast all light and color out of the world. On the last day, they awoke to clear, ice blue skies, and as the sun traversed the azure canvas, its rays reflected off the snow blindingly.

Jenna marveled at this, even as the Sisters covered their exposed skin in linen to protect it from both the effervescent permeating sun and the freezing burning wind. She had grown up in the forests, and being further north, it snowed there often enough. But never had she seen so much accumulation on the ground, as the forest canopy always protected the forest floor from most frozen precipitation. Though that had its own surprises – hearing huge crashes in the middle of the night as the air warmed and the snow lost its perch on the branches up above or worse. More than once she had seen someone enjoying the warmer but still brisk, crisp winter air, and a pile of wet snow simply plummeted down upon them from somewhere above like an enormous, nearly frozen bird dropping. At least it was just water, and usually, the melting during the day was little more than a cold, intermittent rain. If the day warmed enough, it could even feel refreshing.

This had been anything but, and as she shielded her eyes from the sun, with little success as the snow was equally blinding, Jenna gratefully considered the entire affair to be over. Home – interesting how she came to accept Elishia Place as home despite only being there a few weeks – lay just a few miles away across what felt like frozen wasteland, what Jenna thought Isdal must be like every day of the year. It had been three months since Dominica had led them from Soutton, and during those three months, Abrea had moved firmly from autumn and into the depths of winter.

For some reason, Jenna thought that once she and her Sisters cleaned out the pirates that had claimed Portton for even a short while, that the Protectresses would make the return ride to Soutton at once, though perhaps in more leisurely fashion. She had no legitimate reason for thinking this, because after all, this was her first mission as a Protectress, her first anything as a Protectress really. She assumed that they would turn the city back over to its people and leave as soon as they were sure all the trouble was over. Well, not exactly... three months.

They found Master Rall the night of the assault, the night she'd killed three men to include the pirate prince himself, and he had been chained to giant wine barrels in his own manor's cellar. Though roughed up and filthy, he was no worse for wear, and his story of how the pirates arrived and took the town matched up to Madam Rahni's. One of the pirate ships escaped, helmed out to sea within an hour of the battle at Master Rall's manor, but emboldened by word of the Protectresses' victory, the townsfolk stormed and scuttled the other two, overpowering the small handful of men left aboard to defend them. Over the next two days, as the news continued its spread across the score of villages that had melded together to make the city of Portton, remnants of the city watch came out of hiding to join the Protectresses in hunting down stragglers, many of whom attempted to hide across the city. Some were caught and imprisoned, and many more died in attempts to escape or fight back.

But there was a greater problem. Master Rall, an affable but aggrieved man of five and a half feet and the rotundness provided by years and years of good living, refused to accept that a handful of pirates took his city so readily, and he stayed convinced that members of *Hulgre Fratencav* had infiltrated his city long before. He even believed that dozens, perhaps hundreds, of Portton's own residents or sailors from other ships, seized the opportunity to join the pirates in their celebrations, only to slink quietly back to their homes and ships when it was over.

Dominica hadn't been so easily convinced, but Madam Rahni vindicated the man by pointing out one such example – a dockworker who had enjoyed several of her brothel's girls during the occupation, paid for by corsair coin. Rall demanded investigations and arrests, inquisitions and trials, pointing out they had dealt death, rape, and torture to Protectresses as well. Dominica understood the need for justice, but what Master Rall wanted went beyond her mandate. Having already dispatched one rider with a report to Lady Ayn on the day after killing Ghenake, Dominica agreed to sit with Master Rall and pen another message with the good man's beliefs.

Seven days later, they received a message from Lady Ayn, and it read, "Master Rall's concerns seem well grounded, at least worthy of discussion. As I am writing this response, I've already sent a messenger toward Desolation. By the time he reaches the edge, the Convocation will be over, and the Dragonknights returning home. King Rendor will no doubt choose someone to begin these investigations, as well as select a tribunal to judge those accused. Remain in Portton for now and help maintain the peace, but do not act on Master Rall's beliefs until you receive word from myself, Sir Conor, or the king Himself without clear and irrefutable evidence."

Master Rall fumed, and Jenna knew that Dominica felt his anger and frustration in her own heart. Ten Sisters lay dead at the hands of Ghenake and his *Hulgre Fratencav* including Sister Esther, who met the most gruesome death of them all – burnt alive after several of them had... The Sisters wanted revenge, even Jenna to an extent. Though, she only now enjoyed true acceptance, having fought alongside her Sisters and proving herself to them, this acceptance brought with it the seething anger at what had been done to Sister Esther and her squad. But it had to wait, and shockingly to Jenna, Dominica was the one among them who cooled the tempers when they flared.

The next message came not on the back of a horse but from the skies as they spotted an echelon of three of Abrea's dragons flying in from the east. Though more slender and far more graceful than those of Vulgesch, Portton offered no place for them to land within the city itself, as it was once many smaller villages that had grown into each other. The Protectresses, along with Master Rall, met the Dragonknights outside the city as they alit as one, barely making a sound other than the rushing of air from their beating wings.

A sour longing tugged at Jenna's heart as her eyes followed them spiral down out of the clouds above, each one fifty feet long from head to tail with a wingspan to match. Like the Dragonknights of every other nation but Vulgesch, Abrea's sat astride the dragon's narrow neck, just behind the head upon a custom saddle, but unlike a horse, they used no bit or bridle to give the beasts commands. She knew it had to do with the Link, the ritual that gave the riders control over the creatures, and she had always known she was meant for it. She closed her eyes, face still held to the sky as the salty, seaborn breeze blew across the welcoming party, and Jenna swore she could sense the dragons thinking. She said nothing, for no one would believe her anyway, and she opened her eyes as they reached the ground. Sir Malum, Commander of the West, dismounted first, and Jenna felt his eyes linger on her for some reason or another while the other two Dragonknights dropped to the ground. She ignored his gaze dutifully, along with the intense yearning to approach the beautiful creatures behind the Dragonknights, to reach out and touch their giant paws. She thought she could feel... something from them, but she dismissed it to focus on the conversation at hand.

"We are honored, Sir Malum," Master Rall was saying, "but I would have expected Sir Conor or his

240

Dragonknights.   After all, this is his region of the realm."

Sir Malum's eyes had narrowed a bit as he responded, "We all serve where King Rendor requires."

"Of course, I meant no disrespect," Rall replied with a slight bow.

"King Rendor feels that I am more suited to the task of rooting out those among your city who betrayed Abrea. I am to lead the inquiries as well as the Tribunal. We will find and punish those who took part in what happened here.   An attack on the king's people, especially Protectresses," Malum quoted the law with a deferential nod towards Dominica, "is as an attack on King Rendor himself."

Jenna hated the work that followed, and soon after, she noticed that she wasn't the only Sister who felt that way.   The first week or two found over a dozen perpetrators who joined in the piracy but leads grew scarce after that.   By the end of the second month, Jenna and her Sisters along with the city watch, banged on doors and even dragged men out of their homes based on rumors to stand before Malum and his tribunal.   The man doggedly pursued lines of questioning that lasted hours, and eventually, the suspects found themselves so confused they didn't even know what they were admitting to.   The gallows stayed busy, as did the headmen's axes, and bodies of the guilty were crucified, some while still alive, out in the harbor as a warning.

She voiced her misgivings only once, and only to Laina, and her friend cut the conversation off within minutes, warily looking about them to make sure no one else was around or heard.   Laina said in a hushed whisper, "Don't.   *Do not* question the methods or mandate of a Dragonknight of the First Circle, especially one like Malum."

Yes, Jenna felt overjoyed at being back in Soutton, and she would have preferred mucking stalls

241

and cleaning latrines to dispensing justice. As they rode through the sprawling villages and farmsteads and entered the city itself, the dreadful chill dispersed and eased somewhat. Snow didn't coat the streets as it did the plains, and Jenna saw very little of it indeed, except occasionally piled in a corner or alley somewhere away from the ambient heat of the buildings and people clustered so closely together. While they saw almost no one about in the miles leading to Soutton, the city buzzed with activity, though with decreased intensity.

Elishia Place warmed them further with fires burning in the hall and torches throughout, emphasizing to Jenna even more so that she had returned home. They entered the hall through the main entrance, closing the double doors behind them with a softly echoing boom as they loosed sighs and yawns and finally allowed their muscles to slacken and relax. Jenna looked across the hall and saw Lady Ayn in silk robes standing on the dais, and the Sisters approached her slowly, as if these last few steps required too much energy, as if they had nothing left to give.

"Welcome home, Sisters," Lady Ayn intoned solemnly. Her face seemed somehow older by years, even though only three months passed, and her voice held quiet gravity. Yet, it still projected as she spoke, "You have all done well, succeeded, and excelled in the most dangerous and dire of circumstances. I applaud you, Sister Dominica, at success in such difficult circumstances."

The Sisters murmured their agreement and appreciation of their captain, though Dominica's eyes mournfully dropped to the floor. Jenna had come to love the woman's strength – not just bodily, but her mental fortitude as well – and she appreciated that her first outing, her first mission, had been assigned to someone so solidly unassailable. She carried a warmth in her heart for Dominica, amazing to consider how that

242

had changed, but she also acutely felt a sadness from her Sister that she endeavored to hide from those under her command. Jenna sometimes noticed it in the woman's eyes late at night or when she walked away alone to gather her thoughts.

Her guilt showed itself to all as Dominica whispered, "Thank you, Lady, but it was far from successful."

"Is that so?" Lady Ayn asked, cocking her head a bit to her right in mock confusion. "It seems Portton is now free and back under King Rendor's rule. The invaders are dead, or at least gone, including their leaders. I would consider that a success."

"I lost four of our Sisters."

"You did," Ayn nodded shallowly with wide unblinking eyes, and she stepped down to place a caring hand on Dominica's shoulder, "and that is the burden of every leader. I carry that burden as well, Sister. I have lost Sisters in battle, and I have ordered them knowingly to their deaths. I sent eighteen Protectresses to Portton, and only eight returned, a cost that will weigh upon me just as it does you."

Dominica looked back up, looked into her leader's eyes, and Lady Ayn enveloped her in an embrace, completely heedless of the grime and odor common to traveling warriors. She held it for a few moments, and Jenna noted the lone tear that tracked down Dominica's face. The other Sisters looked away or to the floor reverentially, allowing the women their moment.

When she pulled away, Lady Ayn brushed the tear from Dominica's cheek and said, "The grief is something we must deal with in our own way, away from those who follow us. That's part of what it means to lead."

Dominica nodded wordlessly and sniffed once as Lady Ayn climbed back up the steps to the platform and announced, "Sisters, I'm glad to see every one of your faces. Today and tomorrow are yours to do as you please, and the next day we will host a ceremony in Elishia Plaza to mourn our lost Sisters. Go and rest, now."

Thirty nine Protectresses assembled in the plaza under an air warming winter sun that shined cheerily and blindingly despite the melancholy of those outside Elishia Place. They all came dressed for battle, in full armor with sheathed swords, slung quivers and bows held in their calloused hands. At their head stood Lady Ayn, the sun reflecting off her plate armor to make her a heralded heroine out of stories from ages long past. Across the plaza throngs of people by the score or even the hundreds had assembled to pay their respects. A quiet buzz passed around the crowd, and the connecting streets leading to the plaza contained even more of Soutton's city folk.

In the center of the plaza stood a great pyre, its apex reaching to the sky some twenty or thirty feet in the air. It consisted of wooden planks standing on their ends to meet at a point, some of these still damp from the recent snows. They stood on top of a fifteen foot wide, circular iron plate that had a lip around its perimeter to give the planks' ends something to rest against to keep them from sliding downward. Eight iron stanchions about five feet in height rose from the plate and were connected by chains, presumably to warn off anyone curious enough to get too close. Thick hemp ropes completed the pyre, wrapping the planks several times to keep the construction still and steady. Notably, it lacked brush or other kindling. Personal effects filled the space inside the unlit pyre itself. Leather jerkins and shagreen scabbards, books or perhaps journals, small trinkets and even jewelry had been laid lovingly inside before the last boards had been put in place.

Lady Ayn stood perfectly still as the people of Soutton arrived, only speaking once an enormous shadow suddenly flashed across the plaza and was gone.

"My dear Protectresses and people of Soutton," she began, "we have gathered here today to pay our respects to our honored dead. The Protectresses have helped defend the people of Abrea for a thousand years. I have seen only twenty five years as a Protectress, and it has been years of peace and plenty. Few in Abrea have wanted for anything, and we live in peace with our neighbors of Vulgesch and Isdal.

"However, there were some who thought to take advantage of our largess. A band of pirates attacked Portton and took it for their own, knowing the Dragonknights would be in Convocation. The Protectresses, as we always have and always will, answered the call. Eight of the brave women you see behind me fought and slew the pirates and their captains, liberating Portton for King Rendor and the people of Abrea once more."

Lady Ayn took a long, deep breath in as she lowered her eyes for a moment. When she continued, she raised them again to scan the crowd, "But it came at a heavy toll. We lost ten of our Sisters, ten incredible women who represented the best Abrea has to offer. They gave their lives willingly in service to their nation, just as each of us standing before you are ready to do so, and any of us would gladly give our lives so that any one of them could return.

"But such things are the stuff of children's stories and fairy tales, for there is no bringing back what we have lost. The dead have already been put to rest, months ago in Portton. Today is about remembrance, taking the time to mourn them but also celebrate them for the very sacrifice that fills us with sorrow. Within the bonfire are those things which remind us of our lost Sisters, chosen by those of us who knew them best, and we now commit them to fire so they may go to our Sisters in whatever afterlife they find themselves in."

As she finished, Lady Ayn raised her arms to the sky, and a lumbering hulk with leathery wings came into view. A dragon whose scales gleamed in the sunlight, reflecting back hues ranging from dark, smoky gray to blood red, flew low and fast over the buildings of Soutton. This behemoth wasn't as fast as Abrea's green dragons, but it carried with it a physical power born of immensity, for those scales covered a rippling mass of muscle. The creature was twice as thick as the dragons native to Abrea and just as long, and its wings occupied twice as much area, likely necessary to create the lift for such a gargantuan creature. Its rider, in head to toe plate armor, sat further back than Abrea's Dragonknights, almost right between the wings in a leather chair of sorts so that the underside of his boots rested flat on the dragon's back.

Few people in Abrea had ever seen a dragon, or Drakkritt rider, from Vulgesch as each nation kept to their own borders, but the people of Soutton were the exception. So close to Vulgesch, and with Sir Conor originally hailing from that land, made their appearance not so much as commonplace, but not unexpected.

The crowd barely had time to register the presence of the dragon before it swooped over the plaza, a pouring flash of white hot flame pouring from its mouth to strike the pyre. Despite the dampness of the wood and the still frigid winter air, it lit immediately from the immeasurable heat of the blast, and with one mighty downward push of its wings, the dragon lifted away and over the buildings to the east. It was a precision strike, the dragon's equivalent of a bullseye from a hundred yards, and the pyre burned incredibly hot, consuming the keepsakes and mementos within it.

246

As the Protectresses endured as solemn sentinels, some with tears running freely down their faces, some of the folk of Soutton made their way near the bonfire. They threw offerings into the flames – a loaf of bread, a bouquet of winter flowers, a wreath made from a pine bough, even a small cask of wine, or a handful of coins – items they wished to give the fallen for their journeys. Many cried, but no one spoke. Beyond the roar of the consuming flames, little sound broke the solemnity of the ceremony except the wailing of one babe held by its mother somewhere in the crowd.

Chapter 19

Flight of Dragons

"I've never seen one that big before," Jenna mused in fascination.

Dominica, who paused midway through lifting a spoonful of diced and fried potatoes to her mouth, adopted an extensive, mischievous grin and replied, "Then you should get out more, Sister. Maybe Laina can show you the choicer spots around Soutton!"

Laughter exploded around the table, despite the morning's somber ceremony and the subdued activity afterward, as several sisters couldn't contain their reaction. One only barely succeeding in her turning her head as she sprayed wine on the floor beside her, some of it trickling from her nose, while another began to cough uncontrollably, receiving a hard smack in the back from Dominica. Even Laina guffawed at her friend's expense. Jenna of course understood the risqué humor, academically at least, but she didn't really see the need.

"I meant the dragon."

"Oh, the *dragon*," Dominica exaggerated the word, "I thought perhaps you were looking under Sir Conor's fauld again."

"What? I, no," Jenna stammered, and then something struck her, "What do you mean, 'again'?"

"Oh, don't be ridiculous," Dominica chastised, "you look at him the same way all the new girls look at him."

"You're being ridiculous," Jenna accused with a furrowed brow. She shook her head slightly with the thought of it, "Besides, I've seen him literally twice."

"Don't worry, you're going to get another chance tomorrow."

"What?" Jenna asked.

"See, Sisters? That caught her attention," Dominica pointed her spoon across the table at Jenna to another round of laughter. This eruption died down faster, and she explained, "Tomorrow, you will get to see another of Sir Conor's famous duels."

"Against Lady Ayn again?" Jenna asked, and she ignored the slight quickening of her pulse. The last such duel had been amazing to watch, even if it lasted mere minutes.

"No, even better!" Dominica declared, the woman relishing the withholding of information as long as possible.

Laina rolled her eyes and interjected, ruining the fun, "That dragon we saw today was from Vulgesch."

"I assumed. I've heard they're enormous, even by dragon standards," Jenna replied, "but I've never seen one."

"Here in the south, we see them from afar sometimes since we're so close to Vulgesch," Laina explained with a shrug.

It was Dominica's turn to interrupt, not wanting Laina to steal the glory, "That dragon belongs to a Drakkritt named Ser Gogol. He has a keep just across the border in the mountains, and he's friends with Sir Conor."

"Is he First Circle like Sir Conor?" Jenna asked.

Laina shook her head, "No, Vulgesch is different. There's the king, Ser Prath, and the rest serve him. They each have their own lands."

"Oh."

"Anyway, enough with the foreign civics lesson," Dominica glared at Laina in mock annoyance. "Ser Gogol and Sir Conor sometimes duel in the skies just south of Soutton, sort of as entertainment for the people. We know how much you like dragons."

"And Sir Conor," Laina added.

"And Sir Conor," Dominica agreed with as innocent an expression as she could manage, "so you'll enjoy it, you know, with it being your first time seeing it."

"The duel, too!" Laina spouted, and the table again burst into raucous laughter.

Jenna put on an embarrassed smile and looked down at her plate as Laina's arm wrapped around her and gave her a quick squeeze, followed by a push. Back home, she'd heard teenaged boys talk this way, but it never occurred to her that grown women could be every bit as crude. Or perhaps she was prudish? Most young women, before they were her age, had husbands and a child, even children, but the idea never once occurred to her. Love hadn't ever occurred to her because she had other plans in mind. Of course, she understood her Sisters weren't alluding to love.

As uncomfortable as it was, Jenna forced a toe into the proverbial water, for the comradery if nothing else, "I look forward to it."

"Yeah, you do!" bellowed Dominica.

A comfortable crisp day met Jenna as she and several of the Sisters, Laina in the lead as host of the small procession, rode out of Soutton towards the mountains in the distance. Those mountains loomed even at this distance gray, rocky, and jagged, and white caps lay across the peaks of most of them. Three days in a row, the sky remained cloudless, the sun cheerily bringing some small manner of warmth, and combined

250

with a light, warm breeze coming from the south, all the snow had melted away. Icy water trickled down hills into the wind gaps between them, making the ground soft and soggy, as the temperature hadn't dropped enough the previous two nights to freeze it. Despite the sometimes tricky footing, the warming sun and wind felt glorious against the overall chill in the air.

A host of people walked with them, having chosen to make a holiday of the affair. Hundreds of them – sometimes older children on their own or with friends, or even entire families – marched with the handful of Protectresses, and a great many had come early to choose the best and driest hillocks available to view the spectacle. Many carried woven baskets, no doubt containing bread, cheese, or even meat to have a picnic as they watched dragons put on a show of airborne battle.

Jenna could hardly wait for it all to start. She felt like every hair on her body stood on end as if she had just rubbed her feet back and forth on a fur rug, and she felt an incredible urge to lunge forward, not caring if she left her own skin behind in the process. As they rode, she admitted that to herself, but it had nothing to do with the implications thrown toward her by her Sisters. Their jeers and jibes would have everyone believe her reason for going was the Commander of the South, but she felt the truth in her heart – the opportunity to see dragons in combat, even mock combat!

Though, an unexpected observation of Conor, that no one could doubt or argue the quality of his impressive physique or the intensity of those blue eyes, came unbidden to her mind, and Jenna quickly pushed it away as an unwanted distraction.

Laina led them a little further, selecting the top of a long ridge for their vantage point. The land flattened somewhat for the next two miles before turning to earnest foothills in the miles leading to Vulgesch. There were no homes or farmsteads out this way, only a well-traveled road that snaked toward the mountains, and Jenna assumed it had something to do with the old wars. Soutton was the southernmost city of Abrea, the first stronghold of defense if Vulgesch invaded, so the common folk had never sought to build in an invading army's path with so much available land in the other directions of the compass.

"How long will we wait?" Jenna asked, hoping her voice didn't betray her calm demeanor.

"Not long now. Look," her friend pointed.

Jenna shielded her eyes on the left side to block the morning sunlight and squinted far to the south, where at the edge of her vision, she barely spotted a dark speck against the mountainous vista, many miles away. It seemed to grow as she stared, approaching at immense speed, and Jenna realized that it was even further away than she originally thought. As massive as the dragon was, it had to be miles and miles away to appear so small, and yet it crossed the distance and grew promptly in size, indicating a pace she wouldn't have thought possible for such a creature.

"Ser Gogol?" she asked, receiving a silent nod from Laina as a response. "Are the Vulgeschi dragons as fast as ours?"

"Faster," Laina replied with upraised eyebrows, "but it takes them longer to get up to speed."

"Because of their size."

"Yes, well, faster in a straight line," Laina amended. "They're not as deft as ours, as... maneuverable. I'm surprised Ser Gogol agreed to duel today."

"Why?"

"It's cold. Not as cold as it's been, but still," Laina replied, as if it explained everything. Seeing Jenna's uncomprehending stare, she added, "Didn't they teach you anything about dragons back in that village of yours?"

"Not very much," Jenna admitted, "just what everyone knows about them and the Dragonknights. That, and they're practically invincible."

"Even that's not entirely accurate," Laina disagreed, "but, anyway, it's the fire inside them that helps them fly. Can you imagine a bird as big as that Vulgeschi dragon, with as much muscle, being able to lift itself with even those wings?"

"Probably not," Jenna agreed.

"Exactly, it couldn't. Their fire is held inside, and it helps lift them, makes them lighter somehow. I don't totally understand it myself, but it's the same reason why their breath forges such strong steel."

"Which they need because they're also the biggest?"

"Exactly," Laina answered with a quick point of her finger, "but colder days slow them down, especially the big ones."

A lone shout sounded from somewhere behind them, and then it rose into a chorus of voices moving closer to them at a breakneck pace. Jenna turned in her saddle to see Sir Conor and his dragon as they exited his tower, wheeling in the air to let everyone get a good look. The people cheered and clapped, and mothers and fathers holding small children pointed into the sky at the Commander of the South and his mount. The dragon climbed a bit and then turned south, plummeting at the crowds with blinding speed. Some ducked or sought cover, but others confidently stood their ground, as the dragon pulled up mere feet above their heads. The spectators cooed their admiration and laughed at those frightened people who sheepishly wore grins as the dragon swooped above them. Several reached upward, Jenna included as the moment took hold, believing or perhaps fantasizing that her fingertips missed the dragon's belly by mere inches as the rush of air from its passing blew around her. Once past the people, the dragon pulled into a climb, causing Sir Conor to lay on the beast's neck as he went almost straight up. Eventually, he leveled off and eased over the open plain about a half mile past the onlookers, the dragon almost casually beating its wings as it waited in place for its opponent.

"Ser Gogol will strike first," Laina predicted, "but Sir Conor will be ready for it."

Jenna said nothing in return. Her eyes rested on the magnificent creature that seemed to hang effortlessly in midair, the slender wings fanning up and down. It was too far away now, but as he passed overhead, her fingers outstretched in an earnest longing to make contact for the most minute fraction of a second, Jenna's heart beat with a sense of freedom she had never felt in her life. But there was something more – the innate freedom was somehow tempered or held in check by another feeling she couldn't begin to describe. She certainly wouldn't mention it to anyone; they would say it was her imagination. She looked to her friend to find Laina blissfully unaware of Jenna's thoughts and feelings.

Jenna looked back to the sky to find the Drakkritt of Vulgesch had closed the distance incomprehensively quick. She could now make out its scale covered, muscled body, the huge legs, each doubtless larger than a grown man Conor's size and ending in paws with deadly claws, folded up underneath, and the gargantuan wings as they pushed up and down with monumental power. An armored creature sat on his throne like saddle atop the monstrosity, smoke colored plate armor reflecting dully in the morning light.

"Why do the Drakkritt where such heavy armor?" Jenna wondered.

"They do everything heavy in Vulgesch."

"But isn't Sir Conor from Vulgesch?" Jenna asked with a glance at her friend, not wanting to take her eyes from the oncoming dragon.

"He is," Laina nodded once, her eyes searching Jenna's face, and the latter pretended not to notice and labored to keep her face from betraying anything, "but as strong as he is, he favors speed. Recall the duel against Lady Ayn?"

Jenna agreed inwardly, but she neither said anything nor moved a muscle as the larger, reddish dragon continued to speed toward Sir Conor and his own. Aware that her heart thumped so hard that she could feel it in her fingertips, she focused on breathing slowly, in and out, to calm her eager anticipation. A glint of steel flashed from Sir Conor as he drew his sword, perhaps more of a signal of readiness, for she didn't see how such a weapon had much value in this sort of duel. How could one get close enough to use it? The Drakkritt, Ser Gogol, bolted within bowshot and then pulled his mount into a slight climb. Jenna gasped sharply as she realized he had no intention of stopping or slowing his momentum.

"This is it," Laina stated in quiet awe.

As she expected, the huge red surged upward, gaining altitude on the stagnant and unmoving Sir Conor. Less than a hundred yards away, Ser Gogol's dragon dove directly at Sir Conor's. Conor had switched to a bow in those few seconds and fired an arrow that bounced right off the oncoming Vulgeschi dragon's snout. He began to fit another arrow into his bowstring, but he knew his time was up. His dragon lurched forward and dove to the right at once as the big red snapped its jaws in the empty space where Sir Conor had just been. The crowd seemed to choke on its own breath, knowing that death missed the Dragonknight by scant seconds.

As his dragon coursed through the open air, Conor turned in his saddle and loosed another arrow, this one ricocheting harmlessly off the other dragon's flank. The larger red was slow to react and turn about to chase its quarry, and a third arrow dinked off the chest of Ser Gogol's armor. Much lighter and sleeker in the wind, Conor's mount extended the distance, allowing his rider to fire off several more arrows. All but one found their mark, but those failed to find anything to penetrate.

"Why doesn't he aim for the eyes?" Jenna asked, unable to disguise a voice full of concern.

"Because they're not actually trying to hurt each other."

Oriented and surging onward, Ser Gogol's dragon closed the distance. As Laina had said, he was faster at full speed but extremely ungainly. Conor fired another arrow, this one impacting the nose of Ser Gogol's basinet helm, causing the Drakkritt to flinch slightly, and by the time he had recovered, Conor and his dragon had come about to head straight for him! Almost faster than anyone could follow, Conor slung his bow and again brandished his broadsword. Jenna held her breath, certain the two dragons were about to collide in a titanic concussion that would doubtlessly kill both riders. The colossal Vulgeschi red opened its mouth, and a gout of white hot flame lanced through the air at Abrea's Commander of the South. The crowd gasped in awe as Conor's mount turned upside down at the last moment, suddenly folding its wings close to its body, and Conor's sword clanged with a flash as it struck Sor Gogol's armor at the immense speed given it by a dragon.

That impact carried through the air and echoed around the hills below, and Ser Gogol reeled backward in his saddle, very nearly tumbling out of it. His red blasted another attack of its fire, but it struck only empty air where Conor's dragon had once been. The crowd cheered at the struck blow, and even Jenna found herself caught up in it, pounding her fist toward the sky. She ignored Laina's smile, allowing herself to enjoy the moment.

By the time Ser Gogol had himself reoriented, Conor flew back in for the attack. His dragon swooshed by the red's tail and barely grasped it in his jaws, giving the larger dragon a good ignominious yank in so doing and releasing it as he continued, and within moments, he was back crossing the red's path as it brought its head back around to face forward. Conor's dragon tipped towards it, and the Dragonknight gave it a smack on the nose with his broadsword for its trouble. The crowd continued to cheer as the Vulgeschi dragon's rage grew, and it roared in frustration, a sobering and terrifying sound to the high spirited audience.

Pushing his advantage, Conor wheeled and came back again, this time intent to let his mount take a swipe with its own paws at the Drakkritt. He flew in from above, fast as lightning, but Ser Gogol seemed prepared for the maneuver, somehow wheeling his own giant dragon around just in time. However, the larger Vulgeschi dragon couldn't turn quite fast enough to both defend from the attack and avoid the collision, and the two impacted with force unknowable by those watching below.

"Look, mommy," a child called, and people called and cried out to create a cacophony of voices as the dragons seemed to curl around each other into mottled red and green ball, and they plummeted to the onrushing ground below them. They pushed away from each other, managing to disentangle as two small human forms continued to hurtle downward, one in steel armor that glowed in the sunlight.

"No," Jenna whispered, and before she had time to think twice, she urged her horse to gallop forward into the plain.

"Wait! Jenna, come back!" yelled Laina after her, but she paid no mind.

Sir Conor's mount, slender and agile, regained control of itself in the blink of an eye, and it spotted its master as he fell. The creature dove straight down, moving faster than Jenna thought possible, a streak of dark green lightning against blue sky. With a mammoth pump of its wings, he flew faster than Conor fell, angling closer to the Dragonknight. He suddenly pulled up hard, and flying level to the ground, scooped the man right of the air with his front paws.

Ser Gogol's mount floundered clumsily, unable to right himself so agilely to undertake such a feat of aerial acrobatics. The beast tried. It, too, charged downward and let out scorching waves of dragonfire behind it, releasing the internal fire that helped keep the creature aloft, but it reacted too slowly and could not gain speed quickly enough. Jenna's horse rode hard as the steel clad body of Ser Gogol crashed into the plain after falling hundreds and hundreds of feet. The sound of rending steel, cracking bone, and pulping flesh all meshed together to cut the Drakkritt's scream short. Jenna pulled her horse up short, only thirty or so yards away, and turned her face away with tightly closed eyes, hoping she could unsee the poor man's horrible death even as his mammoth dragon alit right next to his body.

Chapter 20

A New Link

The dragon sniffed at the tangled mess of metal, bone, flesh, and blood that was Ser Gogol, unsure what to make of it, and as Jenna approached it raised its mammoth head straight into the air to let free a jet of flame. Only twenty or so feet away, she jumped free of her saddle, whispering consoling, calming words to the horse whose eyes rolled with near panic at the proximity of the terrible creature. She turned toward the dragon, the horse forgotten, and her mount wasted no time galloping back the way it came. Jenna paid no mind, entranced as she was.

The dragon lowered its head again to smell its dead Drakkritt, air flowing noisily through nostrils larger than a grapefruit, and then it suddenly noticed the puny human who had cautiously and stealthily approached within ten feet of it. It turned its head to the side like a bird, considering her with a single eye larger than a dinner plate. A golden iris opened slightly then contracted as it stared at her, and it let out a low growl of warning.

"Get back!" shouted a man's voice from behind her, Conor's perhaps.

But Jenna heard nothing as she looked into that lonely eye, and a tear welled up into her left eye and began to roll from the corner down the side of her face. Feelings overwhelmed her – loneliness and sorrow. It was such an imposing, amazing creature, and yet she knew it felt more alone than anything else in the world. It had seen so much over hundreds if not thousands of years and yet could convey none of those amazing experiences, and the depth of this sadness washed over Jenna even as she continued to place one sure foot in front of the other, her hands held open and empty before her.

Footsteps – boots pounding the ground – rushed up behind her, accompanied by the man's voice thundering, "Don't! It's not safe!"

A woman, Laina, called out, "Jenna!"

Tears flowed down Jenna's face, unable as she was to push back the despair, and then something amazing happened, something that no one who watched from afar or rushed to the scene would have expected. The dragons of Vulgesch, the monstrous reds, were known throughout the kingdoms for their power and ferocity but also their pure angst and unfriendliness (to put it mildly). The Link with these creatures allowed the Drakkritt a measure of control to keep this nature in check, but without his Drakkritt, this red had nothing to restrain it. It righted its head to gaze on Jenna with both eyes, opened its mouth just enough to display rows and rows of jagged and razor sharp teeth, any of which would make a frightful weapon, and then he lowered his head, mouth closed again, to lay it gently on the ground. Only inches away, Jenna laid a tentative hand on his scaly snout, feeling the deep warmth of the flesh underneath.

Everything vanished. The dragon, the plain, the dead Drakkritt, the sun and blue sky, and the voices shouting her name as they came close simply ceased to be. It was completely unlike being in a dark room at night with no light by which to see, for there was nothing there except a sense of being, of darkened existence. Something cracked, like the sound of splitting wood, and an irregularly shaped hole of reddish orange light appeared. Jenna pushed up against it, and her prison of oblivion gave way against her pressure, until she fell onto a cave floor only a few feet from a sea of churning magma.

The cave vanished, this time replaced not by darkness but the bright light of an open blue sky, lazy white clouds slowly scudding their way across it. Air rushed past her, blowing her hair behind her as she traversed those skies, freedom permeating her mind and heart. She knew nothing but the emancipation of flight, passing over jagged mountains and volcanos, spying jungles, swamps, and dark forests to the southeast and hills, plains and deep eldritch woodlands far to the north.

She met other drakks occasionally, mostly thick, heavy creatures of red as she had grown to be, but also black, snakelike wyrms with tiny wings that should not be able to fly and yet do. In the northeast, she found a paradise, a place where all the biomes of the world met, and here she met even more varied drakks – graceful and lovely greens from the deep woods, athletic and aloof whites of the frozen north, and also those from the islands of the far east with wings of white and bodies as azure as the sky and seas.

And also, there were men. Everywhere she found drakks, she also found men. The frail, miniscule creatures spread across the world, first building small crude huts, and over the years their complexity evolved into whole cities with walls defending them. They learned of fire, copper, and iron, and their walls – curious constructs those – were apparently meant to protect them from each other, as the drakks flew carelessly over them. She felt no animosity towards these things called men, except to gobble up the occasional interloper who dared trespass in her cave, but they made terrible, costly war upon each other for reasons she neither comprehended nor cared about.

Until one day, the war was her war. She flew amidst her brothers, drakks dedicated to a land named Vulgesch, a human name, and fought great battles against the drakks of the other parts of the world and their human allies. She didn't know why she did this, except that she had no choice. The Drakkritt upon her back led her into battle, their minds inextricably linked, and they wreaked incomprehensible carnage on their enemies. Dragonfire scorched men, dragons, and the paradise at the center of the world, and when it was done, nothing but a great wasteland was left. The drakks all went home, again led by their riders.

Years passed, Drakkritt came and went, but never did the great wars happen again. The humans died so quickly, so effortlessly, that she lost track of how many she had Linked with, but there was always another, another man to sit in the chair upon her back. After a time, it seemed she had known nothing else. Even now as she looked upon the crumpled mass that had once been another Drakkritt by the name of Ser Gogol, she could not remember another time, and that thought held an agonizing despair that pierced her heart.

An iron grip enveloped Jenna's wrist, yanking her hand away from the dragon's scales, and a raging clamor like that of a wide, thunderous river filled her ears for a moment. She blinked and shook her head as the visage of the enormous dragon filled her view, and dizziness threatened to overwhelm her as she waivered slightly from left to right. A strong, steadying hand found the far side of her waist, and she looked over her shoulder to see Sir Conor put both of his hands upon her in a way that was at once warning and calming. But the dragon released a low growl.

"What are you doing?" Conor asked, and he enveloped her wrist with one hand, a band of force that was almost twice the size of one of her own hands.

"I," she wondered aloud, almost in a daze as if she couldn't make sense of the question, "I don't know. I felt like... she wanted me to touch her."

"You're lucky he didn't eat you with one bite. Now, come away slowly," Conor replied calmly, and he eased backward.

The dragon growled again, more noticeably this time, and Conor stopped moving completely as it glared in his direction, a fire growing in the black slits surrounded by huge yellow irises. Jenna looked back to the dragon, her wrist still encased in Conor's hand, though he'd dropped the hand on her waist, and something passed between her and the glorious behemoth as they met each other's eyes.

"She wants you to let me go," she explained, a fact she knew but couldn't explain.

Sir Conor was not one to bow before anyone, except his king, and though the people of Abrea hailed him as the greatest warrior, the greatest Dragonknight in all of Abrea if not the world, he had made himself so through the wisdom of understanding his enemy and not just lightning speed and massive thews. He would fight to the death if given a small chance at victory, and he had never lost. But he also understood when victory could not be attained under any circumstances whatsoever, and he made a show of not only releasing his grip on Jenna but also displaying his empty hands to the dragon before dropping them to his sides.

Jenna stepped forward toward the creature and soothingly stroked her gigantic muzzle, eliciting another warning from Sir Conor, "Please, don't do that. Come away with me."

"She wants me to," Jenna whispered.

"You can't know that."

"Yes, I do."

"Jenna," Laina's voice interjected, "Sir Conor is right. Come back with us. He's Linked to Ser Gogol, and he's dead. You can't control him."

"*She* doesn't need control," Jenna realized aloud, emphasizing the dragon's correct gender. "She's... so amazing, so incredible, but she's so sad. She has never known... love."

"By the blood of the king, what is she on about?" Laina asked, but she received no answer from Sir Conor.

The Dragonknight stood so silent, so still that he may have been an incredible work of art, a statue carved from marble by the most talented of sculptors ever to grace the world, with every detail displayed down to the emblems on his armor and the rippling of tendons. His expression stayed hard as stone, stern in the face of what transpired before him, and his blue eyes shone while he considered what must be done next, realizing that any wrong move would have him turn into brunch for the dragon.

"Her name," Jenna breathed.

"Is Gighantesk," Conor offered.

Jenna shook her head as her brows knitted together in thought before she replied, "No, that's what men called her. It's Drakkbjorge."

"The mountain dragon," Conor translated.

"Yes!" Jenna cried, and with her hand still on Drakkbjorge's snout, she half turned toward Connor and Laina with eyes wide and alight with newfound reverential understanding and growing tears. She elatedly repeated, "Yes! That's it! Drakkbjorge."

The dragon lifted her head away from the touch, and Jenna let her hand drop to her side. She should have been terrified. Anyone else would have been, certain that Drakkbjorge intended to snap them up into her jaws, incinerate them with her breath, or otherwise flatten them into mounds of squishy jelly with one of her giant

264

paws, not dissimilar to her former Drakkritt Ser Gogol. But Jenna felt neither fear nor terror, or even anxiety for that matter, as a sense of calm expectation washed over her, and her heart pounded with sudden infatuation for the incredible creature as the sun reflected off her red and black scales. The dragon edged her left front paw closer, an intimidating thing, as lying flat on the ground it was over half Jenna's height, and then straightened her foreleg to provide a sort of gentle, sloping ramp toward her back.

Laina gasped inward and murmured, awestruck, "She wants you… she wants you to mount her."

Jenna wasted no time as she stepped in between the dragon's toes and their long, wicked claws and pulled herself up atop the dragon's paw. Sir Conor exclaimed something, something telling her to stop, but as he stepped forward to intercede, Drakkbjorge immediately fixed the Dragonknight with a hard glare and yet another warning rumble. Jenna, standing atop the paw, had stopped and turned to observe this, and as Sir Conor stepped back to dispel the idea that he was a threat, Jenna grinned, nodded at Laina, and turned to climb the dragon's leg. She blissfully ignored the glistening tears that ran down her cheeks. The path was steeper than it looked from below, and the hopeful sunlight nearly blinded her when mixed with the salty drops that hadn't yet fled her eyes. She wiped a forearm across her face once to clear her vision a bit and completed the climb up to the dragon's shoulder.

She saw the saddle, more a chair or throne of polished wood and leather and its heavy straps that wrapped around Drakkbjorge's girth, only a few feet away, situated in the middle of her back, just fore of her currently slack wings, but before she moved closer to it, Jenna turned and looked around. At least some twenty feet in the air, she looked down on Sir Conor and Sister Laina below her, one frowning gravely and the other almost as exultant as Jenna herself. The people of Soutton, as well as the other Sisters who accompanied them, had moved closer in the mere minutes all this occurred, but now they stopped as their eyes alit upon something none of them had ever seen – a woman standing on a dragon, about to take her rightful place.

Jenna swallowed hard, ignoring the lump she hadn't noticed in her throat, and waived at Sir Conor, Laina, everyone. She turned and stepped slowly toward the saddle, noting the gentle but heavy thrumming of Drakkbjorge's heart and the warmth that emanated from her scaly hide. Her soft leather boots sounded almost metallic against the scales, and the dragon had slowed and evened her breathing so as to make herself a more stable platform for unsure feet. Reaching the saddle, Jenna turned again and gently lowered herself into it. It was hard and uncomfortable, not unlike a horse's, boiled black leather upholstering the polished ebon wood. It had been made for a man in heavy armor, as it was at least ten inches too wide for her, and gouges and scratches in the arms and against the back showed that it had been well used exactly so. Jenna's arms found their places, and she appeared as much a ruling monarch on her throne as a woman warrior upon a dragon.

Without hesitation, Drakkbjorge took in a long, deep breath, and her ribcage expanded suddenly as she pulled in air to feed the fires within her. To the cries and exclamations of those watching, including Laina and Conor, she lifted her wings and pushed them back downward again, easing her enormous bulk first, then her legs and tail, and finally her paws from the ground below. As the wings worked into their continuous up and down rhythm, the wondrous dragon ponderously lifting her into the air, Jenna could do nothing but laugh and even weep in near euphoric ecstasy.

Sir Conor, Commander of the South, sighed as he watched the dragon fly off to the east. It had been solely his responsibility to keep an eye on Sister Jenna, but no one, neither King Rendor himself nor the ever conniving Westley, could have expected such a series of events that would lead to this. He looked down at the oozing mass of steel and pulp that had once been Ser Gogol as the dragon's shadow blocked out the sun, Jenna's almost musical elation carrying down to his ears as it flew overhead. Sir Conor found what was once Gogol's left arm and tore the bent and misshapen steel gauntlet from his hand, taking two fingers and no small amount of flesh with it. On the dead man's left ring finger, he found what he sought, and Conor slowly worked the gold ring back and forth a half dozen times before it finally slid free.

Epilogue

A Link Forged

The Dragonknights of the First Circle sat in their usual places, except that King Rendor and Sir Conor were juxtaposed. The former stood next to Conor's seat while the latter took the king's normal place on the platform in the center of the room, relating everything that happened only five days before. Rendor summoned all his Commanders back to Highton immediately, but of course, the Dragonknights of the Second Circle were not invited. Conor told the story that they already heard, but now they heard it directly from the man who was Commander of the South and King Rendor's personal champion.

He explained not only the duel and its aftermath, but that Jenna could communicate with the dragon, that the dragon chose her to be its rider. It took two days for him to rein her in, to convince her to come stay with him in his tower and then to fly with him to Highton, and even then, it was only when she came back of her own volition. She rode her own dragon, able to keep pace with him and command the creature as expertly as any veteran Dragonknight. Even now, she was with the beast in the clearing north of Highton, unwilling to leave it even to sleep. When Conor finished, the room stayed eerily silent, and he took back his seat as the king climbed the steps to the center platform.

"I have my own thoughts on this," Rendor broke the silence, "but I want to hear your counsel on the matter before I make my decision."

"I think," Malum began slowly, "we need some time to digest this."

"Time is a luxury we can ill afford," Rendor disagreed. "Besides, you all knew what happened near Soutton before you made the flight."

"Very well," Malum ceded after a moment, "then return the dragon to Vulgesch and kill the girl."

"How chivalrous," Tullus commented with a roll of his eyes.

"Chivalry? Chivalry is for high minded fools," Malum replied, receiving cold hard stares from Tullus and Conor alike. "We've had peace for a thousand years. Peace and plenty. The girl threatens to upend all of that. What if there are more?"

"More?" Rendor returned.

"Like her."

"Ah," Rendor nodded with raised eyebrows. "Rest assured, there are."

"Then kill her now before word gets out," Malum said, repeating his original recommendation.

"I'll murder no one in cold blood," Conor announced, his blue eyes blazing against his stony face.

Malum sighed and muttered while laying a hand on the hilt of a dagger, "You people and your honor... Then someone with more courage must be found to do it."

"Watch yourself, Sir Malum. Don't dare to question my courage again," Conor threatened.

"Enough!" Rendor interrupted. "Sir Conor, what would you suggest?"

Conor, the left side of his mouth raised in a half snarl at his fellow Commander, released the tension in his face and turned back toward his king, "The dragon does not belong to us. It's from Vulgesch. I will fly with Jenna and turn her over to their king."

"Unnecessarily risky," Malum declared.

"Does she truly control the dragon?" hissed Westley from behind his mask.

Conor lifted his palms upward indecisively, "Who can say? What I can tell you – what I saw with my own eyes – she touched the dragon before I could stop her. She seemed to be... elsewhere, and when I pulled her hand from it, she returned. The dragon *chose* her, and if I had forced her from it, I have absolutely no doubt it would have slain me instantly."

"So, you chose the better part of valor," jabbed Malum.

Conor shot to his feet, aiming a finger at Malum, his bicep bulging with the bend in his arm, "I chose to stay alive to serve my king, something *you* may not have the opportunity to enjoy much longer, you whore rat."

A calming hand dropped lightly on Conor's shoulder, and knowing it belonged to his king, Conor ignored the impulse to wrench its owner's arm out of its socket. Instead, he dropped his own threatening countenance, took a deep breath, and sat back down. Malum seemed to gloat for a moment, practically glowing, but a stern look from Rendor and Conor both ended it quickly.

"Sir Conor brought this back to us," Rendor said when tempers had cooled enough to listen.

He held out his hand. In his open palm lay a single golden ring like those worn by every man in the room. Their reactions varied. Malum shrugged, almost entirely disinterested as he slumped back in his chair, while Tullus leaned his head backward in a long, slow motion and then nodded once. Westley leaned forward suddenly, the motion showing interest and emotion that none of them often saw as his expressions stayed hidden behind his wooden mask, and a hiss of taken in breath accompanied it.

270

"We have an opportunity here, Highness," the man's words snaked out, "an opportunity never before seen by anyone."

"Explain, Sir Westley."

"Give the girl what she has always wanted. Make her a Dragonknight."

Malum jumped to his feet faster than anyone thought possible, considering his utterly relaxed and almost slovenly posture. He shouted a nearly unending string of obscenities at his fellow, not the least of which questioned his parentage, choice of lovers, and his favorite animals. Westley smiled from behind his mask, as he found the display amusing, while King Rendor sighed in annoyance and rolled his eyes toward the ceiling.

Finally, the king tired of the display and roared, "Malum, shut the fuck up!" It had the desired effect, as Rendor avoided raising his voice or using profanity. One might think this was the case because such behavior was simply not regal, un-kingly as it were, but truthfully, Rendor had just matured past the point of feeling the need to use such words and methods. Mostly. He turned back to his most trusted advisor and said, "Please, go on, Sir Westley."

"First, let us all understand," Westley said in a wheeze, "I do not suggest this lightly, but think on it for a moment. Sir Malum is right; things have been peaceful and plentiful for longer than any of us have lived, but we have the chance to have more – more power, more strength, a stronger hand with which to negotiate at the Convocations with our Dragonknight brothers from Vulgesch, Isdal, Azgua, Raucrud."

Rendor began to nod in understanding as Westley continued, "We will have two more Dragonknights than our southern neighbors in Vulgesch and one more than the other three. We will be positioned to demand... more."

"This isn't honorable," Conor grumbled.

"It isn't dishonorable," Westley countered. "In fact, we were looking out for the safety of all by Linking the dragon with Jenna. Who knows what chaos she could wreak unbound and free to roam with a rider who cannot control him. And think of the other benefits. We now have our own way to produce the steel for which Vulgesch smiths command such a premium."

"The dragon is female," Conor almost mumbled, "and has its own name – Drakkbjorge. Sister Jenna told me."

"How did she know this?" Westley hissed back, and Conor shrugged as if neither the question nor the answer had any importance.

"Will the Link even work on her?" Tullus asked, at once changing the topic and ignoring any implications of Conor's words.

Westley shrugged and offered, "There is only one way to find out, but there isn't any reason to think otherwise. The other nations will clamber to gain our favor."

The king furrowed his brow slightly as he considered this, asking "You think one dragon will upset the balance so much?"

"I do," Westley replied, "Do this, and we grow in power and can further control the girl who would be a boy who would be a Dragonknight."

"I still say we should kill her. Keep the dragon or return the dragon to Vulgesch, I care not. But kill the girl. We can ill afford word of her spreading across Abrea or all of Nahrea for that matter," reasoned Malum.

"It is too late for that," Westley replied with an almost imperceptible shake of his head. "Word of my once friend's daughter and her exploits already spreads like infection. We cannot stop it, but we can control how it spreads."

272

"And whose command would she be under?" Malum asked dejectedly. Knowing that King Rendor almost always took Westley's advice, he returned to his characteristic slump.

"I would suggest," Westley responded, "Sir Conor."

"Ha! Because he has done so well when all he had to do was look after the girl!"

"I can twist your head off your neck with my bare hands, Malum," Conor warned.

"If you can catch me, you undergrown rhino."

"Regardless," Tullus loudly boomed, interrupting the insults and threats, "under Sir Conor's command makes sense to me."

"How is that?" Malum sneered.

"Because he won't murder her in the night, and he will do exactly as King Rendor commands, regardless of how he feels about it," Sir Tullus explained with an honoring nod. "Also, it will keep the girl in the south, where the people already know of her."

Conor returned it solemnly and said, "I don't agree with this course of action, but as I'm certain mine is the minority opinion, I prefer it over Sir Malum's. I will abide your word as law, Majesty."

"Sir Tullus," Rendor called with a look at the towering Dragonknight, "you haven't offered me your counsel on this."

Tullus sighed and looked to the floor for a moment with pursed lips before looking back to his king, "I have nothing else to offer, Majesty. My Brother Commanders have laid out the options. I agree with Conor's thoughts, but I see how fortuitous this could be as Westley said. I will not endorse murdering the girl."

"Even though it's the only thing that makes sense?" Malum asked, his voice slightly higher pitched than normal.

"Even though," Tullus nodded with a sullen sigh.

"Even though it threatens to upset everything we've built in Nahrea for a thousand years?" Malum incredulously pressed on, but Tullus only shrugged.

Rendor looked from face to face, making eye contact with each Dragonknight of the First Circle to be certain none had anything else to add before deciding, "Very well. Sir Conor, deliver the news to Sister Jenna that tomorrow morning at sunrise she will undergo the Link ritual with her dragon. She is to be a Dragonknight of the Second Circle and under your command. I trust you will keep her... controlled."

"I will, Majesty."

"Then go, all of you," Rendor commanded, the tone of finality contained within that command brooking no further response.

He watched as they filed out of the room and to the tree's stairway beyond. Sir Conor was the first to exit, even though he sat furthest from the door, exiting with the purpose filled stride that he used everywhere he went whether he had a task or not. Malum was the next to leave, his posture defeated and his face a mask hiding his thoughts and emotions. Tullus came right behind him, dropping a friendly hand on the shoulder of the man who stood over a foot shorter than he, leaving only Sir Westley still in the room. The masked Dragonknight said nothing, only wheezed slightly as he bowed deeply, turned, and left Rendor alone.

Certain they were gone, the king dropped heavily into Conor's chair. He chose it for no particular reason except that he loved his champion like a son, though he took far more advice from Westley. Conor the warrior, Westley the politician, Malum the sneak, and Tullus the leader. They all had their strengths and their weaknesses, and as King Rendor reached back into his pocket and held the late Ser Gogol's ring aloft as he watched a torch flicker through the middle of it, he wondered what strengths and weaknesses his new Dragonknight would bring to Abrea.

End of Book 1

Jenna and the world of Nahrea will return in Book 2 in 2025.

Who is Martin Parece?

I'd really rather you not ask me questions like this! Well, are you asking who I am or "Who am I?", because the latter is a completely different question that forces one to look deep into the heart and mind. It is the question humankind has been asking since there was humankind.

Who I am, on the other hand, is just some guy who loves to read and tell stories. As I look back, I have always been a storyteller, from my first short stories to my first faltering attempts at playing Dungeon Master. I still love TTRPGs, all sorts of fiction, heavy metal, and horror movies. In fact, this last will be readily apparent should you read my anthology <u>Tendrils in the Dark</u>. A lot of shout outs, homages and influences there...

I returned to my creative endeavors around 2009 as my business of seven years began to burn down around me during the recession. I suppose adversity causes growth, and though I shelved my projects for a few years, I returned to them with the publication of <u>Blood and Steel</u> in 2011. Regardless, people seemed to enjoy the world of Rumedia, and I returned to it with five more novels.

In the end, I'm just a guy who loves to tell stories, read other persons' stories and head bang in the car. I have so much more to come, and I hope you'll join me on the journey!

Turn the page for an excerpt from

The Dragonknight Trilogy
Book 2

Coming 2025!

A shadow over a hundred feet wide sped across the landscape, bathing the foothills separating Vulgesch from Soutton in darkness despite the early morning light. A traveler was caught in that shadow for just a moment, peering upward into the blue, cloudless sky in wonder, and by the time he had done so, the dragon quickly shrank into the distance. A sudden and instantaneous buffeting of wind was the only remaining sign of the dragon's passage, and even that was gone just as quickly. The giant beast from Vulgesch, its steel clad rider safely secured in his almost throne like saddle, flew far faster than anyone would believe such an immense dragon to be capable of. On his eastern flank, the cold morning light glittered off of deep red scales, casting a scintillating ruby reflection off his hide even has his enormous leathery wings worked to keep him both aloft and speeding onward. He'd been flying since before dawn at the urging of his *Drakkritt* who carried a message from the king of Vulgesch himself.

Ser Radun squinted slightly through the visor of his helm, forged as was the rest of his plate armor from the fires of his own dragon's breath. Miles distant, the city of Soutton had already begun to glow its orange hues, made so by the stone from which the city quarried nearby. Just a speck on the horizon, it grew as his *drakk* crossed three miles with each passing minute, and he started to make out finer details, such as the river that divided the city into north and south districts, the ancient castle of gray granite that housed the Protectresses of the South, and the homes and farms that spread out to the north past the city.

There was also his destination – the monstrous tower that stood hundreds of feet over the rest of the city.   Abrea and King Rendor committed significant resources to its construction for Sir Conor, whose fighting prowess was beyond compare or reproach. Radun had seen Conor fight many times, even engaged with him in a mock duel years ago before either men had been linked to dragons, and he had nothing but respect for King Rendor's Lord of the South, though some *Drakkritt* from Vulgesch almost viewed him as a traitor to his homeland.   Radun knew they simply didn't understand; had Conor stayed in Vulgesch, he surely would have been a *Drakkritt* and perhaps even king of the nation one day. The tower was certainly fit for a king – casting a brilliant host of reds and oranges in the morning light, it's stonework and façade featuring a fresco of a giant blacksmith on one rounded side and a dragon on the other.

Ser Radun wondered if Conor would be King of Abrea one day and would that drive the two nations apart or closer together? He shrugged as he supposed that would depend on who sat upon the throne of Vulgesch when that day came.

A hint of warning tingled in the back of his mind, bringing Radun back to the present as Drakkarnix spotted three green wyrms rising deftly into the air from the plains just east of the city. As their dark wings unfolded, their sleek, emerald green bodies defied the ground more easily than his own mount, shooting into the air as bolts fired from a crossbow. Though not as impressive or powerful as Drakkarnix, Radun knew them to be far more agile, as proven by the recent falling death of Ser Gogol where Conor's own *drakk* had managed to save him. To be fair, Ser Gogol often eschewed the safety harness built into their riding chairs, so sure of his own might as he was.

Regardless of his confidence in Drakkarnix, Ser Radun knew he could not hope to defeat three of Abrea's Dragonknights, but battle was not on his mind, at least, not yet. That day may yet come, depending on how his message was received.

The three Dragonknights came straight for him as an echelon, and as they closed within bow range, the two on the flanks picked up speed and swung wide. He slowed Drakkarnix almost to a stop, the enormous dragon expending immense effort to stay aloft though barely moving, as the three dragons flew in a lazy circle around him still several miles away from Soutton. If they intercepted him, it could only mean that Sir Conor was not present. Otherwise, Abrea's Lord of the South likely would have let him come all the way to alight at his tower.

"Down!" called a dragonknight as he passed in front of Radun and Drakkarnix.

Radun felt his mount's ire rise, felt the creature's desire to burn. He wanted to loose the hottest flames ever felt in Nahrea on these errant, impertinent, tiny man-things that rode its brethren, and Radun exerted his will to tamp these infernal urges down. And down he took the dragon, the creature exhaling a bit of flame as it did so, slowly almost hovering its way down to the hills below. He landed gently on the top of a grassy, rolling hill, and Abrea's Dragonknights did likewise with one directly in front of him and the other two on opposite flanks.

"Why do you impede me?" Ser Radun almost roared, though he knew the answer.

The Dragonknight in front of him responded, and Radun knew him. Fair haired and light skinned with high cheekbones, he was slender and fit in the normal black leather armor worn by most of Abrea's Dragonknights. His name was Sir Quent, and his northern heritage lent him a beauty that sparkled in his bright blue eyes. Moreover, the man knew he was beautiful, and more than once Radun wanted to break every haughty bone in his body.

"This is not Vulgesch, Drakkritt," Quent said with a smirk that demanded to be struck from his pretty face. "Your visit was neither expected nor welcome. Return home."

"I am on the king's business."

"Your king holds no sway in Abrea."

"I am here," Radun growled, and again the dragon urged to be let loose to destroy, "with a message of the utmost importance from *Dreg Drakkritt* Lukon to your King Rendor. Let me pass."

"Leave the message with me, and I will pass it on to Sir Conor when he returns."

"It cannot wait. Let me be on my way to Highton," Ser Radun demanded, and he did not miss that the Dragonknights on his flanks had drawn their bows. Their dragons seemed restless, so he softened his tone, "I mean no harm to you or Abrea, but I must deliver *Dreg Drakkritt* Lukon's message to King Rendor. Escort me if you wish."

Sir Quent raised a hand aloft and replied, "On your honor as a *Drakkritt*?"

Slowly so as not to spark a conflagration, Ser Radun lifted his open hands to his helm and gently removed it from his head with a scraping of the steel on his chain cowl. He lowered it to his lap and held his own hand in the air as his deep brown eyes locked with Quent's. He knew he must look old and ugly with his graying beard, the broken nose that had never healed correctly, and the scar that ran vertically from his forehead over his right eye to the cheek below. The bandit who struck that blow had been killed with his own axe after Radun had wrenched it from his own cleaved helm and face.

"On my honor as a *Drakkritt*," Radun affirmed.

"Then, follow me to Highton, ser," Quent replied as he lowered his hand, and his other Dragonknights lowered their bows. To them, he said, "Return to Soutton."

As all four dragons took to the skies, Quent's waiting patiently as Radun's larger mount ponderously lifted upward, the *Drakkritt* from Vulgesch placed his helm back upon his head. He'd expected whomever met him to demand to relay the message to their king, but Quent was one who viewed all Dragonknights as men of particular honor. He privately thanked whatever gods may exist for this, even though he thought it generally misplaced. Regardless, he'd have done so if required, because today was not the day to begin a war.

If King Rendor did not return the dragon Gighantesk at once to Vulgesch, to its rightful owners so that they may link it with one of their own... Ser Radun dared not contemplate the destruction and terror such a war would bring to Nahrea.

Turn the page for an excerpt from

BOUND BY FLAME
THE CHRONICLE OF THYSS

Coming July 2024!

"I do not understand. How have you yet to find her? I have paid you well. You are the best tracker in my lands, and yet you have no news?" the priest questioned angrily as he stared down at the man who stood before him.

Mon'El eagerly awaited news for weeks, and so had no qualms about interrupting breakfast with his wife, demanding his servants bring the tracker up to their suite atop the palace straight away. As King, High Priest and Chosen of Aeyu, He whom ruled the air and winds, Mon'El could have commanded the man to locate his daughter without any compensation at all, so the priest felt extraordinarily generous in offering a sum of gold that would buy the tracker an estate on the river itself.

Much depended on Thyssalia's safe return. Thyss, he reminded himself.

The suite sat atop Mon'El's massive pyramid that stood in the center of his city and consisted of a large, central room with four open archways that led to others at each point of the compass. These all had grand balconies to allow Mon'El to look down on his people and to allow the currents of his god to pass freely through his abode. He and his wife maintained separate bedrooms to the north and the south, though they seldom slept alone, and the room to the east comprised Mon'El's private temple to Aeyu. His wife Ilia kept the room to the west, there indulging in whatever her heart desired.

Standing three or four inches taller than Mon'El, the ranger known as Guribda had smartly dropped to his knees upon being brought before the priest and king. It would have done him no good to physically overshadow a man who could send him to his death with a mere flip of a hand, but even kneeling, he felt himself shrink before Mon'El's ire even as the king seemed to grow and darken.

Guribda feebly replied, "Well, Highness, I have some news, and I will find her. I swear it."

"What news, then?" Mon'El demanded impatiently.

"Your daughter recently was seen in a village to the north, bordering on the great jungle there. I tracked her to the edge of it where she was joined by at least six other people before they entered the jungle," he explained, leaving out the part where he was sure Thyss had been accosted and taken prisoner.

"And what of the jungle?" Mon'El pressed, idly adjusting his robes. He had been told that Guribda returned to the city alone, so he opted for more blue in his robes than white, hoping that the calm wisdom of Nykeema would embrace him in the face of bad news.

"I... I did not pursue them."

"What?!" Mon'El's voice smashed the interior walls, carried by a gust of wind as thunder cracked in a cloudless sky. Silk tapestries blew from the walls to the floor, and the plates of food on the table behind him rattled and moved about. One fell to the floor with a shatter, causing his wife to sigh. He lowered his voice to a dangerous growl as he pressed on, "Explain carefully."

The tracker's eyes shot quickly around, lolling almost like that of a panicked animal as he assessed his chance of escape should he choose to run. There were four very large, heavily muscled men at each corner, excluding the one who had moved up to be but six feet behind him. All were armed with the best scimitars the city of Kaimpur could produce, and while the tracker was no stranger to swordplay, he doubted he could take out one before the others were upon him. And then he had the priest-god's magic to contend with. No, escape was not an option.

With hands open before him, almost in supplication, he responded meekly with a bowed head, "That jungle is well known to be cursed, Highness. There are monsters in that place that defy time, that predate the rise of men, and I admit to being a coward. Surely, you would have no fear with your immense power. You are blessed of the gods, but I am but a man. I beg your forgiveness.

"Highness, I have other taken steps, however. The jungle borders the sea to the north, and a vast, lifeless desert stretches from its southern edge all the way to your lands. If she doesn't return to the village, she has little choice but to travel to King Chofir's city on the other side. I have paid for eyes in both places. She will not escape me."

Mon'El's anger seemed to abate as the man spoke, for the priest did remind himself that most men were in fact weak and powerless. So few of Dulkur's people wielded the power of the gods, and Mon'El was one of those Chosen few, arguably the greatest of them all. The tracker's words placated him enough, and he nodded at the mention of Chofir. He knew the king well, and a smile touched the corners of his mouth at the thought that the fat merchant-king might try to impose his will on Thyss.

"Very well," Mon'El replied calmly after a moment. "See to it that she does not. She has been gone too long, this time, and I demand her presence. She must be at my side in one month or much may be lost. Go."

The tracker turned to leave, just as the guard returned to his post in the corner, and as Guribda made his way down the steps that would lead him down the outer wall of the pyramid shaped palace, Mon'El surely heard the tracker issue a relieved sigh. Mon'El clenched his fists, anger brewing again, but not aimed toward the man who had just left. No. Yet again, his daughter tested his patience and his will, as she had for the last ten years or more, and it could no longer be allowed. What was soon to happen would have repercussions throughout all of Dulkur, and she was the integral piece on the gameboard.

"Must you scheme so?" Ilia, called from behind him as he began to pace.

Turn the page for an excerpt from

Wolves of War
A John Hartman Novel

Coming October 2024!

Darkness filled the ancient woodland, permeating everything around Hartman just as much as the frigid air chilled him to the bone. Nothing about his slow, quiet trek through the forest felt pleasant, and a sense of foreboding hung heavily in the air, tempting him to abandon his mission and start hoofing it back to France. It wasn't the first time he longed to be back with the regular Army, taking it to the Jerries in a straight fight, but this was different. John just couldn't shake the pervasive dread he felt as he ventured deeper into the German wood.

He shouldn't be alone out here. It was one thing to undertake a solo operation, a task he had accomplished many times in the past. But this time, he was supposed to have a guide with him who knew the woods better than he, but his contact failed to show up at the designated rendezvous. Maybe the he had gotten held up by German soldiers, or maybe he had to hunker down somewhere. After a while, John decided he couldn't wait any longer, steeled himself and went on with the operation.

For the fourth or fifth time, John wished he'd procured a heavy coat to keep the damp cold at bay. He found a tiny break in the eldritch canopy, through which shined a beam of pale light from the full moon overhead. He stood in this welcome dispeller of darkness long enough to unfold his map and become certain of his bearings. He had only a few miles left to traverse until he broke from the forest into the open where he would have little protection from watchful German eyes, and yet, he would breathe more easily once free from this place.

A shiver ran through Hartman, and he thought, *Damn, it's cold!* He began to fold the map back into itself, but his hands seemed to slow with each progressive crease. Surely, they were cold, but it wasn't the near freezing night air that made them react so. He slipped the map into a jacket pocket, and his motion slowed to a complete halt. He stood perfectly still, and the hair on his neck and arms would have stood on end were it not for his appropriated German uniform.

Narrow set, disembodied red eyes materialized out of the gloom some distance in front of him, seeming to glow with an inner, baleful light. They hovered perhaps a foot off of the ground, but Hartman couldn't for the darkness be sure if they were five feet ahead of him or twenty five. He knew only that he stood transfixed by that hellish glare, apparently frozen to inaction while they regarded him. He needed to act, draw a pistol and shoot at those eyes, ready a knife, something, but his limbs wouldn't obey his brain's commands. The entire encounter felt eerily familiar. He had been in some freezing German wood at some point before and had seen those eyes there and then as well, but this was also different. Hartman was alone, and the darkness and cold were all pervasive, not simply offensive to the senses. And there was only one set of eyes, though he remembered, on that other occasion that other attackers had come at him from the sides.

Hartman broke his paralysis just in time to see a silver and black streak from the right as it caromed off of the back of his legs. The energy from the blow knocked him off balance, and it was only his superb athleticism that kept him from tumbling to the forest floor. Just as he regained his footing, another rush of dark motion attacked from the other direction, but this one drew blood. A fierce snapping of unseen jaws severed tendons in his left leg, causing Hartman to collapse, and as he clutched the wounded limb, warm, steaming blood coated his hands.

Either out of a preternatural sense or pure luck, he managed to get his left forearm up just as a huge wolf of silver and black lunged at him. A mouth of wicked, yellowed teeth opened wide in anticipation, and Hartman wedged his arm as far into the mouth as he could. Like a dog whose chewing bone had gone too far backward, the wolf chomped its jaws trying to dislodge him. The power of those jaws wrought tremendous pain, and Hartman felt the teeth puncture the skin of his arm even through the layers of his jacket and sleeve. But it also bought him precious moments. His free hand reached for his knife, but before he could find it, another beast charged from his right. This canine minion of Hell he caught by the neck, and it took all of his might just to hold the thing at bay as it snapped at his face, rancid carrion breath caressing his face. If he could somehow manage to get his legs underneath the creature in front of him, perhaps he could launch the beast just far enough to access his knife or gun. Then, he could turn this fight around.

This glimmer of hope flickered in his mind only to be extinguished in an instant as a third monstrous wolf stood less than a foot away to his left, mouth agape and tongue hanging low out of its mouth. It panted softly, but seemingly out of anticipation rather than exhaustion, and Hartman knew he couldn't hold this one off; he was simply out of arms. It lunged toward his face, and all he could see was teeth and then darkness as the wolf's jaws clamped around his face.

Hartman bolted upright, his clothes and the bedsheets of the hospital bed soaked in sweat. As his heart and breathing gradually slowed, his head cleared so that he could regain his bearings. Two nurses moved around the room, drawing back curtains to allow in the first rays of the autumn sun, which told Hartman it was around seven in the morning. There were only six men in the score of beds in the room, and of them all, he was the only one unwounded. He was vaguely aware of a rifle toting guard that stood in a gray uniform next to the room's entrance.

One of the nurses glared his direction as he watched them, and as she made her way across the room to his bedside, he reached down and rubbed at his ankle, which was shackled to the metal frame of the bed. She stood to his right in her uniform - a dress of narrow, vertical white and blue stripes under an apron of white. Her collar, also white, contrasted against the dress, and was pinned closed severely by an emblem of the Third Reich. A black German eagle clutched a red cross in its talons, though the cross had been extended and resembled an inverted Christian cross.

"Gut morning. Nachtmares?" she asked in a hodge-podge of English and German. She wasn't pretty in the least, but she hadn't been unfriendly to him despite their nations' adversarial nature.

"*Es ist nichts*," Hartman replied in perfect German, "*Danke*."

"Nothing? It's nothing you say? You come into my country, my Fatherland, and kill my sons and brothers, and it is nothing?" she asked, her English becoming clearer though accented. Her eyes began to glow with an unholy red light as she continued, "You come here to fight a war that doesn't belong to you. You kill thousands of good men and deprive the Fatherland what we are owed by right. You do not know what you face, what this Old World can unleash upon you!"

She seemed to grow as she spoke, her uniform tearing at the seams as her bones popped and elongated. By the end of her tirade, her words were nearly unintelligible as her human mouth reformed to that of a wolf's toothy maw under bright red, demonic eyes. Hair, fur of silver and black had sprouted across every inch of her, and razor sharp claws extended from each of her fingers. The room grew dark, as if her very presence alone blotted out the light of the rising sun.

John shouted in alarm and leapt out of the bed as if a great spring had been compressed underneath him, except the shackle around his ankle prevented him from going too far. His back slammed hard onto the cold floor, and he would've cracked the back of his skull as well were it not for his flailing arms somehow breaking his fall. His leg remained suspended in the air, attached as it was to the bedframe, with the hospital bed acting as the only barrier between Hartman and the monstrosity.

"Captain Hartman?" a worried voice said in his ear, and cool hands cradled his sweaty face. "Captain Hartman, wake up."

John Hartman blinked his eyes and shook his head once to dispel and clear away the fading image. He indeed lay on a cool floor, but it was that of the Army field hospital in France. His left leg was propped up on his bed, his ankle wrapped up in bedsheets so twisted to be as strong as thick rope. The room was dimly lit, except for the warmth of a soft glow emanating from the hallway beyond the door. Somewhere in the next room, he heard a muffled announcer's voice calling a baseball game. It sounded like the World Series that just ended two days ago with the St. Louis Cardinals beating the St. Louis Browns.

"Captain Hartman are you all right?" the brown haired night nurse asked.

"I'm fine," he replied with a hardened face as she helped him stand and get back into bed.

"You know, I could find something to help you sleep," she offered, likely referring to whiskey or some other such spirits; being an officer had its privileges.

"No, thank you very much," he replied as he laid his head backward to stare wide awake at the ceiling. "I've slept enough."

Made in the USA
Middletown, DE
28 February 2024